"I didn't realize how much I needed this," Tehani said.

"That's what you have me for," Wyatt said easily. "I'm on a mission to give you new memories. I do have one question, though. Have you gotten over your fear of heights?"

"It's not a fear," she countered grumpily. "Just a healthy distrust. Why? Would that change your plans?"

"No." He shrugged. "Just creates a new level of challenge. If you're up for it."

She'd always enjoyed her sunset time spent with Wyatt, but before now she'd never noticed how cute and entertaining he could be. How lucky was she that he chose to gift her with these surprising reminders of everything life had to offer. "I'm feeling just reckless enough to say yes."

He smiled and she smiled back.

She looked down to where his hand had settled over hers. She turned her hand over, entwined her fingers with his. "This is nice, Wyatt. Thank you. For thinking of this." *For thinking of me.*

Dear Reader,

There's something so magical about the Christmas season. The one I spent in Hawaii when I was eight is by far the holiday that holds the fondest memories. The explosion of colorful flowers and the continuous music somehow sank into my cells. That time was the primary inspiration for my Hawaiian Reunions series for Harlequin Heartwarming.

It makes sense, therefore, that it's Tehani Iokepa's story that takes place in December. It's a moment of remembrance and promise, of moving on and looking back. New mother Tehani is feeling trapped and uncertain about how to move forward. Tehani is surrounded by the best friends, including neighbor Wyatt Jenkins. Wyatt has long harbored feelings for Tehani, feelings he's never felt confident to act on. His devotion to Tehani and her son, Kai, opens up new opportunities for both of them. All they need is the strength to see them through. These two friends are about to discover the healing power of love as they build a new life together, as a family—as Ohana.

I hope you enjoy.

Anna

A HAWAIIAN
CHRISTMAS ROMANCE

ANNA J. STEWART

HEARTWARMING

Harlequin®
HEARTWARMING™

Recycling programs
for this product may
not exist in your area.

ISBN-13: 978-1-335-05134-9

A Hawaiian Christmas Romance

Copyright © 2024 by Anna J. Stewart

 Harlequin Enterprises ULC
22 Adelaide St. West, 41st Floor
Toronto, Ontario M5H 4E3, Canada
www.Harlequin.com

Printed in Lithuania

MIX
Paper | Supporting
responsible forestry
FSC® C021394

Bestselling author **Anna J. Stewart** honestly believes she was born with a book in her hand. After growing up devouring every story she could get her hands on, now she gets to earn her living making up stories and fulfilling happily-ever-afters of her own. Her dreams have most definitely come true. Anna lives in Northern California (only a ninety-minute flight from Disneyland, her favorite place on earth) with two monstrous, devious, adorable cats named Sherlock and Rosie.

Visit the Author Profile page
at Harlequin.com for more titles.

For Bree Hill, whose love of the romance genre is almost unparalleled. Thank you.

CHAPTER ONE

IN THE TWO months since Kai was born, Tehani Iokepa had come to one inescapable conclusion: her son had been born with the most perfect timing ever given to an infant. And also the worst.

In either case, he was currently working his way through an unblemished record of knowing precisely when she was wearing a brand-new or even a clean top. Even now, Tehani could feel his latest feeding dribbling down the back of her shoulder.

"Perfect aim as always, *mae-mae*." *Beloved.* Cuddling him close, Tehani turned her lips against his head and pressed a kiss to the soft cap of dark hair. The holiday ukulele music plinking out of the office speakers tinged the late afternoon with the promise of a perfect island Christmas that was fast approaching. She'd missed this place. Her friends. The work they did. So much so that she'd come back earlier than she'd planned. "How do you always miss the towel?"

"Because that takes talent and my nephew is the most talented baby that was ever born, aren't you, Kai?" Sydney Calvert made familiar baby noises and rattled one of Kai's favorite toys behind Tehani's back. Tehani's friend and boss at Ohana Odysseys—Hawai'i's premier tour and excursion company located in Nalani—circled around, her arms outstretched and fingers wiggling in excited anticipation. The adoration on Sydney's face when she looked at her nephew had remained unchanged since the moment Kai was born in very late September. The undeniable love Tehani's son received from her Ohana, her family and friends, almost eased the ache of loss that continued to cling to her.

Sydney's long sun-kissed dark blond hair was tied in a knot on the top of her head, no doubt an advance move to keep Kai from grabbing a clump and sticking it in his mouth. The khaki multipocketed shorts she wore, along with the bright red tank top, spoke of the holiday season they were quickly barreling into now that Thanksgiving was behind them. The town was already putting on its holiday show with its boughs and holly, pineapples and poinsettias.

"Give him here and go change," Sydney ordered gently. "Or you're going to be late."

Tehani kissed Kai again and handed him over, a tiny part of her silently wailing at the momentary loss. The only thing that tempered the emotion was knowing her son could not be in safer or more loving hands. Being constantly surrounded by her loved ones had been such a blessing as she traversed these first months of single motherhood. Despite having lost Kai's father earlier this year, everywhere Tehani turned in her hometown of Nalani, she found open hands, open arms and, most importantly, open hearts.

She and her son were blessed to have so many people looking out for them.

Tehani closed her eyes for a moment, letting the fading sorrow of losing Remy so unexpectedly wash over her. Embracing his loss, acknowledging it, accepting it, had been the only path to coping. The pain of his death would never completely go away, but she was gradually learning to incorporate the new normal as she moved forward. Despite the secrets she still carried.

"There are some clean shirts in my locker." Sydney snatched the still pristine burping cloth off Tehani's shoulder and expertly draped it over her own. Kai cooed and babbled a bit as he heaved an infant-sized sigh and rested his cheek against his aunt's shoulder.

"I've got some of my own," Tehani admitted and earned a grin of amusement from Sydney. "I learned my lesson last time. Give me two seconds."

"Take your time." Sydney rubbed Kai's onesie-covered back. "No rush. We're in the calm before the storm portion of the tourist season. Enjoy it while you can."

Tehani ducked into the locker room, tugging her holiday-inspired strapped blouse over her head. Served her right for wearing white. She really needed to reevaluate her wardrobe now that she had no control over what ended up on or down her shirt.

Her ankle-strap sandals slapped against the tile floor as she pulled open her locker and, after sorting through the handful of backup clothes she'd stashed inside, chose a bright blue flowy tank top she'd been saving for a special occasion. She pulled her long hair free and gave the shirt a quick tug and smoothed it over her still slightly rounded stomach. The last of the baby weight would take care of itself, but personally she liked the added curves she'd more than earned.

Coming back to work right after Halloween had ended the most amazing time of her life, but she'd been anxious to find her new normal as a single mother. She'd followed the long-held island tradition of staying home with her son for the first month after his birth. She'd wanted for nothing as neighbors, friends and family delivered food and offered emotional support so she could keep all her attention not only on Kai but also herself. Whatever immediate bond she'd felt with her child upon his birth had only strengthened in those weeks. And it was only after that time that she'd finally come to terms with losing the love of her life.

That didn't mean her new reality didn't have her struggling to find her footing. Every day she found herself stumbling a bit, readjusting, even as she came face-to-face with countless memories. But every day got a little better. How could it not when she had the most perfect baby boy? Remy's son. Even now, the guilt she felt over not having told Remy about the baby before he'd died clung to her. There was nothing she could do about that decision now and while Remy might never have known about his child, she had no doubt he was out there, watching over both of them. If only that brought her as much peace as she needed.

"Hey, T?" Sydney poked her head into the locker room and waggled Tehani's cell phone in her outstretched hand. "Your phone keeps ringing. Caller ID says it's Aimita Haoa from the Hawai'i Ocean Education Foundation."

"Oh." Tehani reached for the phone. "Thanks." She glanced at the screen, gnawing on her lower lip until the call went to voicemail. Tehani knew the reason for the call; Aimita was on the board of the HOEF, a nonprofit organization, and was responsible for putting on the annual Surfing Santa Charity Championship in Kona. Remy had been one of the founding board members of the organization and he and Tehani had attended the event every year. No doubt Aimita was calling to see if Tehani planned to come this year.

Tehani took a long, slow breath and set her phone down on the shelf in her locker, then noticed her hand was trembling. Tehani clenched her fist and rode out the new wave of grief that crashed over her.

The two-day event had been close to Remy's heart since it first began six years ago. The various activities, including the crowd favorite Surfing Santa Charity Championship, raised money for the HOEF, which was dedicated to promoting marine environment conservation by sponsoring numerous school programs and community events along with sponsored surfing lessons and water education.

As with everything he'd been passionate about, Remy had taken an active role in the HOEF and had acted as a sponsor and a judge, and even participated in the competition a time or two. No one could pull off board shorts with a Christmas-light pattern while wearing a long Santa beard and surfing the waves quite like Remy Calvert.

Tehani reached up and touched the photo-captured smile displayed on the door of her locker. She traced her finger over Remy's handsome, laughing face. She could almost feel the soft dark curls that matched those of their son.

"'E kala mai ia'u." I'm sorry.

She knew it was cowardly not to take the call from Aimita, but attending this year was out of the question. Especially after last year. Her heart twisted to the point of pain. She wasn't sure she could ever go back.

What she wouldn't give to go back in time and handle that situation with Remy differently. But she knew, even if she'd told him about the baby, it wouldn't have changed anything. What she could do was focus on the happier times, all the years they'd shared together. Like the one displayed in the image on her locker door of Remy straddling his board, breezing through life with his ever-present "hang loose" signal on full display.

"Everyone sees you in Kai," she whispered to the photograph. "Everyone says how much he looks like you." And everyone was right. The moment Kai had been placed in her arms, she'd looked into eyes she never thought she'd see again. It had been a blow of sorts, how undeniably Kai's features resembled his father. For a while she'd worried that her son had been born beneath a shadow he might never be able to walk out of. That Kai would feel as confined and limited as she had for a good portion of her life. She'd spent a lot of years doing the expected, not wanting to rock any of the boats she had access to. She'd walked on tiptoe for what felt like forever. She'd make certain her son never once felt that way.

The most important thing for Tehani to do as a mother was to make sure Kai was his own person, that he didn't feel intimidated or beholden to a man who unfortunately he'd never know. She had every intention of telling Kai about his father, what he'd stood for, the kind way he'd lived his life by always putting someone else first. But she needed to do that in a way that didn't overwhelm her son with the same grief so many others carried around Remy's death.

The gentle tinkle of the door opening broke her free of her melancholy. She shook her head as if dislodging the cobwebs of loss and brushed her finger over Remy's face before she grabbed her phone and shut her locker door.

After she quickly rinsed out her stained shirt

and left it hanging on the drying rack near the window, she splashed some water on her face. The sound of laughter and familiar voices from the main office area brought a smile to her lips. Upon her return to her desk to gather her purse, Tehani found her next-door neighbor and local handyman Wyatt Jenkins along with surfer and dinner cruise operator Keane Harper lugging in a seven-foot Christmas tree.

"Trees finally made it from the mainland," Keane announced like a stressed-out Santa. "Delivery one of six now complete."

Tehani covered her mouth to stop the laugh from escaping. It was such an island sight to see: surfers—hair dripping and toned, taut bodies encased in black wet suits that zipped up the back. The two men were definite stellar examples of the male species but trying to shift a giant tree between them was clearly a comedy of errors. They managed to get the tree upright and wedged against the front corner of the office, where it would await its decor.

Wyatt stepped back, slapped his hands together and turned his million-watt smile on Tehani.

"Hey, T." Wyatt's sparkling eyes always managed to light up any space far brighter than a strand of Christmas lights. His positivity, his encouragement and his unwavering calm had played a pivotal role in Tehani moving into this new life with her son. Her gratitude for Wyatt's friendship grew exponentially every single day. There wasn't a time he hadn't made her smile. She couldn't, not for one moment, imagine life without him.

Wyatt stood a few inches shorter than the six-foot-plus Keane, and carried at least twenty fewer pounds, but with that mass of brown curls on his head and an attitude that never, at least to her knowledge, needed adjusting, he fit in wherever he went. Kindness personified. Something that was becoming a rarity these days. And something she definitely did not take for granted.

"You look pretty," he told her. "All set for your dinner?"

"Yes, thanks." Tehani's cheeks warmed and she found herself looking away. Wyatt was like the sun. If she looked at him for too long, she began seeing—and feeling—things that weren't there. Sunspots of a sort.

Smoothing her hand once more over her stomach, she inclined her head, gazed at her son and sighed. She'd actually miss her quiet dinner on the sofa, gently rocking her son's carrier with her foot as they both dozed off watching TV. "I guess I'd better get going."

"Got a date?" Keane's eyebrows almost disappeared under his crop of damp and over-grown dark blond hair. The former champion swimmer and ladies' man had turned in his bachelor's card this past summer after getting knocked off his feet by a vacationing Marella Benoit. Marella had been in Nalani for her sister's wedding and, to hear Marella tell it at least, the island magic worked its spell on the two of them. The couple had just settled into their new home in time to celebrate the Christmas holidays with a visit from Marella's family. A family that included Pippy, Marella's spitfire of a grandmother, someone Tehani couldn't wait to see again.

"Not a date," Tehani told Keane. "Just dinner. My friend Maylea's here from Maui for the hospitality seminar they're hosting at the Hibiscus Bay." She glanced at her watch. "I have to get a move on." She glanced at Wyatt. "You're still okay watching him this evening?"

"Pfffth." Wyatt waved off her concern. "No problem."

"I didn't realize you were meeting with Maylea." Sydney patted Kai gently on the back. "Should we be worried?"

"About what?" Tehani frowned at the three of them as they exchanged knowing—at least to them—looks.

"Because the last time you talked with Maylea, she tried to steal you to work at her fancy schmancy Maui resort hotel of hers," Keane said.

"Oh. That." Tehani stopped herself from flinching with guilt. "That wasn't anything." Just a huge decision she'd made without talking with her friends. Fortunately, the job fell through before she'd broken her lease or quit her job. "I'm happy here and so is Kai." She reached out and tugged on Kai's onesie. "Besides, I don't think he'd ever forgive me for taking him away from you all. Don't worry," she assured a still-skeptical-looking Sydney. "Nalani is my home. I'm not going anywhere."

"Well, that's good to hear," Sydney said. "Right, Kai?" She did her now-practiced jiggle walk as Kai snuggled deeper into her shoulder. "See?" Sydney aimed a triumphant look at Tehani. "He totally agrees with me."

"He's two months old." Tehani rolled her eyes. "He hasn't learned how to argue yet."

"Anytime you want to revisit the conversation about becoming a partner in Ohana Odysseys—" Sydney swayed back and forth to keep Kai asleep "—you just say the word. It's long past due."

"Sydney's gotten pretty good at the paperwork," Keane added with a wide, charming grin. "First me, then Daphne, the more partners the better if you ask me."

"I appreciate that," Tehani said carefully, even as conflicting emotions raced through her. Remy had made plans to make his college friends his partners, but not Tehani. It hadn't hurt exactly. She'd understood his desire to bring his sister and college friends to Nalani, to have everyone he considered family close, working side by side, in what he considered paradise. Offering them partnerships in the business was a natural plan for a man like Remy, whose greatest talent lay in bringing people together. And of course, once she and Remy were married, she'd have become an automatic partner by default. Doing so in another way now seemed…wrong somehow.

"I have to admit, my brother made a big mistake not making you one from the jump," Sydney said. "I'm more than willing to correct that."

Tehani simply nodded. The uneasiness that circled whenever her and Remy's relationship was put under a microscope returned. She was well aware of the picture-perfect portrait the two of them had made for the ten plus years they'd been together. And she'd loved him with her whole heart. But no relationship, especially hers and Remy's, was all sunshine and jasmine. Particularly those last few weeks before his death. "I really need to go." She slung her cross-body, clutch-sized purse over her head, and stopped long enough to touch her hand to Kai's head. "Be good, *mae-mae*."

"We'll take excellent care of him," Sydney assured her.

"You're Ohana. I know you will." Tehani headed out the door and was down the stairs before she heard Wyatt calling her name. She spun and saw him hurrying toward her.

"I just wanted to make sure you're okay," Wyatt said when she met his gaze. "I know talking about Remy and the business isn't your favorite thing."

Only because she was trying so desperately to move on. Before she was forced to reveal the truth. She shook her head and offered a tempered smile. "It's fine."

"No, it's not. It's just—" Wyatt stopped, frowned, an expression so unfamiliar that Tehani wasn't sure how to process it.

"What?" She reached out, touched her fingertips to his bare arm and felt a kind of charge shoot up her own. Unsettled, she tried to shift her focus. "What's wrong?"

"It's silly, I guess." Wyatt wasn't a man prone to uncertainty. He was a rock of stability and assuredness and had been the strongest shoulder she'd had to cry on since Remy's passing. "You really are planning to stay in Nalani, right? Maylea didn't ask you to dinner to tempt you with another job offer, did she?"

"I doubt it, but even if she does, I'm not interested," Tehani assured him.

"I seem to recall you telling me Maylea doesn't like being told no."

"She's just not used to it is all." Funny, she always seemed to end up defending Maylea in some way. "Doesn't affect my ability to say the word."

"Okay." Wyatt seemed convinced. "Just remember, she usually has ulterior motives when she pops up. You said it yourself. You tend to see her only when she wants something."

Of course Wyatt had actually listened to her and remembered what she'd said. "I will. But honestly, we're just going to catch up. She's gotten engaged so I'm sure most of what we'll be talking about is wedding related. Besides—" she quickly squeezed his arm "—there's nothing she could ever say that would make me want to leave." *Not anymore anyway.*

"Good. Okay." He shoved his hair out of his face and nodded. "That's good. Nalani wouldn't be the same without you. And Kai," he added quickly.

Tehani's smile relaxed. "That's sweet."

"Yeah, well, that's me," Wyatt said with a bit of an edge in his voice. "Sweet, harmless Wyatt Jenkins."

"It's good to know you aren't trying to get out of emergency babysitting duties," she teased.

"Never. I love taking care of Kai." Something odd flashed in his eyes, something she couldn't quite identify. "I love him. We all do." He blushed. "Besides, you and I have an agreement. Who else am I going to sit out on the front porch steps with to watch the sunset?"

"My guess? Anyone you'd like." Their nightly routine that had begun shortly after Remy's death quickly became one of if not her absolute favorite parts of the day. Spending time with Wyatt had eased so much of her pain and helped her come to terms with everything that had changed. He was, truly, a good, kind man. A good *friend*. "You listen. You admit when you're wrong." Which wasn't that often, not that she was going to add that comment. "Plus, you're awfully nice to look at," she teased. "You know very well there are many women in Nalani who'd like to hang out with you, Wyatt. All you have to do is say so."

His cheeks went pink before he ducked his head. "I'm a one-woman kind of guy."

"All the more reason you're popular," Tehani

laughed. "Seriously, Wyatt. You're a great catch. Any woman would be so lucky to have you."

"Any woman, huh?" He looked hopeful. "You think?"

"I don't think." She reached up to touch his face. "I know." Her fingers warmed. Instead of a quick gesture, she found herself transfixed, as if she'd fallen into something she wasn't entirely sure how to climb out of.

Wyatt reached up and caught her hand. "Tehani—"

"I'm sorry." She tugged her hand free and stepped back, uncertainty and something akin to alarm slipping through her. "I really have to go. I'll see you when I pick Kai up. And then sunset tomorrow, yeah?"

"You bet." He offered a quick smile, one that didn't quite reach his eyes. "Of course. Sunset tomorrow. Wouldn't miss it."

WYATT WATCHED TEHANI make her way down the hill from the Ohana Odysseys office into town. His bare feet scrunched against the asphalt, toes scraping. He flexed his hands, uncertainty pulsing through him.

The relief he'd felt after Tehani's job offer fell through over the summer had long since faded, only to be replaced by the nagging worry something else was going on with her. He had no doubt she was still dealing with the overwhelming loss of Remy; they'd been together since she was sixteen. More than ten years. That wasn't something someone just got over. But he couldn't shake the feeling there was something more going on. Something...she wasn't ready to talk about yet.

"Or maybe you're just imagining things," Wyatt muttered to himself. He'd learned at a very early age to be prepared for anything. This could just be his own anxieties needing some kind of workout. Or the feelings he'd squashed down surging to the surface. *Don't worry until there's something to worry about.* That was the lesson he needed to remind himself of.

The end of November breeze ruffled the decades-old palm trees arching and swaying overhead.

Store windows were alight night and day with blinking bulbs, and full green boughs were wrapped in colorful flowered ribbons accented with bright orchids and glittered poinsettias. Branches swayed almost in time to the soundtrack of the ocean lapping and rolling on the other side of the office. The reinforced bamboo structure of the building Remy himself had rebuilt was one of Wyatt's favorites in Nalani as it looked like a throwback to the traditional homes once so prevalent in the area.

Remy's vision for the physical home of Ohana Odysseys had been carried out with Wyatt's then fledgling expertise. Wyatt, who had always been a hands-on learner, had developed a good chunk of his construction abilities thanks to that job. Now, as the go-to handyman, construction consultant and all-around fix-it guy in Nalani, there wasn't much Wyatt wasn't able to tackle. And all because his friend Remy had believed in him. He'd also taken his friend's advice by never settling, never becoming complacent and always being willing to accept new challenges.

In the past few weeks, he'd gotten a crash course in solar power installation thanks to Keane and Marella's recently purchased system for their new home. But this building, Remy's dream project, remained one of Wyatt's best accomplishments.

"Hey!" Keane shouted from the top of the stairs, holding up a huge tangle of holiday lights. "You up for getting the Christmas lights up before you head off with the kid? We can get ahead of things for once?"

Wyatt plastered a smile on and faced his friend. Like Tehani had said, it wasn't like Kai could argue with a change in plans. "Sounds good."

He took his time heading back inside, wanting to stop his mind from spinning. He wanted to enjoy the coming season. Christmas was his favorite time of year and, with it being Kai's first and everyone's first without Remy, he planned to do his best to keep the mood elevated and the holiday stress-free. Remy had always made everyone feel like a friend, even strangers. If Wyatt could step into those shoes, even a little bit, he'd consider that a suitable tribute to his friend.

Shifting Tehani into the center of his focus had taken some adjustment. For so long, he'd kept himself at a bit of a distance, afraid his long unrequited crush would either be noticed or he'd make an utter fool of himself. But after Remy's death, Tehani and he had gravitated toward one another naturally; after all, they'd lived next door to one another for years. It had started with just a quick daily check-in that progressed to text messaging throughout the day, to him dropping by in the morning with breakfast—malasadas most of the time as the Portuguese-inspired fried donuts were her absolute favorite.

Then, one night about a month after Remy's death, he'd gotten home just as the sun was beginning to set. He'd found Tehani sitting out on her front porch, drinking mango lemonade and watching the sky. He'd joined her, and from that night on their meeting had become a ritual. The day simply wasn't complete without watching the sun set with her. He'd watched over her as her pregnancy progressed and even driven her to the hospital at one in the morning when her water finally broke.

He'd be forever grateful to whatever powers in the universe had put him in the right place at the right time to be the first person to hold Kai when he was born. He would never, ever forget the power of that moment. Of being able to whisper a welcome to the world even as his heart twisted in grief over missing the friend who should have been there.

Placing Kai in Tehani's arms had been the privilege of his life.

It had changed everything for him, but instead of giving in to his feelings, he'd become even more determined to keep them to himself.

He'd shifted his attention to Kai, became an expert diaper changer, an even better swaddler and an on-call babysitter. He'd even gone so far as to buy himself a selection of baby items for his own house, including a baby sling so he'd always have one handy. Now? He couldn't imagine his life without the baby boy.

Or without the boy's mother.

Upon stepping back into the office, he spotted Sydney on the phone, struggling to hold a conversation and keep a now squirming, irritable Kai securely in place.

. With the sound of Keane shuffling through boxes in the storage room, Wyatt swooped in and scooped Kai into his arms. "I've got him."

"Thanks." Sydney sighed in relief and rotated her shoulder as she headed to her desk.

Wyatt expertly extricated the infant from his aunt's hold and, tucking him into his arm, earned a toothless, drooling smile of approval.

"You're seriously earning cred as a baby whisperer," Keane told him as he carried out two clear plastic bins filled with holiday decor. "Good to know."

"Why?" Wyatt arched a brow. "You and Marella thinking about having a baby?"

Keane shrugged. "Maybe." He disappeared back into the storage room for more decorations. Wyatt was tempted to observe that they tended to overdo it with the holiday cheer, but he didn't believe that was a thing. "We'll have a whole houseful of them if Pippy has anything to say about it."

The mention of Marella's grandmother had Wyatt's heart squeezing in its usual reminder of grief. He missed his grandmother—and his grandfather—every day. His mother's parents had given him a home when his mother passed and his father had been incapable of dealing with a grieving teenager. Not only a home, but a family. A life. Everything turned around the moment he stepped foot in Nalani.

Losing them two years ago within months of each other had felt like a double kick from life, but he'd witnessed their love. After more than fifty years of marriage, they hadn't been meant to be here without one another. Tethered, his grandmother had told him frequently. In the best kind of way.

Speaking of tethered…

"I bet all these thoughts of babies is your doing, little guy," Wyatt murmured to Kai. "Once upon a time your uncle Keane couldn't even imagine having a family. Now?" Now Wyatt had the strong suspicion Keane and his wife would be filling up those empty bedrooms in their new home in short time. "I'm betting you will end up with lots of little cousins running around."

Sydney hung up, looking a bit dazed.

"What's wrong?" Wyatt asked as Keane stuck his head out of the supply room.

"That was Mano," Sydney said slowly. "Something's going on with our sponsorship for the Surfing Santa Charity Championship." She went to her desk to gather up her belongings.

"Something?" Wyatt asked as Kai squirmed in his arms.

"Don't know." Sydney frowned, looking toward the locker room. "Aimita Haoa called Tehani earlier. But Tehani would have told us if something was wrong. Especially with the event so close. Wouldn't she?"

Unless Tehani hadn't answered the phone. Wyatt kept his focus on Kai. He knew Tehani's method of dealing with emotionally fraught subjects was to avoid them as long as possible. He had no doubt even thinking about the charity event she and Remy had always attended together brought up a whole bunch of feelings she didn't want to cope with.

Perhaps that's what he'd been picking up on with her earlier.

"We need to get some more information. I'm going to head over to the Hibiscus Bay and get into it with Mano. You okay to close up the office?" she asked Keane.

"No problem," Keane confirmed. "I'm done with surfing lessons for the day, so my schedule's clear. We're going to get going on the decorating. We don't want to let the rest of Nalani beat us to it."

"Great." Sydney looked relieved. "That'd be great, thanks. And you're good with—" She gestured to Kai.

"Perfectly." Wyatt looked at the baby in his arms. "His carrier's right over there and we've got a dinner planned of sushi for me and for-mula for him." He kept a supply of Tehani's preferred formula at his place for when she couldn't feed him herself. "He can supervise us putting up the Christmas lights. Don't worry," he added at her hesitation. "You go figure out what's going on with the Surfing Santas. We'll have ourselves a guys' night, right, Kai?"

Kai blew a big spit bubble in his sleep.

"Looks like a yes to me," Keane said.

"I wonder what's going on," Wyatt mused after Sydney took off and he set Kai into his cushioned carrier. "That event's been Kona's biggest fundraiser for years."

"Mano and Sydney will get to the bottom of it," Keane said as he popped open the top bin and pulled out yet another tangled string of lights. Tehani's brother had connections all over the islands. If he couldn't get a straight answer from the charity, he was going to find one elsewhere. "Something tells me we might be here all night."

Wyatt chuckled and grabbed his own hand-ful of colorful strands. Given what other en-tanglements he found himself pondering these days, Christmas lights might just be the least of his worries.

CHAPTER TWO

"I'M SO SORRY I'm late." Tehani approached the beach-view table in the Southern Seas restaurant with a strained smile that eased when her dining companion jumped to her feet and embraced her in a warm hug that ended with a quiet squeal. Had Tehani not been in a rush, she would have stopped to take in the giant eight-foot tree in the lobby of the Hibiscus Bay along with the blue and white lights blinking happily. "These days, getting away isn't as easy as it used to be."

"Don't apologize," Maylea Hapai assured her as she stepped back and motioned for Tehani to sit. "Gave me extra time to enjoy the view. Although I have to admit I'm a little disappointed."

"In the view?" Tehani teased as she took a seat across from one of her oldest friends, a friend she had seen in person only a handful of times the past few years. College seemed an age ago but she and Maylea had been determined not to lose touch.

"Please." Maylea rolled her dark eyes and flicked a finger in the air. "Nalani never disappoints." She cast her gaze beyond the patio cordoned off for a private party, to the ocean lying just on the other side of the full-story window. The evening tide was tumbling in just loud enough for the roar to add to the restaurant's atmosphere. "I was hoping you might bring Kai with you."

"Yeah, as much as my brother adores his nephew—" Tehani adjusted the straps to her blouse "—I don't think Mano would appreciate Kai serenading the fancy dinner crowd with his overactive lungs. That said…" She reached into her purse and pulled out her cell, tapped open her photo app and handed it to her friend. "Enjoy."

"Oh." Maylea gasped and swiped through the most recent pictures. "My gosh, he's just gorgeous, T. Look at those eyes of his. And that hair!" Maylea offered that now all too familiar sympathetic head tilt. She pouted a bit. "He looks just like Remy, doesn't he?"

"Yes, he does," Tehani murmured with practiced ease. "If you have time before you head back to Maui, maybe you can stop by the house and see him in person."

"I would love that." Maylea sighed as she handed the phone back. "But I'm grabbing an early flight out in the morning. Scott's scheduled a last-minute party for New Year's Eve and he needs me to help plan it. Next time for sure, though."

"How is Scott?" Tehani sipped her ice water.

"Perfect as ever." Maylea leaned her chin in the hand that displayed the huge square-cut diamond engagement ring she'd texted a picture of to Tehani weeks ago. "We finally decided on a holiday wedding next year. You wouldn't believe all the work that goes into something even this far out."

"Sure, I would." Tehani's lips twitched. "Remy's sister is getting married New Year's Eve. I know exactly how much work's gone into that and it'll be small compared to yours." Miniscule was more like it. If there was one thing Maylea excelled at it was putting on a spectacle.

"Three hundred wedding guests." Maylea shook her head. "Can you imagine?"

"I cannot," Tehani said honestly. The last thing she'd have wanted was an event like that. Simple. Subdued. With a few friends and family members. She wouldn't have needed more than that. But Maylea had never been simple. Or subdued. "Can I assume since you're telling me all about it that I'm on the list?"

"That's why I wanted to see you in person." Maylea bounced once on her seat. "You aren't just on the list. I want you to be one of my bridesmaids. I figured asking you in person would make it harder for you to say no."

Tehani bit the inside of her cheek. Honestly, the last thing she wanted to be part of was this showstopper of a wedding, but as a perennial people pleaser, she didn't have the wherewithal to refuse. "I'd love to."

"Oh, thank goodness." Maylea heaved a sigh of relief. "Scott's family is insisting on at least six attendants. I originally thought of you for my maid of honor…" She hesitated. "But Scott's sister is really hard to say no to. I decided to let her have it. At least I know she'll throw me a spectacular bridal shower."

"There's the silver lining." Tehani tamped down on the surge of relief. She'd only met Maylea's fiancé, Scott Forrester, once since he and Maylea began a whirlwind romance a little over a year ago. Seeing her friend so blissfully happy had gone a long way to tempering the unease Tehani felt upon her and Scott's initial interaction. Suffice it to say, Scott wasn't close to the top of Tehani's favorite people list.

He was handsome and charming, but also came across as very practiced and calculating and more than a little superior. Slick was the word Tehani had come up with later. She tended to judge people on how they treated those in service jobs: the restaurant servers, hotel receptionists, cashiers. She hadn't picked up on a modicum of respect emanating from Maylea's intended. Not that Tehani's opinion mattered. She wasn't the one who was going to marry him, and while she and Maylea were still friends, it was becoming more clear with every get-together that their lives had diverged onto two very different paths.

"We have so much to catch up on." Maylea reached out and grabbed Tehani's hand for a brief moment. "I hope you don't mind that I wanted to eat here. I just love the view." She looked around to take in the holiday decorations that had gone up the day after Thanksgiving.

Southern Seas, located in the lobby of the Hibiscus Bay Resort, was the fanciest restaurant in Nalani at any time of year but with Christmas only a few weeks away, the elegant space had been transformed into a twinkling, poinsettia-laden wonderland. White, pink and red flowers lined the window ledges and baseboards while smaller plants dotted the cloth-draped tables. The solitary votives shimmering through their glass holders offset the thousands of tiny fairy lights strung overhead. Once the sun set, the entire restaurant would be cast in gorgeous flickering shadows.

"I'm more than happy to eat here," Tehani said. "I think this might be my first grown-up meal since having the baby. Aloha, Turi." Tehani greeted their server, a middle-aged man who had worked at the Hibiscus Bay for as long as Tehani could remember.

"Ah, Tehani." Turi bent down and bussed her cheeks. "So good to see you. How's the little one?"

"Perfect." Tehani used Maylea's word because it suited. "Almost sleeping through the night, thankfully."

"Good, good." Turi nodded. "You must bring him by for a visit. You know we're taking bets on how soon he's surfing those waves like his father. We're hoping he got Remy's love of the ocean."

"Well, Kai is named after it." By now her response felt well rehearsed. "I guess we'll see."

"What can I get you to drink?" Turi asked.

"Just sparkling water, please." While she was working on transitioning Kai to formula full-time, she still nursed him on occasion.

"Of course."

"Wine for me. That yummy house white?" Maylea said when he looked to her.

Turi nodded in approval.

"What specials has Hema created this evening?" Tehani asked.

"Oh!" Turi's expression brightened at the mention of his wife, the head chef of Southern Seas. "Well, she's outdone herself if I say so myself. I highly recommend the ahi tuna tartare…"

Tehani opened the menu and scanned the offerings as he went on, giving her a moment to push aside the uncomfortable emotions that still descended whenever Remy's name was mentioned. It had been nearly a year and there were times, like now, that she still felt…stuck. Mentally. Physically.

Emotionally.

She really wished she could figure out a way to fix that, but how did one get over the loss of a love that ignited at sixteen and still continued to burn, however more dimly?

At least she wasn't alone in her grief. She and Sydney had developed a kind of verbal shorthand that cut straight to the core of their unsteady emotions. They understood each other, sometimes without even saying more than a few words. Daphne, Ohana Odysseys' nature guide, had become one of her best friends and even with her new chaotic life as stepmother to two kids, provided a frequent sympathetic ear and an encouraging smile.

But it was Wyatt who had become her main confidant in the past eight months. Wyatt with his easy way of listening without judging, commenting without lecturing. And when he smiled at her, she was reminded that everything was going to be all right.

For a moment, Wyatt's face shimmered into focus ahead of Remy's, filling her with a lightness she hadn't felt in an age. Her breath caught heavy in her chest, panic shifting through her. Mentally, she struggled to keep hold of Remy, but it seemed the tighter she tried, the less clear he became.

And the brighter Wyatt glowed.

"And for you, Tehani?" Turi turned expectant eyes on her as she blinked out of her trance.

"Ah." She tried to relax her mind and swallowed her discomfort. "I'll have my usual—the lobster pasta with fennel and hearts of palm."

Turi nodded with approval. "And of course you will both save room for the *lilikoi* cheesecake, yes?"

"If we have to," Maylea sighed dramatically, then laughed as Turi left to get their drinks. "If I'm not careful I'm going to gain ten pounds before I head back to Maui. Reminds me of that first year in college when…hey." She waved a hand in front of Tehani's eyes. "Where'd you go?"

"Sorry." Tehani plastered her shaky smile

back on to her face. Maylea might be a friend, but she wasn't the type who inspired confidence when it came to discussing emotional upheaval. "Tell me all about the wedding."

"Oh." Maylea waved away the request even as her eyes glinted. "No. We don't have to talk about that. I don't want to...you know." She winced. "I don't want to make you unhappy or upset you."

"Weddings do not upset me, nor do they make me unhappy," Tehani assured her. "If anything they remind me how wonderful life is. I might not have gotten the life I wanted with Remy, but I had enough time with him that resulted in our beautiful baby boy." Now all that remained was pivoting.

After their drinks and a complimentary ahi appetizer were delivered, Maylea went full steam ahead in regaling Tehani with the wedding plans, all of which made Tehani's practical-minded head spin. There was nothing like a wedding to set the expenses to flowing. The cost of Maylea's custom-designed gown—which she was happy to share pictures of—could have paid for a significant amount of Kai's schooling. That said, the conversation did provide the benefit of making Tehani grateful for the low-key event Sydney and Theo Fairfax had planned. And gave her second, third and even fourth thoughts about agreeing to be one of Maylea's bridesmaids.

"Sounds like you're going to have your hands full getting everything arranged," Tehani said once their entrées arrived. "The invitations and seating issues alone sound daunting. I can't believe you aren't hiring a wedding planner."

"I feel like my job the last few years has been training for this day. I've spent most of my life dreaming about my wedding," Maylea said. "Not to mention I've planned dozens of weddings at Mount Lahani. I'm not trusting anyone else with this but me, and besides, Scott loves the idea of me taking care of all the details." She picked at her food, glanced at Tehani with an all too familiar spark of guilt in her eyes. "But since you brought up how busy I'm going to be… I guess it's time to admit why I'm really here."

"Because you were hungry?" Tehani teased as she bit into a succulent piece of butter-bathed lobster.

"I mean in Nalani. The hospitality conference thing was just an excuse. I mean, it's been good and fun and all that but…" Maylea sighed and set her fork down. "I'm really sorry that job didn't work out for you earlier this year."

"Don't be." Tehani shook her head to wave off her concern. "Seven months pregnant had not been the right time to make a life-changing decision like that." Her hormones had been leading the charge and they definitely hadn't been heading in the right direction.

"Well, you aren't pregnant now," Maylea hedged.

Tehani blinked. "I don't understand."

"You're right. I can't juggle all this wedding stuff and my job. And since Scott is planning on making his official announcement about running for state senate right after the wedding—"

"State senate, huh?" Tehani dropped her gaze to her food. Why was she not surprised?

"Scott's father thinks he's a shoo-in for the party's nomination, but the family's traditional, you know? Scott would prefer to have his wife at his side, working on his campaign, doing all the things—"

"You do at the resort only without being paid?" Tehani wasn't known for snark, which probably explained Maylea's look of surprise. "Sorry. I'm filterless these days. So you're going to quit your job after the wedding?"

"Oh, before. Way before." Maylea straightened in her chair and puffed her chest out with pride. "I've already submitted my resignation, effective January 15. And they've agreed to accept my recommended replacement." She paused and eyed Tehani. "You!"

Tehani's fork froze halfway to her mouth. "Me?" She blinked. "But last time—"

"That job fell through because the owners wanted to give first chance at those jobs to Maui residents who lost everything in the fires. Besides, you were massively overqualified for that position."

"Funny you didn't mention that before," Tehani observed.

"Because I was being selfish and wanted to work with one of my best friends. You totally underestimate what you're capable of, Tehani. You built Ohana alongside Remy. Heck, he couldn't have done half of what he did with the business if it hadn't been for you. And I'm sorry, but you're wasted as a secretary."

Tehani's temper caught. She always gave Maylea a long way when it came to her snobbish tendencies, but this was one comment too much. She took a deep breath, set her fork down and folded her hands in her lap. "First." She spoke slowly, deliberately, and made certain to look her friend straight in the eye. "There is absolutely nothing wrong with being an *administrative assistant*."

"Oh." Maylea jumped a little, clearly realizing she'd crossed a line. "I'm sor—"

Tehani held up her hand. "Second, if you're going to give me a title, it's office and operations manager and just to be clear, not being anything more than that has been my decision. Sydney's offered me a partnership multiple times and I've said no."

Maylea's eyes went wide with shock. "Why on earth would you do that?"

Maylea might be a great dinner companion, but she'd long ago stopped being a friend Tehani felt comfortable confiding in. Besides, she couldn't really explain why she couldn't bring herself to accept Sydney's partnership deal, let alone make it clear to anyone else. "Because," Tehani said slowly, "I've got a newborn baby, which means schedules and predictability have gone out the window. He comes first now, Maylea. And he will for a very long time. Besides, I'm happy helping run Ohana without a lot of the other responsibilities. I love the people I work with and the way we introduce the islands to our clients. We're expanding our offerings and our promotional program's been going gangbusters thanks to our new PR person."

"Marella Benoit, right?" The way Maylea dropped the name made Tehani suspect she'd been waiting just for this opportunity. "Her sister Crystal is a megastar online. Buttercup-

Doll is one of the biggest voices in the fashion and—"

"Crystal's focused more on travel now," Tehani cut Maylea off before she veered too far off the subject. "And for the record, she credits Ohana and her time in Nalani with her shift in focus, actually." A very profitable shift. Crystal and her new husband had sponsors coming out of their constantly growing portfolio.

"Oh, I know, I know." Maylea nodded. "I follow her everywhere on social media. That was something else I wanted to ask you about. Do you think there's a chance she might be open to coming to my wedding? The exposure—"

"Feel free to ask her," Tehani cut her off, refusing to be baited. "I know she checks her DMs regularly."

"Oh." Maylea frowned, clearly disappointed. "Sorry. I thought you two were friends. Is there any chance you could ask her? Maybe put in a good word for me?"

"I know Crystal," Tehani clarified slowly. "I wouldn't say we're friends." Irritation scraped along her nerves. "Is that the real reason for dinner tonight? Because you want me to get you close to Crystal Benoit?" Blast it. Wyatt had been right, hadn't he?

"Don't be silly." But Maylea's laugh sounded strained. "It was just a spur-of-the-moment idea is all. Truly." Maylea shifted in her seat and drank a good amount of wine. "Let's forget about Crystal and talk about who you might bring as your date."

"Considering I only said yes to being a bridesmaid a few minutes ago, I haven't given it much thought." Where on earth was this conversation headed?

"Maybe you don't have to. Three of Scott's groomsmen are single and they're all drop-dead gorgeous. One of them's even a doctor. I'll send you some pictures and you can tell me which one—"

"I'm not going to play spin the bachelor at your wedding, May."

"Why not?" Maylea looked truly perplexed. "I mean, you're single again what with Remy being out of the picture—"

"Remy *died*, May. He died," Tehani repeated as her skin went clammy. "He didn't move to another country or take off with his administrative assistant. He died."

"Right." Maylea blinked quickly, then cringed as if realizing she'd gone too far. "Wow. That was just so… I'm sorry, Tehani. Really sorry. I seem to be making a complete mess of things tonight."

Tehani pursed her lips and chose her words carefully. "It's funny. I knew we were different, but I always believed there was at least some mutual respect between us. Remy isn't someone I can just forget existed, Maylea. We were together for eleven years. We might not have been married—" and things might not have been great between them at the end "—but that doesn't mean our relationship wasn't important. Or that I can just pick up and move on with someone new. I'm raising his son." A strange cyclone of uncertainty took root in her stomach. "Remy's not replaceable, May."

"Of course not." Maylea ducked her head. "Once again, my words got ahead of my brain. My head's just all over the place with the engagement and the wedding and my job… But that's no excuse. I'm sorry, T."

Tehani nodded, unable to come up with any words to reassure her friend. "Accepted."

"I know I'm difficult," Maylea said. "I know I'm obnoxious and trying to do better a lot of the time. I don't mean to be, it's just…" She shrugged. "I'm just a lot to take. I need at least one friend I can trust. Please don't give up on me."

Despite the temptation to do just that, it wasn't in Tehani's DNA to turn her back on anyone. Not even someone who apparently looked down on Tehani's entire life. "I'm not going to give up on you, May. Not tonight at least." She attempted to make a joke.

"I guess this is why I don't have a lot of friends," Maylea admitted quietly. "Or Ohana. I'm sorry if I upset you by pushing you to move to Maui or to start dating again. I'm just so happy, I guess I want everyone else I know to be this happy, too. That said—" she paused "—sometimes I feel like I'm spinning and I can't stop. Then I'm afraid if I do stop, everything will fall apart."

"I'll get over it. But as far as the job or you setting me up with a date?" She shook her head. "I don't need any of that. I won't lie. It's rough doing this mom thing without Remy, but I've got an incredible support system here and there's no way I'm going to take my son away from that. I'll assume your job offer came from a good place, but I won't be accepting it and I do not want to be fixed up with anyone." She pinned Maylea with a determined look. "I'll understand if that changes things and you'd rather I not be one of your bridesmaids."

"But you have to be." Maylea shot forward in her seat again, that strange panic filling her gaze. "I need you to be in the wedding." Whatever mask she'd been wearing until this moment slipped and tears filled her eyes. "I know I haven't been as good a friend as I should have been, and okay, tonight I've been beyond obnoxious, but you've always been someone I look up to. Someone who's always had it all together."

Tehani gaped and snorted. "Please."

"No, seriously," Maylea insisted. "Everything's always come so easily for you, but I feel like I've had to claw my way to where I am. Sometimes it just feels impossible to hold on."

Everything came easy for her? It was like they were having two different conversations. Unlike Wyatt, Maylea clearly didn't listen. "Maybe you're trying too hard."

"Maybe." Maylea didn't sound convinced. "You've always been the one person I could count on. I need that now. Maybe more than ever."

It was the desperation in her voice that had Tehani's anger abating. Mainly because she couldn't shake the feeling something more, something deeper, was going on beyond bridezilla behavior and wedding jitters. "Do you really love Scott, Maylea? Like to your marrow love him? Is this marriage really what you want?"

Maylea nodded. "He's what I've been looking for all my life."

That didn't exactly sound like an answer. As sour as she felt toward Maylea at the moment, it was clear her friend needed someone in her corner. "All right then. So let's focus on you and your wedding and stop trying to change my life. If you can promise me that—"

"I can," Maylea insisted. "I absolutely can!"

"All right then." Tehani took a deep breath and reached for her water. "I'm still in."

"You are?" Maylea's mood lifted.

"Someone has to keep your head on straight." She'd probably regret it, but she didn't want to be the type of friend she accused Maylea of being. Besides, the wedding was a full year away. A lot of things could happen between now and then. "Why don't you fill me in on my bridesmaid duties and we'll go from there." She signaled Turi and asked him to refill their bread basket.

Something told her she was going to need all the carbs she could get.

CHAPTER THREE

WYATT HEAVED OUT a sigh. Watching the sun set with Kai but without Kai's mother left a lot to be desired. Instead of commenting on the colors and reminiscing about their day, Kai was far more interested in trying to shove the entirety of his stuffed octopus into his drooling mouth.

A Technicolor sky, apparently, held little appeal to a two-month-old. Especially when Christmas lights were strung on nearly every house in sight.

Perched on the top step of Tehani's porch, Wyatt situated Kai's carrier against the porch post and tugged the hem of the green hand-knitted cap down on the baby's head.

"Bah bah bah."

"You said it, dude." Wyatt leaned back on his elbows, perfectly willing to agree with whatever brilliant pronouncement Kai had just made. While he had yet to discover his hands, the kid was a championship chewer.

As the last of the color vanished behind the wall of dark sky, another day slipped into the past and tomorrow's adventures presented themselves as bright and promising.

"I bet you're going to take your mom on all kinds of adventures, aren't you, Kai?" He reached over to where Kai sat in his carrier, rested a hand against the baby's chest. The gurgling, amused noises the baby made were a new kind of soundtrack Wyatt had found himself favoring as of late. "Don't worry. She'll be home soon."

Wyatt had always made it a point to maintain a distance between being Tehani's friend and unofficial guardian. He wasn't responsible for her; she'd be offended at the very thought. But he was her friend and friends watched out for one another. He knew the effect Maylea tended to have on Tehani. He'd witnessed it often enough over the years. But today had been the first time he'd said something out loud about it.

Whether that was a mistake or not remained to be seen.

Maylea was the woman who seemingly had it all with her fancy job, rich partner and upscale life far removed from the small town of Nalani. She was sparkle and glitz and while Wyatt didn't know her particularly well, she'd often struck him as someone who never quite lived in the reality others did despite her trying desperately to fit in.

So yeah, Wyatt was concerned about the mood Tehani would be in when she got home. It was that concern, he told himself, and nothing else that had him waiting out here. But if the temperature dropped another two or three degrees he was going to use his key and get Kai settled into his crib for the night. He knew how much joy Tehani took in putting her son to bed, but he didn't want to take the chance on the little guy catching a chill or staying awake too far past his bedtime. Especially since he was so close to a regular sleeping schedule.

As the stars popped out against the blackening sky, Wyatt leaned his head close to Kai's as he pointed up. "First star, Kai. You want to make a wish?" He felt the warmth of the infant's skin against his cheek. Not for the first time, he found himself caught in that emotional trap between heartache and joy.

Joy that he was a part of this baby's life.

The heartache came when he was reminded that his best friend, Kai's father, would never be witness to the tiny miracles Kai created every day.

Wyatt's heart constricted in the all too familiar sensation of loss. Remy had often talked of his dream about being a father, but it was always in reference to the future. He had plenty of time, Remy had always joked. Plenty of time to start a family.

In the end, he'd been wrong and Wyatt had been left behind to wonder if he'd missed the signs of his friend's illness. Had there been something he should have seen, something he'd missed, a step he could have taken to prevent his friend's death?

He'd never know and those questions haunted him to the point of bringing back painful memories of having been left behind.

Only with Remy, the pain seemed so much more profound—probably because Remy, unlike most of Wyatt's other family members, had been such a positive influence in his life. How different his life would have been had he not met Remy on his first day of school in Nalani. Remy had, from day one, been a kind of safety net for when things went wrong.

And now he was gone as well.

"I can hear you thinking all the way out here."

He hadn't noticed Tehani approaching. She made her way down the stone steps to her cozy little house that was a near duplicate of his own next door, her smile brighter than the solar lights lining her walk. With only a small courtyard separating their houses, there was never much distance between them.

But it wasn't distance that was foremost in Wyatt's mind at the moment. It was the entertaining view of Tehani coming toward him, a relaxed smile on her face.

"You look happy." *And beautiful. So beautiful.*

"This, my friend, is me feeling grateful. Oh, so very grateful."

The moon shone down on her, her black hair glistening like high polished obsidian. Thoughts he should never have of his best friend's girl circled inside his mind. Thoughts he couldn't quite reconcile nor deem acceptable and yet…

Tehani had always been striking—the personification of an island princess—with her soft curves, long, long hair and dark eyes that seemed to have the power to see into a person's soul. Her smile could wield more power than the sun at its zenith, and the way her full lips curved when she was amused or happy simply made his heart sing.

But now that she was a mother? He didn't think there was a more beautiful person in the world.

"Grateful for anything in particular?" he asked as she sat beside him.

"That I'm me. That I'm here, with you and

Sydney and Keane and…everyone." She took a long, deep breath and closed her eyes. "And that I am not like Maylea, jumping through hoops to make her life seemingly perfect."

He could feel the warmth of her body radiating against his bare arm. It triggered an ache so deep inside him he had to bite back a groan of pain.

She reached across him to touch her fingers to Kai's head. Her baby looked up at her and his face broke into the biggest, most brilliant smile imaginable. "Hi, *mae-mae*. I missed you."

"Did you walk all the way home?" Wyatt asked.

"Yes, I did." She dropped a finger on Kai's round nose. "I wanted to take my time and enjoy Nalani in the quiet." With her leaning across him, he could smell the fragrance of her shampoo. "It's the perfect night for stargazing," she noted.

Any night in Nalani was, Wyatt thought. He'd spent what felt like half his life with his head in the stars. Out there, everything seemed possible. Whatever problems he had lost importance beneath their twinkling brightness. "So?" He had a pretty strong suspicion what the answer was going to be, but he asked anyway. "How was your dinner with Maylea?"

"*Dinner* was delicious." Irritation flashed in

her dark eyes. "I'm sad to say you were one hundred percent right. My *friend* definitely wanted something."

He leaned back and decided not to take any pleasure in this admission. There were times he loathed being right. "She hit you with another job offer, didn't she?"

"With both barrels." Tehani sighed. "She also asked me to be one of her bridesmaids."

"Did she?" It was one more thing that didn't come as a surprise. "What did you tell her?"

"What do you think?" she grumbled miserably.

Wyatt resisted the urge to tuck a loose strand of her hair behind her ear. "I think you're a nice person and you couldn't bring yourself to say no."

"Guilty as charged." She stared at him for a few beats before glancing away. "She tried to fix me up with one of the groomsmen. A doctor, I think. But that wasn't even the worst part."

Given the way his heart skipped a beat, it sounded like the worst part to him.

"I'm pretty sure she only asked me to be her bridesmaid because of Marella's sister."

"Crystal?" For the life of him, he couldn't piece those two bits of information together. "Why on earth—"

"Maylea would like Crystal to come to her

wedding," Tehani said. "Probably assumes if she does, then the entire event will go viral."

"Yeah, well." Wyatt shrugged. "That's not a bad assumption to make. Crystal does have a gift when it comes to social media. The video she made of the dinner cruise went viral. Keane's got bookings from now until the end of time thanks to her." Wyatt rubbed Tehani's back. None of this came as any surprise, either, but oh, how he wished he'd been wrong. "What did you say to that?"

"I told May to ask Crystal herself."

"Did you?"

Tehani nudged him with her shoulder. "Don't sound so surprised."

"What about the doctor?" Had he really just asked about that?

"I told her to cut out the matchmaking. I let her know I'm happy with my life just as it is and that I don't need a man to make it better."

Wyatt nodded slowly and smiled in relief. "Well, good for you."

"You know what? There's something...I don't know, maybe energizing about standing up for myself? It felt good establishing boundaries."

"It usually does," Wyatt agreed.

That spark in her gaze faded and she sagged a bit. "She's really hard to be friends with, Wyatt. Even she admits it."

"Self-awareness is always a good thing."

Tehani grinned. "You're so nice." She scooted closer and rested her head on his shoulder more comfortably. "Even now, you have every right to say I told you so but you don't. You just smile and nod and stay nice."

"It's my default setting." He'd learned a long time ago that getting angry or upset or even triumphant or petulant didn't bring anything other than misery. But it also meant he frequently didn't get everything he wanted. "Any other revelations occur to you on your walk home?"

"A few. May's marrying a jerk."

"This is my shocked face." Which it wasn't.

She laughed and brightened his evening even more. "I swallowed that observation with my dinner and most of our dessert. I should have brought you home some leftovers. Sorry about that."

"I picked up sushi at Luanda's." The main market on Pulelehua Road was a one-stop shop for residents and tourists alike; everything one might need from beach-friendly clothing and surfing equipment to a phenomenal selection of island delicacies. Even freshly made sushi could be found there. "Kai on the other hand stuck to his bottle since he can't have raw fish until he's at least five."

"You've been reading that new parenting blog again, haven't you?"

He smiled. "Maybe."

"Is there anything you don't know?"

"Tons." Like how to tamp down on feelings for this incredible woman who should be off-limits. Like how to maneuver around his desired romantic relationship with someone who had become his best friend?

"Do you know I have secrets?"

Wyatt's stomach twisted. "We all have secrets, Tehani."

"I bet you can't guess mine." The smile that spread across her mouth felt like a punch to his solar plexus. She smelled like honeysuckle and summer and the promise of everything he could never have. "No. Don't try to guess." She held a finger up to his lips and nearly short-circuited his brain. "I'll show you."

She leaned forward, just a little bit, tilted her chin up and kissed him.

Firm, determined, tempting. She sat up a bit straighter, lifted her arms and rested her hands on his shoulders, her lips clinging to his. Wyatt froze. There wasn't a part of him that wasn't on full alert. His hands flexed at his sides before he rested them on her waist and stared into her eyes. Eyes that went wide as she shifted closer and he resisted the overwhelming desire to take the kiss deeper.

"Tehani," he murmured as her mouth softened and she let out a soft gasp. "What are you doing?"

She blinked as if coming out of a trance. "Probably making a mess of things." She sat back and looked at him with questions in her eyes. "I shouldn't have done that, should I?" Instant regret shone at him. "Oh, jeez. Why do I mess everything up?"

"You haven't messed anything up, T." His heart swelled. He caught her hand in his, turned it over and pressed his mouth to her knuckles. Before mentally taking a step back. "I think Kai's ready for bed." He forced himself to look at the baby. "You have your key?"

"Yes, I do." She dug into her purse, standing up and moving away from him at near lightning speed. "Can't believe I did that. I'm going to blame May. She got me all twisted around. I think I need some coffee. And sugar. You want some?"

"Sugar?"

She finally looked at him again.

"Sorry," he laughed. He wasn't entirely sure why he was enjoying this moment, but he couldn't recall the last time he'd seen Tehani frazzled. Kissing him had frazzled her.

This might just be the best night of his life.

"Go ahead and brew the coffee," he suggested as he followed her inside. "I'm going to get Kai settled in his crib."

"Okay." She practically bolted into the kitchen as Wyatt headed for the nursery, wanting, needing to put some distance between them so his head—and heart—would stop spinning.

The layout of the bungalow was nearly identical to his, but with a larger, open kitchen. It was a change he intended to make in his own house as, like Tehani, he wasn't a fan of walls or feeling boxed in. Too many walls made him feel claustrophobic and he definitely had too many walls in his life.

"You ready for bed, Kai?" Once in the nursery, he set the carrier on the floor beside the changing table and quickly retrieved a clean set of footed pajamas from the tall dresser painted with a wood-grained effect that made it look like a tree. He could hear Tehani singing to herself at the other end of the house and for a moment, he was back on the porch, feeling her mouth against his.

He'd wondered for far too long what it might be like to kiss her. To hold her. And now that he had, he was faced with a new truth: the fantasy of her hadn't come close to the reality.

His insides were buzzing as if she'd awoken

something inside of him. Something he'd been perfectly happy to keep dormant.

"Your mama doesn't know it, but she just gave me a gift," he told the giggling baby as he quickly changed Kai's diaper and snapped him into his sleeper. "Time to hit dreamland." He rested his hand on Kai's chest, gave him a bit of a jiggle, and earned a series of kicks and baps from the baby's hands. "Okay, let's get you into bed." He scooped up Kai, cradled him against his chest and turned to the crib.

It still surprised him that Tehani had veered away from a full-on ocean theme for the nursery and opted for a more rainforest feel. There were still water elements, but the space definitely felt more like Tehani than Remy, who had practically been born riding the waves.

While Remy's ancestry wasn't Hawaiian, he had been born in Nalani after his parents moved here shortly after getting married. Remy and his younger sister, Sydney, had grown up in this town; they knew every inch of it almost from the time they could walk and, while Sydney thrived in the sky as a pilot, Remy's talent in the water had been second to none. He could have turned professional, like Keane Harper had attempted, but Remy's love for this town had kept him grounded and determined to make the most of the island.

With varying hues of green against a pale blue sky on the walls—courtesy of a local artist who earned quite a good living selling Nalani landscapes to tourists and residents alike—standing in Kai's nursery was a bit like stepping into a floral paradise replete with various native animals and insects sneakily painted into the scene. And on the windowsill, created in 3D, were painted images of Noodles and Zilla, two island geckos who lived in one of the guest cottages owned by Ohana Odysseys.

The ivory-colored crib was accented with forest-toned coverings and bumpers. The rocking chair in the corner sat beside a small bookshelf filled to overflowing with storybooks and framed photos, including a few of Remy and Remy's late parents, Kai's grandparents.

But it was the group shot taken only a few months ago at Daphne and Griffin Townsend's wedding that maintained a special place in Wyatt's heart. Their happy gang of friends surrounded Daphne and Griffin—Griffin's two children, Sydney and her fiancé, Theo, Keane and his wife, Marella, Tehani and her brother, Mano, the sheriff Alec Malloy along with his surfer girlfriend, Jordan Adair, and Wyatt—toasting the happy couple with sparkling champagne, their glasses raised in the air.

Wyatt's irrational fear that he'd somehow be

left out after Remy died had never fully materialized. With or without his friend, Wyatt felt included and that, he'd quickly accepted, had been the real present Remy had given him. Family. Ohana.

Remy's death had bonded them all in a way they'd never been before. If there was anything good to come out of losing Remy, that had been it, without any doubt.

Kai babbled and kicked as Wyatt set him on the mattress, his peddling feet finally slowing a little. He clicked on the overhead mobile and set the birds silently soaring through the nursery sky while a favorite island lullaby plinked softly. There wasn't a place in Wyatt's heart that wasn't occupied by this little guy. His love for him had been instant, tempered only by Wyatt's determination to remember that Kai was not his.

Neither was Tehani.

Wyatt waited for Kai to focus on the mobile before he stepped away. He clicked on the nightlight, double-checked the baby monitor light and quietly backed out of the room, switching off the overhead light and leaving the door slightly ajar.

He found her rummaging through the refrigerator. "He went down perfectly."

Tehani stepped back, a glass container in

her hands, a giant cookie sticking out of her mouth. She nudged the fridge door closed with her hip and spun, freezing when she saw him standing on the other side of the counter. She bit through the cookie and let it drop onto the container, chewing and swallowing quickly. "Great. Thank you." She reached into the container and pulled another cookie out to offer it to him. "I call these crisis cookies." She handed him a large white chocolate macadamia nut cookie. "Want one?"

"Thanks." He had to admit, her taste in cookies was second to none. The play of brown sugar against the sweetness of the white chocolate and crunch of roasted nuts was perfection.

She took another bite of hers but didn't close the container up, as if she wasn't quite done with it yet. "I'm really sorry," she mumbled.

"What for?"

She arched a brow. "We aren't going to talk about me…?" She pointed to the door, and the porch that lay beyond. "You know… What I… Okay." She held up a hand in surrender. "You don't want to talk about it—"

"There's no reason to be embarrassed, Tehani. I told you—no harm done." Pushing his disappointment aside, he walked over and sat on her sofa, then watched as she joined him but sat in the flowered upholstered chair across from him. "But considering you want to blame Maylea for it, did something else happen tonight with her?"

She waved off the suggestion. "Not really." But there was something. He could see uncertainty lurking behind her eyes. "I think I'm feeling guilty."

"Hence the cookie?" Wyatt resisted the urge to ask for clarification.

"Hence a lot of things." She kicked her bare legs up over the arm of the chair.

"Do you want to tell me what you're feeling guilty about?" Wyatt recognized someone needing to be nudged.

"Not really." She ate more cookie, still avoiding his gaze. "But I'm afraid if I don't tell someone I'm going to end up eating an entire batch of these things." She took a deep breath. "I told you all that Maylea offered me a job in Maui earlier this year. What I didn't tell you—" she hesitated "—was that I accepted it."

Wyatt's stomach dropped straight to his toes. He'd suspected as much, but the confirmation felt like actual pain.

"I was…" she went on. "Sometimes, I still feel like I'm floundering, you know? Like everything around me is spinning out of control and I can't make it stop. Taking the job calmed things down. Gave me something different to focus on. For a while, at least."

He broke off a chunk of cookie, if only to give himself something to do. He wished what she was telling him was a surprise, but it actually made sense and confirmed his nagging suspicion she was dealing with something she didn't want to talk about these last few months. "What changed your mind?"

"Nothing." She stared into her lap. "They rescinded the offer after the fires in Maui. They decided to hold the job for a local who needed the work. I didn't anticipate how relieved I was going to feel when they called, but it took until then for me to realize what a huge mistake I'd be making if I left Nalani. If I left all of you."

He couldn't quite reconcile the emotions swarming inside of him. "I'm sorry you didn't think you could come to us. To me. I thought—"

"It was a panic move," Tehani said quietly. "I was embarrassed I let it get that far. I don't know... I don't know if I can explain it well."

"Try," he urged. "No judgment, T." Never any judgment.

"Okay." She seemed to pull her thoughts together and shifted in her chair. "Let's take tonight. After dinner. With everything that Maylea and I discussed, I just wanted to get out and clear my head. Just go for a walk, sit at the marina and enjoy the lights. It's always so beautiful during the holidays, with twinkling lights on the railings and even on most of the masts of the boats. But…" She frowned, the cookie forgotten in her hands. "Instead, all I could think about was the last time Remy and I went out sailing. It was like I could see us, walking down the gangplank to the catamaran, replaying each moment of that day." She leaned her head back, tears sparkling in her eyes.

"That happens all the time, Wyatt. I loved Remy. I always will. But how can I move on when he's everywhere I look? Every part of my life was tied up in his and now that he's gone… I don't think I know who I am. Everywhere I go—shopping, the beach, even just getting a stupid shave ice from Seas & Breeze—I see Remy or a memory of the two of us together. It's him or it's us and it's never…" She took a shuddering breath and looked into Wyatt's gaze. "It's never me. I think part of me thought that if I could start over somewhere new, some-place that didn't have many memories of him, I could finally find myself. If for no other reason than to make certain Kai has a solid footing in life. But that's selfish. I can't take him away from the one place his father loved, but I have to be secure in myself if he's going to thrive. Please tell me that makes sense."

"Of course it does." It made entirely too much sense.

"You're not just saying that because you're a nice guy?" Tehani challenged.

"I'd never lie to you, Tehani." Right now, secrets didn't count. "It absolutely makes sense." He'd arrived in Nalani around the time Remy had discovered Mano's little sister was more than an irritating tagalong. Barely sixteen and scrambling to survive emotionally. With his mother gone and having been left with a father Wyatt constantly struggled to connect to, he'd landed on the island as if he were starting over. He'd been done the instant he'd spotted her. His new best friend's girl. But he'd been included in every sense and therefore content with friendship from those in Remy's circle. Including Tehani.

He'd watched her and Remy's love for one another bloom and witnessed them change and grow. All from the sidelines. But Remy's powerful personality had the tendency to overwhelm everyone around him. It had happened to Wyatt. Of course it would have had the same effect on Tehani.

"I guess we found something good that came out of the Maui fires," he said quietly. "They stopped you from leaving."

Her smile was quick. "I don't think Sydney

or Keane or Daphne would be quite so under-standing if they knew the truth. Something tells me they'd all be ticked I made that decision without talking to them."

"I think they'd be more disappointed you didn't feel you could talk to them about it in the first place." He should know. "You don't have anything to feel guilty about," he assured her. "At the time you thought you were doing what was best for you and for Kai. The last year has been pretty hard on all of us. We've had to do what was necessary to protect ourselves. No one can blame you for that." He stopped, choosing his next words carefully. "What about to-night? Were you tempted by her new job offer?"

She shrugged. "The job itself sounds pretty amazing, but then I realized she wasn't offering it to me because of me. She needs someone to step in because she wants to quit to get married. As soon as I figured that out, I knew I wasn't going to take it. She called me a glorified sec-retary." Tehani ate more of her cookie. "I mean, there's absolutely nothing wrong with—"

"Doesn't matter what name you put on your job, Ohana Odysseys would fall apart without you," Wyatt said without hesitation. He'd never met anyone with the organizational skills and controlled temperament to keep dozens of cus-tomers and tours on track for months at a time.

"Jordan managed pretty well while you were gone, but..."

"But what?"

Wyatt considered Jordan Adair, Ohana's most recent hire and a good friend. She was fun and funny, impulsive and entertaining, and she always found the bright side of things. That said? "Jordan's too much like Keane. She's got her head in the waves most of the time. She managed. They all did." Because they knew Tehani was coming back. He frowned, thinking on something she'd said. "Is this why you haven't accepted Sydney's offer to become a full partner in Ohana? Is it because the business is tied too closely to Remy?"

"I don't know." She rubbed a hand across her stomach. "It's just that every time she brings it up I feel sick and that tells me it's not the right move. I'm content where I am, Wyatt. For now, at least. I know this is where I belong even if I don't necessarily know where I fit in." She finished her cookie, slapped her hands together and shoved to her feet. "Listen to me. I think tonight's main takeaway should be I was right to keep this to myself."

Wyatt shook his head. "Sometimes you can't work this stuff out on your own. Sometimes it takes friends."

"Remy did that for you, didn't he?" Tehani's

question caught him off guard. "That day you met in school. He brought you home that night for dinner, pretty much locked on to you and dragged you out of yourself."

"Pretty much," Wyatt agreed. "He was most definitely a force to be reckoned with."

"It would just be nice…" She aimed a pointed look at him. "To be able to start over without having to…start over." She shook her head, then covered her face with her hands. "Ugh. I can't believe I'm going to have to be a bridesmaid next year in that wedding!"

As Wyatt himself was a master at avoidance, he fell in line with her changing the subject. "Do you think Maylea will make you wear neon-pink taffeta?"

"You really need to stop binge-watching old sitcoms." Tehani's soft laugh shifted them back on track. "But you bring up a good point. Knowing Maylea, it's going to be classy, which means expensive. I should probably start budgeting for that. Thank you for the reminder."

He stood, brushed the crumbs off his shirt and followed her into the kitchen. "You're welcome."

"No, I mean it." She turned and apparently didn't expect to find him quite so close. She lifted a hand to his chest and tilted her head up. "You're always such a stand-up guy. You took care of Kai for me tonight, you listened to me complain and then put up with my stupid kiss—"

He lowered his mouth to hers, stopping whatever regretful protest lurked behind her lips. Wyatt wasn't a man prone to taking chances, but sometimes life didn't leave him any other choice. Her kissing him had been one thing, a surprising thing, but now he kissed her the way he'd always dreamed of kissing her.

When he broke contact, he rested his forehead against hers, kept his eyes closed for fear of seeing doubt or even rejection in hers. "There's nothing stupid about a kiss," he whispered. "And before you think that to death, that was me evening the score. Now." He ran his hands up and down her arms. "I'm going to head out before either one of us overthinks this." A small, hopeful smile curved his lips. "Good night, Tehani."

"Yeah," she whispered as he walked out her front door. "Good night, Wyatt."

CHAPTER FOUR

ELBOWS RESTING ON the kitchen counter, head in her hands, Tehani focused on taking deep, calming breaths. Her current muddled state and general confusion should have been the result of too much wine. Instead, it was filled with too many thoughts of Wyatt Jenkins.

She'd crossed a line and, last night, on complete impulse, kissed her best friend. She groaned, feeling guilty and regretful. She didn't want to believe she had made a mess of one of the best relationships in her life.

She rocked back on her heels. "Except then he kissed you." And that kiss had blown the one she'd given him out of the water like a depth charge.

Wowza. When Wyatt put his mind to it, that man could kiss! Her face went hot at the memory.

What was she supposed to do now? What would happen when she saw him again? Would they talk about it? Try it again just to confirm the sparks weren't a fluke? She shot up straight and blinked into the brightness of her kitchen at sunrise. Maybe that was just her. Maybe she'd been so far off-kilter that she'd have felt sparks with one of Haki's *Menehunes*?

At least the passing thought of Haki hunting down one of the islands' most infamous invisible tricksters took the pressure off. If only she could think of *Menehunes* all day long instead of worrying about what would happen the next time she saw Wyatt.

She'd come to rely on him for so much—most importantly an objective ear. She hadn't realized how much she'd needed to be listened to or how completely present he always was with her. He…appreciated her. Liked her even. She caught her lower lip in her teeth. Maybe…

She jumped at the sharp knock on her door. She could see Wyatt's outline on the other side of the drawn curtain. Barefoot, hands twisting together, she hurried across the floor and pulled open the door. Her voice cracked when she said, "Hi."

"Hi, yourself." Wyatt pushed past her and strode inside, then turned and offered a bright pink box as a gift. "Thought you could use a pick-me-up this morning. Fresh off Maru's cart." He waggled the box and his eyebrows. "I got your favorite. Pineapple custard."

In the background, the coffee machine spat and sputtered, spreading the caffeine-laden aroma throughout the house.

She accepted the box even as her stomach reminded her of all the cookies she'd eaten before she'd crashed into bed. "Thanks." She waited a beat. "Coffee?"

"Absolutely. Hey, Kai."

While she retreated into the kitchen, Wyatt went over to the stuffie-filled playpen, leaned over and tweaked Kai's footed-pajama-covered toes. Kai squealed, kicked his feet and waved his hands as Tehani poured Wyatt's coffee and pried open the bakery box.

"My savior." She inhaled deeply. The aroma of fresh fried dough jump-started her system. She plucked up one of the plump malasadas and bit in. The mix of tangy pineapple and sweet crunchy sugar melted on her tongue.

Wyatt glanced at her over his shoulder, his gaze dropping to her lips as she licked the crumbs off. Her face warmed as he asked, "He sleep through the night?"

"Depends on your definition of night." She flipped the open box around as he approached and he reached in to grab a malasada of his own. "He was up at four, so we're still working on figuring out what constitutes morning." She poured Wyatt some coffee, slid the mug across the counter to him, and shook her head in mild disbelief as he added cream and then three sugars. What was the point of diluting coffee, especially *Kona* coffee, like that?

"Four a.m., huh?" Wyatt grinned and shook his head. "That's just mean."

If only she could blame Kai for her lack of sleep. Nor was it her stressful dinner with Maylea. Nope. Her inability to rest at night had everything to do with this man and the unexpected pair of kisses they'd impulsively shared.

She took another bite of her breakfast, eyeing a fresh-faced Wyatt. "You're looking bright-eyed this morning." Clearly he hadn't suffered the same aftereffects of their kisses that she had.

If there was ever a better example of the perfect boy next door with that charming, eye-twinkling smile permanently etched on his round face, she certainly hadn't seen it. She could smell soap and sawdust drifting off his skin, a telling combination that she appreciated more every time he was near. His damp mass of dark brown curls made her fingers itch, an impulse she tried to stop by flexing her hands. This new awareness of him made her feel uncomfortable and a bit panicked. She didn't need any more challenges or changes in her life!

"I take it you got your full eight hours," she accused him over the rim of her mug. She couldn't decide whether she should be irritated or relieved that he hadn't brought up last night.

"Only my usual six." Wyatt beamed at her absently before he turned his attention back to Kai. "You feed him yet?"

"I was just about to. Bottle's in the microwave." She waved behind her. "Feel free."

"Cool." He glanced over his shoulder as he retrieved the bottle.

As much as she'd wanted to breastfeed exclusively, it had become obvious shortly after Kai's birth that he was going to need additional nutrition. She still fed him a few times a week, but they were gradually moving toward a full formula routine. Besides, he gobbled down his formula like a champion and he'd gained almost four pounds since his birth. Clearly her son wasn't suffering any caloric deficit.

"Since you're still in tortoise mode," Wyatt said as he reheated the bottle, "I take it you haven't checked your cell phone lately."

"Hmm?" Eyes closed, she hummed a bit over the rim of her coffee mug. The sugar was definitely starting to kick in. Her head was beginning to clear. "My cell? No. I turned it off when I got home. Why?"

"Sydney sent out an SOS around ten last night."

"She did?" Tehani sighed and turned to grab her cell off the charging station on the back counter. "Is everything okay?"

"She's called an emergency Ohana meeting at her place before work. Asked me to come, too, so it must be something big."

"Man." She waited for the phone to power back up. Her stomach sank when she read the message. "The meeting starts in less than an hour."

"Go take a shower and get dressed," Wyatt said as he pulled out the warmed bottle. "I'll feed him and get him ready."

"Yeah?" She sighed in relief. "You don't have a job to get to this morning?" She knew his handyman business kept him busy.

"I'm installing some shower bars in Benji's bathroom today, then I'm helping him decorate his golf cart."

Tehani smiled. "What's this year's theme?" Benji, one of Nalani's most popular senior citizens, along with pretty much everyone else, jazzed up his vehicle for the holidays.

"He's keeping it a secret," Wyatt said. "But

word at Luanda's is he's bought up every Christmas flamingo they had in stock."

"Flamingos." Her smile shifted into a laugh. "That ought to be amusing. Good luck."

"Thanks. Other than that, I just have to stop at The Hawaiian Snuggler and install some shelving in Shani's storage room. She is expecting an influx of quilts for the holidays." Wyatt flashed a quick smile. "No set schedule, though. Here you go, Kai." He scooped Kai up and, cradling him gently in one arm, tipped the bottle into the baby's mouth and earned a drooling grin of thanks in return.

Tehani's heart all but took flight. She had to remind herself to breathe. He was so, so good with her son. She touched a hand to her chest and blinked back tears.

"Seriously, go get ready for work, T. Do you care what he wears?" he asked as she headed into her room, coffee and donut in hand.

"Ah." She stopped, tried to recall what day it was. "The dolphin outfit. That reminds me, I told Delaney I'd stop by Luau Lullabies sometime next week so she could take a picture of him in it for their website."

"You taking up modeling, little man?" Wyatt teased. "Look at you already earning your keep."

"Yeah, well, Delaney gives me a great discount, which will come in handy since it looks like he's going to outgrow his latest newborn size in the next week." Even before she'd gotten pregnant, Tehani had long admired her high school friend's eco-friendly baby and toddler clothing creations. In the hopes of supporting Delaney and other local businesses, Tehani purposely hadn't registered anywhere for her shower and instead asked everyone to shop local and Big Island small. She'd also taken her time meticulously filling Kai's nursery with Hawaiian-produced products that added to the island economy.

A fond smile curved her lips as she thought of the dinners she and Wyatt had shared while he'd assembled said furniture for her. Wyatt Jenkins was a magic man when it came to easing her heart and making her smile and once again, she found herself filled with gratitude that their friendship was as solid as it was. And she'd stupidly put it all at risk by kissing him.

She inclined her head, watching Wyatt attempt to keep the bottle steady for Kai while he reached back blindly for the last of his malasada.

Or had she?

On that thought, she retreated into her bedroom and closed the door.

She made quick work of the shower and did

her best to drag a comb through her tangled hair. When she emerged, fully awake, she stopped short. The sight of a shirtless Wyatt strapping a changed and dressed Kai into his carrier had made her jaw drop.

"Um." She'd seen a half-dressed Wyatt hundreds of times over the years. In bathing suits, for a start. No big deal. They'd practically lived on the beach during their summers and surfing was always a way of life in Nalani. Board shorts and wet suits were everyday wear in Hawai'i. Avoiding his gaze, she quickly headed to the sink and let out a slow, deliberate breath. What on earth was happening to her?

But the truth was that the sight of Wyatt at this particular moment, with him caring so beautifully for her son, flipped a previously unidentified switch inside of her and left her fighting a deep sense of longing for the man. "Everything, um, everything okay?" she choked out.

"Oh, yeah." Wyatt turned his telltale grin on her. "He missed the burping rag. The second I started to pat his back he let me know how much he appreciated his breakfast."

"He is a champion spitter-upper," Tehani confirmed.

Wyatt carried his coffee mug over to the sink, washed both his and hers, and set them in the rack. His dark green board shorts hung low on his waist, exposing those toned hip muscles and the six-pack he'd earned. Had he always looked like this? Obviously he didn't need a workout regime when his job required so much physical activity. "I just need to run home and get a clean shirt."

Don't do so on my account. She barely stopped that comment from escaping. Instead, she said, "I'm so sorry." She hurried past him, trying helplessly to identify these weird feelings circling inside.

"Hazards of the job, right? It's just baby puke. Nothing to worry about." He grabbed another malasada before heading to the door and bit in. "Back in a sec," he mumbled around a full mouth.

Tehani eyed her son, who wore a huge smile as he chewed on his fist. "You aren't doing that on purpose are you, *mae-mae*?"

"Bah!" Kai blasted as he pedaled his bare feet like he was going for the gold in cycling. "Bah bah bah bah bah!"

"You said it." She needed a distraction. Wyatt was a friend. Her *best* friend. She was stepping right off the deep end by looking at him in this different light.

"Because you're stressed and you're trying to lead yourself away from real-life issues by creating a new problem." Everything else in her life seemed to be heading into a tailspin. Why not add her one solid unshakable relationship into the mix? "Looks like we're starting our day a bit unexpectedly this morning, Kai." In more ways than one. "But on the bright side, you're about to be the center of attention at your auntie's house!"

She cleaned up the kitchen and indulged in a second malasada, mainly because she knew there would be more of them at Sydney's and she didn't want to be tempted. She was licking the last of the sugar off her fingers when Wyatt returned.

He stood in the front doorway and, as had happened earlier, his gaze dropped to her mouth. This far away, she couldn't tell if she imagined his blue eyes darkening or if there really was something there. Maybe…maybe whatever this was between them wasn't one-sided?

"All ready?" he asked as she turned to wash her hands. "Clouds seem to be taking the day off. Nice for a walk if you're up for it."

"Ah, sure." The Calvert house was barely a mile away and it had been a while since she'd taken the walk over there.

Growing up, that house had been a second home to all of Remy's friends, Tehani included.

Remy and Sydney's parents had been so welcoming and supportive, acting like second parents to a lot of them. Tehani and Mano included.

Her childhood years had been fraught with anger and tension, usually brought on by financial strains. The frustration over not being able to hold down a straightforward job had eventually driven their father out of the house and into the unknown, leaving their mother heartbroken and barely able to cope.

It had been her brother, Remy and Wyatt who had filled the void and rebuilt the trust she didn't realize she'd lost. The three of them together, along with Remy's parents, had given her the stability she craved. She'd found another home, somewhere else she belonged. It meant everything to her.

Tehani had gone out of her way to avoid the house Remy had taken over since his parents had passed. She wasn't entirely certain why; with all the changes Sydney and Theo had made to the place in the last few months, it didn't even really look like the house Remy had called home. Maybe it was just because it was supposed to be her home after she and Remy got married. Seeing it now reminded her of the life she should be living rather than the one she had.

There she went again. Tehani squeezed her

eyes shut. Why, *why* couldn't she even think of a house without thinking of Remy? *Because he's still here. In spirit and in memory,* Tehani reminded herself silently. Irritably. *Because every corner you turn, you can still see him, hear him. Feel him.* And try as she might, the issue wasn't getting any better.

"Want me to take Kai?" Wyatt's hand collided with hers when they both reached for Kai's carrier.

She leaped back as if burned. "Sure, um, yes." She grabbed her small purse, phone and keys, then stopped on the porch long enough to slip into some walking sandals. Wyatt snapped the carrier into the matching stroller and together they lifted it off the porch. The cool morning breeze welcomed them as they made their way to the street, turned and headed into town.

Currently the streets were caught between getting ready for Christmas and fully embracing their decorations—half-strung lights and mishmashes of florals and baubles. It wouldn't be long before everything came together.

Their path took them down to Pulelehua Road and when they turned left to head up the hill toward Sydney's home, Wyatt gestured to the old abandoned theater that had originally opened its doors back in the early seventies.

Tehani didn't realize she'd slowed her pace until Wyatt stopped and backtracked toward her. She gazed up at the marquee that read, as it had ever since the day it closed, Aloha and Mahalo.

"Seeing this place shut down always makes me so sad." She had such vivid, pleasant memories of it, of hanging out with her friends, watching classic movies on Thursday nights and eating popcorn until she thought she might pop herself. The classic theater was a throwback compared to the modern movie houses in Hilo or Kona, neither of which held much appeal for her even now. She missed going to the movies on a regular basis but going anywhere else felt like a kind of betrayal. "It's such a waste to have it sitting empty."

"Mmm." Something in Wyatt's response had her looking at him.

"What does that mean?"

"Nothing." He shrugged. "Nothing specific," he clarified at her narrowed eyes. "I should say nothing *official*."

"Oh, come on! Spill!"

He chuckled. "Suffice it to say I may have heard something about a possible new owner for the theater. Again, it's not written in stone," he insisted as he held up his hands in surrender.

"But my information definitely comes from a reliable source."

Unexpected hope bloomed inside of her. "You can't leave me hanging like this."

His mouth twitched. "I'm sworn to secrecy." He motioned to zip his lips together. "But you might not have to be sad about that empty theater for much longer. Morning, Mrs. Olivio!" Wyatt waved at the woman wearing a long wild-print muumuu and sweeping her porch. She waved back and the growing smile on her face made Tehani's cheeks warm.

"I definitely made the right decision to stay in Nalani if the theater is coming back." Tehani felt an unexpected lightness at the news as they moved on. "I can't wait to see what they do with the place."

"So nothing about Maylea's offer last night tempted you?" he prodded.

"Not really. Maybe." She tried not to sound too enthusiastic. "I liked the idea of doing something a bit different. Working with longer-term clients sounds appealing to me. And working on bigger events rather than just daily plans, you know? Especially for clients with more extravagant needs."

"Do you feel like that's missing with your job at Ohana?" Wyatt asked. "Wealthier clients, fancier events and more money to play with?"

"Doesn't everyone want more money?" she tried to joke, but she could see by the sudden lines marring his brow that this wasn't a subject he found particularly amusing.

"No," Wyatt said. "Not everyone."

Tehani pressed her lips into a thin line. "You're thinking about your father, aren't you?" Despite not knowing a lot of the details of his family life—he'd never liked talking about the time before he'd moved to Nalani—she did know his one remaining parent was a sore subject.

"Hard not to when the subject of money comes up," he admitted. "It's been all he's cared about for a very long time. I get why it's foremost in most people's minds. Finances can be stressful whether you have money or not."

Tehani remained skeptical on that front. Her parents had fought over money, mainly because neither of them had been capable of keeping a steady job. That experience had definitely altered her perception not only on the role money played in marriages, but in relationships in general. Remy might have been responsible for some of the challenges he and Tehani had faced, but she was more than willing to accept responsibility for others. Trust wasn't easy for her. Especially when it came to family matters. "I get what you're saying," she told him. "But

Mano's and my childhood might have been a lot different, a lot better probably, if financial stress hadn't had a seat at the dinner table."

"Or," Wyatt countered, "you might not be living the life you are now if all that hadn't happened. My father is consistently horrified that I live job to job, but I have what I need. I don't need more than that. Especially from him."

The only time she ever heard bitterness in his voice was when he spoke of his father. A father who, according to what little Remy had shared, was incapable of affection or even giving attention to his only child. "Have you heard from him lately?"

"On my birthday. And I'll get a Christmas card in about a week," Wyatt said. "Probably signed by his administrative assistant." He flashed a quick smile as if to remind her of their conversation last night. "It always has the same message. That the offer is still open."

"What offer is that?"

"To take over the family business. It's a construction firm, ironically enough, only instead of building things, he demolishes them." He let out a harsh laugh. "I have no doubt the irony is lost on him."

"So a deconstruction firm." She wanted to lighten the mood and it worked. He smiled a little.

"After my mother died," Wyatt said, "the only thing he cared about was financial success. He neglected to anticipate that that focus left him with an alienated son who wants nothing to do with either the business or him."

"Sounds like your father and mine could start a club." At least she didn't get yearly reminders of how detached her father was from his two children. She'd never really considered her father's absence and neglect as a blessing before. "I know it sounds selfish, but I'm glad you came to Nalani to live with your grandparents. They were always very nice to me."

"Thanks," Wyatt said. "Yeah, they were pretty great."

"I remember your grandmother always trying to feed me."

"It's what aunties do," he said. "Besides, she loved to cook and the more people she could feed, the better."

"I still try to replicate her fried rice." Her mouth twisted. "Never seems to come out the same."

"Try adding some vinegar next time," he suggested. "Then let me know. So, um, tell me something."

She arched a brow.

"Do you have any plans in the near future to

start Kai off with swimming lessons? Or surfing classes?"

"Don't tell me." She laughed and shook her
head in relief at the change of subject. "You
went in on that stupid betting pool, didn't you?"

"On whether Remy Calvert's son would take
after him when it came to the water?" Wyatt
looked aghast even as his eyes twinkled. "Of
course not."

"Well, you aren't going to get any inside information from me," she told him. "At least not
yet." She'd only taken Kai to the edge of the
ocean so far. As much as she couldn't wait to
witness his first experience in the water, she'd
decided to hold off until he was at least six
months old. The extra time would also give her
a chance to balance out her feelings about the
obvious comparisons he'd receive to his father.
He was not Remy and she didn't want him to be.

"You should reconsider," Wyatt said. "If only
to increase the pot. If the locals see you taking
Kai for a swim, the betting's gonna launch into
the stratosphere."

"Ha. They're going to have a long wait for
a payout. I'd prefer Kai to know how to walk
before he even steps foot on a surfboard. And
even then he'll do so only under Keane's guidance."

"Ugh!" Wyatt pretended to pull an invisible

knife out of his heart. "I'm offended. I can surf well enough."

"Keane won awards," she reminded him.

"As a swimmer, not a surfer," Wyatt argued and the lightheartedness of the banter eased her mood. "But I suppose you have a point. Keane'll get him up and riding those waves a lot faster than anyone else."

"In the meantime, I'll turn Kai over to Daphne occasionally for rainforest hikes when he is old enough." They veered right at the top of the hill. "I wouldn't want Kai to think he has limited options."

"No limits," Wyatt assured her. "You'll make sure of it."

Yes, *she* would. Because when all was said and done, she was alone in raising Kai. She glanced over at Wyatt as he leaned down to adjust Kai's blanket protecting her son from the cool morning air.

She couldn't help but wonder, perhaps even hope, if maybe she and Kai weren't nearly as alone as she thought.

CHAPTER FIVE

"EARTH TO WYATT? You in there?" Theo Fairfax dropped a hand onto Wyatt's shoulder, breaking his unintentional focus that he'd had pinned on Tehani. Kai had been whisked away by Daphne and Marella, both of whom wanted serious baby time while Tehani chatted with Sydney and Keane's protégé Jordan Adair, who, per her usual way, chose to sit on the floor rather than take up one of the chairs.

Jordan wore her long, pale blond hair in twists and braids, decorated with various baubles and beads. Her black cat, Nama, short for Namaka, was a constant companion and traveled around with Jordan in a specially made shoulder bag. Right now, Nama seemed inquisitive about Kai and was trying to find a way to curl up in the carrier with the baby.

The expansive porch railing had been strung with colorful holiday lights, and potted poinsettias were placed equidistantly apart along the floorboards. Overhead, icicle lights draped and dripped, giving a bit of frosty tint to an otherwise brilliant sunny morning. It was, Wyatt thought to himself, a beautiful scene to start the day with. Almost as beautiful as seeing Tehani and Kai first thing after sunrise.

"Here." Theo pushed a mug of coffee under his nose. "Looks like you could use this."

"Thanks." At this point, Wyatt was probably going to float away on the ocean of coffee he'd been drinking since well before dawn. He hadn't lied about the six hours of sleep. They'd just concluded around the same time as Kai had apparently woken up. He turned from the window overlooking the back patio of Sydney and Theo's home.

Meeting at the office was always an option, but Sydney preferred having them all meet at her house whenever possible. As a part-time fill-in for various Ohana guest excursions and activities, Wyatt was considered part of the group, something he'd always appreciated. His grandmother had always said he'd find his own way and she was right. How he missed that gentle, patient guidance she'd provided.

As he cast his gaze around the very kitschy holiday decorations strewed about the kitchen, including a stuffed hippo wearing a very sparkly Santa hat, he had to wonder if Theo Fairfax's idea of holiday decor needed a bit of… editing.

"You just about ready for the wedding?" Wyatt asked Theo when he leaned back against the kitchen counter.

"Not even remotely," Theo said, then laughed and shook his head. "Everyone else seems to be. My parents and sister and her family are coming out early for an island Christmas, so that'll be some added chaos." Given his expression, he was looking forward to the visit. "It'll all be fine. We have plenty of room here at the house and my sister's little boy is a few months older than Kai. Marella's using her super-organizational skills to help Sydney put the last bits and pieces together for the wedding. In the meantime, I just do as I'm told."

"Smart man," Wyatt agreed.

Mainlander Theo had become an island transplant earlier this year when he'd been sent by his then employer, Golden Vistas, to oversee a financial audit on Ohana Odysseys. The purpose at the time had been for Golden Vistas to buy out Ohana, but Sydney soon realized that selling her brother's beloved business went against everything Remy had been trying to build. She hadn't sold the business, but she did gain a fiancé in besotted Theo, who was quickly becoming one of Wyatt's favorite people in Nalani. The man might not have much natural island sense but he made up for it with enthusiasm and a horrible idea of fashion. Case in point: the neon-green parrot shirt he currently wore.

Wyatt glanced up as Keane strode in. "Morning."

"Morning," Keane grumbled and ran a hand down his whiskered face. "Had my heart set on a morning run on the waves. Thanks." He accepted his own coffee without having to ask. He took a long gulp, winced, then drank some more. "You think this SOS from Sydney has something to do with her meeting with Mano last evening?" He glanced at Theo, who shrugged and turned away.

"Man's a wall of silence," Wyatt said good-naturedly. "I'm assuming it does." He'd refrained from specifics with Tehani just in case he was wrong. He knew what the Surfing Santa event meant to her and Remy. No need to pile on more emotional baggage if it wasn't necessary.

The front door opened and closed, and seconds later, a barefoot Mano Iokepa, wearing a fine tailored dark suit, entered the kitchen. "Sorry I'm late." He tugged at the tie around his neck, loosened it and unbuttoned the collar of his silver shirt, exposing hints of the tattoos he had.

His bare feet slapped against the bamboo flooring. "Had just enough time to grab a shower and change of clothes."

"Long night, then?" Keane asked, the exhaustion around his eyes fading when they got a look at Mano. It wasn't normal for the six-foot-plus part owner of the Hibiscus Bay to look as haggard and stressed as he did at the moment. His large stature, dark hair and equally dark eyes made him a standout but today it seemed for all the wrong reasons. He kept his longish hair tied back in a tail at the base of his neck. While he'd spent his share of time on the waves and working around the community, he was as professional and business-minded as they came.

Over the past decade, he'd taken the Hibiscus Bay Resort from a semi-struggling local hotel to a destination resort that continued to garner buzz and excitement in the island tourist industry. He, along with Tehani, had always felt a kind of ancestral responsibility to the town where their family had lived for generations. That said, Mano was the kind of man who thrived on chaos and his ability to smooth out the rough edges. Right now, it looked like his edges were as sharp as a shark's fin.

"I've had better nights, that's for sure. Mahalo," he said to Theo as he accepted a mug of coffee. "Don't suppose anyone brought—"

"Jordan stopped at Maru's malasada cart on her way in," Theo told him. "Caught her just as they were setting up. There are two full boxes out on the patio so help yourself."

"Great. Gentlemen. If you'd join us, please." He led the way onto the patio, gesturing for Keane, Theo and Wyatt to follow, each wearing a varying form of curiosity on their face.

"Aloha, Tey." Mano bent down and knocked his forehead gently against his sister's before setting his mug down and immediately crouching to capture his nephew in his hands. *"Kulia i ka nu'u hokū, keiki hanauna."* He bowed his forehead to the baby's.

"Mahalo, *kaikaina*," Tehani whispered. *Thank you, brother.*

"I'm still learning Hawaiian," Theo murmured to Keane and Wyatt. "What did he say?"

"Strive to reach the highest stars, nephew," Wyatt said, grateful that Tehani's one steadfast family member was playing such a vital, parental role in Kai's upbringing. To say Mano was taking his responsibilities as an uncle seriously was an understatement. But then, fewer things were as important to Mano as family. Although, that hadn't been the case a while back and his marriage had ended as a result. Not that regret shone brightly on Mano Iokepa's face. The man had an expression of granite most of the time.

A gentle mew sounded as Mano set Kai back in his carrier. Jordan's sleek black cat immediately jumped free and circled around to curl up on the bag that acted as his transport.

"Whatever this meeting is about," Daphne said, "I'm in charge of set decorations for the grammar school's Christmas pageant." She checked her watch. "I need to be at the school theater pretty soon."

"I've got a chopper tour at ten thirty," Sydney added. "This won't take long."

"I'll try to keep this short." Mano retrieved two malasadas and, after eating one in three bites, set the second one aside on a napkin. "Rather than have this information dispersed in some weird version of telephone, we thought it best to present it to you all at the same time." He drank more coffee, then eyed Sydney, who got to her feet.

"SportsFlex Apparel filed for bankruptcy last week," she told the group. "They've pulled their support from the Hawai'i Ocean Education Foundation, or HOEF, as well as their sponsorship for the Surfing Santa Charity Championship. They're liquidating."

Wyatt grimaced, but his gaze shot to Tehani, who visibly swallowed.

"But SportsFlex has sponsored the event every year since it started," Daphne said as if she didn't believe it. "Their donations cover almost everything, from the T-shirts to the snack bar to…to the trophies."

"Which means if the organization wants those items," Sydney clarified, "they're going to have to come up with the money to pay for it themselves."

"But how can SportsFlex just do that?" Jordan asked. "There's only like three weeks until the event!"

Wyatt kept his eyes on Tehani, who seemed extraordinarily quiet. She touched a hand to her stomach and looked slightly ill.

"Can the event even go forward without its main sponsor?" Marella asked.

"That's the big question," Sydney said. "Mano and I spent most of yesterday and a lot of last night on a video call with Aimita Haoa." Sydney glanced at Tehani. "That's why she's been calling you, T. She knows how important this event was to Remy. She wanted you to hear this from her personally."

Tehani winced and Wyatt's heart pinched. Jordan reached up and rested a gentle hand on Tehani's knee and offered a sympathetic smile.

"If it was just the main sponsor pulling their support, there might be a way to salvage the event," Mano said. "Unfortunately, once word got out about SportsFlex, a lot of the other sponsors have followed suit. Including the host hotel in Kona."

"Most of the smaller businesses are hanging in for now at least," Sydney added. "The event brings them a lot of customers. It's one of their best weekends of the year, but they can't afford to lose what they've invested. If the event is in jeopardy, they have every right to ask for their money back."

"No one can blame them for that," Mano agreed. "There is one bit of good news."

"Finally." Jordan picked up Nama and cuddled the cat close against her chest. Even from across the patio, Wyatt could hear the telltale sound of the feline's purr.

"So far, the hotel pulled its support for the event only, they're still offering to keep their reservation room block open for attendees and competitors," Mano said. "That means that as of now, those people at least have a place to stay. But that's all they have. The hotel won't be hosting any of the events as planned. No pre-event luau or post-event breakfast. It'll be room discounts only. And that's only if the event goes on. They've given Aimita and HOEF until end of business tomorrow to give them an answer as to how they plan to proceed."

"So the hotel is hoping to make a profit on an event they aren't willing to subsidize any longer." Theo let out a low whistle. "That's cold. Especially for an island business."

"You said it." Mano nodded. "They don't see a way around losing the sponsors but they aren't looking at the big picture. Nor are they thinking about all the people on this island who need this event to succeed. This event funds dozens of educational programs and opportunities throughout the year. Those local businesses who have yet to pull their sponsorships…they're holding out hope there's a solution, so we need to give them one." He drew his gaze around the room. "We don't have a minute to lose. Let's start brainstorming and come up with as many ideas as we can."

"Before tomorrow evening?" Marella asked without looking up from where she was tapping on her tablet. "That's a big hurdle to jump."

"But not impossible." Wyatt heard the worry in Sydney's voice. "We can't just give up."

"I really hate to add to the doom and gloom of the situation," Keane hedged. "But can I just make a comment? If this year's event is canceled, it'll be near impossible to ever bring it back in the future. It's hard enough to get a charity event off the ground in the best of circumstances. Restarting it after a blow like this… I just don't see how that'll happen."

"This can't be how the Santa Surfers ends,"

Jordan said. "I've been looking forward to this event since before I got here. I planned to compete next year. I can't be the only one."

"Jordan's right. She won't be the only one who's disappointed," Daphne agreed. "And just think for a moment about the people planning to attend or compete? They've trained, they've practiced. Booked their flights, made their plans and on and on. Canceling the event wouldn't be fair to them. And what about Aimita and her staff? They work so hard all year to make this event happen."

"Points taken," Mano agreed. "And Keane's correct. Aimita admitted the HOEF might not survive if they can't find a way to salvage this year's event."

"We aren't going to let that happen." All eyes shifted to Tehani as she leaned down and picked up a suddenly fussing Kai. "Stop circling the solution and just land on it, Mano." She gently patted her son on the back. "You know what we have to do."

"And what do we have to do?" Mano asked.

"Simple." She pinned her brother with a look. "We need to move the entire event to Nalani."

It was as if someone or something had taken possession of her vocal cords. Tehani couldn't quite reconcile what she'd said despite thinking almost immediately that moving the entire event to Nalani was the only real answer.

She held Kai close, felt his tiny heart beating against her own chest as he fussed and wiggled in her arms. Inside, it felt as if there were a tug-of-war going on. As determined as she'd been to avoid attending the Surfing Santa Charity Championship and even Aimita's calls, the idea of the event being canceled altogether was simply out of the question. She could not stand by while the HOEF, an organization Remy had poured his heart into, went down in flames. It was as if a little angel Remy had perched himself on her shoulder to nudge her in the right direction.

"There's too much at stake for us to all just walk away." Tehani's gaze slipped around the room, skimming over the faces of the friends she considered Ohana. While her brother's face remained unreadable—Mano had never been anything remotely close to an open book—Sydney seemed a bit overwhelmed. Daphne and Marella and even Jordan all wore expressions Tehani chose to interpret as intrigued. Keane and Theo nodded in encouragement while Wyatt...

She swallowed hard. Wyatt's eyes were filled with compassionate understanding and, if she wasn't mistaken, pride.

It was the latter that had her stiffening her spine and diving in, pushing through the grief that still wrapped around her heart. "The logistics will be a challenge, but it should be doable with some dedicated attention and the right person running things. Aimita knows what she's doing. We just have to help her shift the location and fill in the details. There are some big questions to address of course," she went on as her mind raced. "Like how many rooms at the Hibiscus Bay would be open to take in the reservations from the Kona hotel?"

Mano's brows rose. "You don't think we should bus the guests—"

"No." Some things were crystal clear. "No. If the hotel doesn't want to put their full support behind the event, then they shouldn't profit from it. Luaus and parties we can handle. Heck, we throw one a week in this town and we do it better than anywhere else on the islands."

"One call to Poluno and Akahi and that's a done deal," Keane said of the best caterers in Nalani.

"Akahi's up to it?" Wyatt asked, recalling that the older woman had been dealing with serious health issues over the past year.

Keane nodded. "New medication regime is working great. Seriously. If we do this, consider those events taken care of."

"Once word gets around that it's either host the competition ourselves or let one of Remy's dreams die, we'll be overwhelmed by support," Tehani mused. "The trick will be organizing everything. We'll give Aimita all the support we can."

Sydney and Mano glanced at one another.

"What?" Keane asked. "You two keep looking at each other as if there's another shoe waiting to drop. Better drop it before we get into this too far."

"Aimita's pregnant," Sydney said.

Tehani's heart lightened. "That's—"

"She's also on mandatory bed rest as of two days ago," Mano added before she got too excited. "No way is her doctor going to approve her coming out here to oversee things. And most of her employees are volunteers with real jobs in Kona. They work at the charity on the side."

"Tehani can do it." Marella looked to Tehani as Tehani's face drained of color. "You've been to this event in the past. You know what it's supposed to be about. How it runs. All you need are the right people around you and like you said, Nalani's going to get on board. And you've got us. Use us."

"I—" Tehani's breath hitched. Her heartbeat picked up speed. "That wasn't what…" Panic

surged into her throat. Her hold on Kai tightened. This was Remy's special event. Not hers.
How could she even consider…? "I don't think
I can…" Her gaze flew to Wyatt, silently plead-
ing for help.

Kai wailed, reached out a tiny fist and
dropped it against her chest. She tilted her chin
and looked down as her son raised his head and
blinked open sleepy eyes. Eyes that were so
much like his father's that Tehani's heart threatened to break all over again. Her fear couldn't
matter. The decision had already been made
without her.

"You won't do this alone." Wyatt's voice
broke through the doubt and dread and, for want
of a better term, fear. "Marella's right. We're
here for you. We just need direction."

"Absolutely," Sydney confirmed. "We've all
got your back. You need an army to pull this
off? You've got one."

"We're all in," Jordan confirmed. "Even if it
means I have to handle the front desk at Ohana
Odysseys again."

"Let's not get ahead of ourselves," Sydney
said in a way that earned a round of laughter.

Tehani's gaze remained on Wyatt, who nodded not only in agreement but what felt like
encouragement. He had faith in her. She could
see it in his eyes. Real or projected, she couldn't

help but embrace it. Maybe…maybe instead of trying to outrun her past, it was time to simply step out of it.

"Okay." The second she said the word, Kai calmed. He heaved a sigh, dropped his head onto her shoulder and fell instantly asleep. She continued to rub his back and looked around at her friends. At her Ohana. "Okay, I'll do it. Just remember it'll mean lots of extra babysitting hours from all of you."

"Deal!" everyone in the room responded. Before they all laughed again.

CHAPTER SIX

"SO THAT'S THIRTY-TWO competitors confirmed," Tehani said as she typed the additional information into her new spreadsheet. The last couple of days had passed in a blur. One huge number-crunching blur. But they'd made their pitch. Pending final approval of the town council, the HOEF Surfing Santa Charity Championship was officially coming to Nalani. In less than three weeks.

"And what were your projected numbers for attendance this year?" She glanced up at her second monitor where Aimita's round face was displayed. Her dark hair was knotted on top of her head and she glanced back and forth from her screen as she tapped on her own computer. She was holed up in her bedroom in Kona, feet up, trying to relax. An impossibility considering everything that was going on. Tehani was determined to lift the weight off the woman's shoulders by the end of this call.

"Ah. Attendance." Aimita frowned and leaned closer to the screen, then rattled off a number. Behind her, a shimmer of tinsel caught against the light streaming through her bedroom window. "That was a conservative estimate based on the increase over the past four years."

"Okay." Numbers brought Tehani a certain kind of peace in the midst of chaos. Numbers made sense. They always added up. When they didn't, she enjoyed the challenge of finding the error. "What about the ticket sales for the pre-tournament sunset luau and post-award celebration?"

"Two hundred and twenty-two registered for the luau." Aimita clicked on her keyboard. "That includes two free themed cocktails per adult ticket." She winced. "Is that even doable—"

"We've already got someone working on that." Tehani waved off her concern. Keane had let her know Poluno and Akahi were definitely interested in hosting the luau and post-tournament beach breakfast. Locals rarely turned down the opportunity to show off Na-lani. "I need solid numbers to present to… And that's Mano again," she said when her phone buzzed. Across the room, Kai babbled in his playpen. His feet kicked at the low hanging mobile she'd set to spinning to keep him entertained. "Give me a sec?" She muted her laptop and answered her phone.

"Mano." She tucked her cell against her shoulder and scanned the growing spreadsheet. "I'd think in the last couple of days you'd have learned I can get all this done a lot faster if you'd stop calling me." She glanced at the clock over her kitchen sink. She still had another ninety minutes before she was meant to be at his office with a final plan of action. Getting the council's approval wasn't mandatory in order for the event to happen, but doing so could free up some town funds to help with costs.

"You thrive on multitasking," her brother said. "Main thing the council is interested in is the breaking even numbers and a projected income for local—"

"Got it." She held up a hand even though he couldn't see her. He needed evidence-based optimism. "You'll have it."

"One thing. I'm getting questions about insurance," he barreled on, without giving her a chance to finish a thought.

"Insurance. Yeah. I've got that right…" She closed her spreadsheet window and clicked open one of the attachments Aimita sent over. She'd been running at top speed ever since she'd walked out of Sydney and Theo's house earlier in the week. "HOEF is already covered, but they've got a liability rider for the surfing event. The premium's already been paid and, near as I understand it, change of venue doesn't void it so we shouldn't have to start over with it or apply for a new one." She did, however, want to take a closer look at the actual coverage wording just to be safe.

"Great. I'll let the council know. How about registrants? Any estimation of how many will cancel if we move it?"

"Okay, stop." Tehani sighed and turned away from the monitor. "First, I'm not psychic and neither is Aimita. I've got information coming at me at light speed, half of which I've barely had a chance to dive into. I'm still playing catch-up, Mano, so please just leave me alone to work." The silence on the other end made her wince. She resisted the urge to apologize. She had nothing to apologize for other than her tone. Instead, she sighed again and said, "Based on the information I've gone through, the majority of attendees are from the Big Island and Kona in particular. It's a big local event, but it does draw from other areas around the island. There will be a drop from last year. I don't see how there won't be, but that doesn't mean it won't be a success. Does that help clarify anything?"

"It does," Mano said slowly. "Gives me a direction to spin things. I will now leave you alone."

Promises, promises. She spun on her chair at the knock before her front door popped open. Wyatt poked his head in. "Hey." She waved him inside. Seeing him always brought her a sense of relief. Forever the calm in a storm, for her at least. "I'll be at your office by noon," she told her brother. "Any other questions can wait until then. Bye." She hung up before he could respond.

"How're things going?" Wyatt stopped at the playpen, knocked the mobile into spinning again and set Kai to babbling.

"Good. Well, okay." She still had a lot of figures she needed to reconcile. "Oh." She clicked off her mute key. "Sorry, Aimita." She frowned at the other woman's expression. "What's wrong? Do you feel okay?" Being put on bed rest was something Tehani was exceedingly grateful for never experiencing. She couldn't begin to imagine the strain the other woman had been under as of late.

"Physically, I'm fine." Aimita sat back with a heavy sigh. "One of my volunteers just took a call from SurfsUp Swag. They heard about SportsFlex and want to know what they should do about the order they've already started to fill?"

"SurfsUp." Wyatt frowned. "They're the printing company, yeah? They're on Oahu?"

"They are," Aimita confirmed. "We've used them the last three years. They're a small operation, locally owned. Never given us any trouble and are always the first to jump on board."

"Great," Tehani muttered as she sorted through the printed papers for the invoice. "They were supposed to do the T-shirts, water bottles, caps and..." She squinted and leaned closer.

"Bracelets," Wyatt added, pointing to the additional notation on the paper.

"Right. Bracelets." Tehani frowned. "Those slap bracelets that fit everyone?"

"Yeah. They were really popular last year, but all of these items were also supposed to have SportsFlex's website printed on them. All the designing has already been done and... I don't know." Aimita was sounding more dejected by the minute. "Maybe we should just—"

"We aren't giving up." Tehani set her papers down, blinking back the tears at the expression on her friend's face. It made her hate what was happening even more. "Aimita, listen to me. We are in this together and I'm not giving up." The memory of Remy haunted her. The last thing she needed to do was give his spirit an excuse to come back and hound her about this. "Printing is fixable. Food is fixable. Everything on our list is fixable. You need to trust us on this."

She felt Wyatt's hand on her shoulder. She

reached up and covered his hand, squeezed and felt a surge of renewed energy.

Aimita shook her head. "It just feels hopeless."

"Nalani has your back," Tehani insisted. "I have your back. And I come with a whole lot of support. We still have time, Aimita. We just need you to hang in there with us for a little while longer."

"You look like you need a break," Wyatt said over Tehani's head. "Why don't you log off for a while? Leave this with us."

Grateful for Wyatt's confidence and positive attitude, Tehani nodded in agreement even as she breathed a bit easier.

"Okay." Aimita's smile was weak. "I'll just send you over the rest of the contracts and files so you have all the official details and information we were working with."

"Get some rest," Tehani ordered gently. "You need to take care of that baby and yourself. We've got this."

"Thanks." Aimita's lips trembled. "You know, I wasn't sure the HOEF could survive this. Now I think I might have just enough hope left to believe you."

"Hope is Nalani's specialty," Tehani reassured her. "I'll get in touch when I have some solid plans, okay?"

Aimita nodded, then swiped her fingers under her eyes to catch her tears. "Okay. Thank you." Her smile was watery and sad. "I know this must be hard for you what with Remy—"

"You're Ohana, Aimita." And Ohana overruled everything. Even her own heartache. "Remy considered you family and so do I. That's all that matters."

"Thank you." Aimita waved. "Mahalo, Tehani. Mahalo, Wyatt."

After Aimita ended the call, Wyatt remained where he was, behind Tehani, his hands braced on the back of her chair. "You doing okay?"

"Oh, I'm fine." She began clicking on new e-mails popping into her inbox, sending each of the graphics to the printer. Now wasn't the time to dwell on anything that might send her spiraling. "I need to get a handle on all these numbers and print everything out for Ma—" Kai let out a shriek that had them both jumping. "Right on schedule."

"I'll get him."

"No." Tehani caught his hand when he moved away but quickly released it when she felt the flash of warmth shimmer against her palm. "Thanks, but we've found a rhythm the last few days. I need to keep the balance in check." He stepped back as she got up and picked Kai up out of his playpen. A quick check confirmed he needed changing. "I'll be back in a second."

It was more like a half hour—everything took longer than expected with an infant, but she'd spoken the truth earlier. She and Kai were finding their way together. Even with the long hours and chaotic situation, they were doing okay. When she returned, she found Wyatt sorting through the mess of papers from the printer while he talked on the phone.

"I appreciate you hearing me out." He waved her over. She set Kai into his carrier. "I think that's more than fair. Let me get back to you on an exact pickup date, okay? Great." His smile smoothed the rough edges of Tehani's heart. "Yeah, thanks again. Talk soon." He clicked off.

"Who was that?"

"That was the owner of SurfsUp Swag."

Her brows went up.

"Sorry if I overstepped," Wyatt apologized. "Just felt like I needed to do something."

"And what did you do?" She wasn't worried necessarily. There didn't seem to be a way the situation could get much worse.

"I wanted to know how much product had already been run. Fortunately for us, they hadn't started yet. And doubly lucky, SportsFlex hadn't paid their deposit. Which means if we still use them, we just need new designs, without any reference to SportsFlex."

"Why do you have that gleam in your eye?" Devious, she thought. Sheepish, too.

Wyatt grinned. "According to Mrs. Takalga—"

"The owner?" Tehani guessed.

"Exactly. According to Mrs. Takalga, she was under the impression SportsFlex rolled the dice and assumed the HOEF couldn't get a new design in time so they'd still get the publicity."

"Publicity for a failing company," Tehani grumbled. "Typical."

"Mrs. Takalga said she's seen it before. This time it really ticked her off. Hence her call to HOEF this morning." He rubbed his hands together. "I took my own chance and played off her bad mood. We worked out a deal. SurfsUp will produce the bracelets, water bottles and caps as agreed to, but they'll sell them to the HOEF for cost in exchange for being listed as one of our sponsors. We just need to coordinate with them on the revamped design by the end of the week."

Tehani blinked. Blinked again. "That's… I think this is actually doable." Suddenly all the work and semi-sleepless nights this last week felt worth it.

"It'll still be a chunk of change, but…" Wyatt handed her the amended invoice. She looked down at the new number he'd circled in red. "It'll be a lot less than what SportsFlex was going to pay."

Tehani stared at the printout. "That's…amazing." And from the accounting sheets she'd looked at, completely within reason. "But what about the shirts?" According to the list, they needed multiple colors and sizes with various designations to cover all the volunteer jobs the event would require.

"I was wondering about your friend Delaney," Wyatt replied. "The one who makes all the baby clothes with the cute animals and catchy sayings? Aren't you taking Kai in for some photos?"

"Delaney." Tehani squeezed her eyes shut and dropped her chin to her chest. "I totally forgot about seeing her this week."

"Week's not over." Wyatt checked his cell phone that buzzed. He pocketed it almost immediately. "I need to get back over to Shani's shop and finish installing those shelves. Do you think Delaney might be willing to do the shirts? Keep it local to Nalani, maybe in exchange for being listed as a sponsor?"

"That's a great idea." Offering local businesses the chance to get involved where others had walked away. "I'll check with her today and see." She frowned at the invoice. "What's this? SurfsUp is covering the shipping costs for their items as well?"

"Ah, no." Wyatt scrubbed a hand across his chin. "I know you like to cut costs as much as possible, so I asked if we could pick up the items. As I was organizing the invoices and orders from Aimita, I noticed there were a number of items on Oahu. I was thinking maybe Sydney and Theo could take the chopper and do a pickup?"

He knew her. Maybe better than anyone did. "Did Mrs. Takalga give an estimate on when the order might be finished?"

"They need at least ten days once they have the new design." Wyatt winced and looked a little uncertain. "I seem to recall you mentioning some kind of chartered flight in a couple of weeks? Maybe they could coincide?"

"I think you're..." She nudged him out of the way and pulled up the current bookings for Ohana Odysseys. "Yeah. There's a tour and transportation flight booked for a couple on their honeymoon around then. I'll double-check with Sydney, but I think we can make that work. You..." She stood up so quickly she nearly knocked her head into his chin. She turned, grabbed his shoulders and kissed him full on the mouth. "Are brilliant!"

Oh, boy.

Tehani swallowed hard and stared into his eyes as she tried in vain to ignore the warmth winding up through her toes. His hands rested on her hips, his fingers flexing into her flesh. In the background, she could hear her computer humming and Kai giggling, but it barely rose above the hammering of her heart.

"I, um." She struggled for control. "I can't believe you remembered that booking."

"I remember everything you say." He stepped back, gestured to the stacks of papers on her desk. "You've only got an hour before you need to head to Mano's office. I'll keep an eye on the kid while you finish getting that report of yours ready."

"I thought you had to get to Shani's shop?" The handmade quilt, blanket and accessories shop was one of Nalani's biggest success stories.

"I'll text her that I'll be a little late. She'll understand. It'll be fine."

The heaviness on Tehani's heart began to lift. As impossible as this feat felt only moments ago, thanks to Wyatt, she was beginning to think they might be able to pull this off after all.

"This is good." Mano flipped through the pages of her hastily put together report and nodded slowly. "This is really good, T."

"Thanks." Tehani wasn't certain why she felt as if she'd been called in to be disciplined by the principal. Normally her brother's office at the Hibiscus Bay Resort gave her a feeling of comfort, mostly because of the multitude of traditional Hawaiian artwork acting as the main decor. But today she was an unexpected bundle of nerves. With its deep, rich wood-paneled walls, streamlined furniture and exceptionally large hand-carved desk, this space told anyone who stepped into it that it was for a respected position.

She took a quick glance around, noticing that the familiar commissioned painting of the Nalani shoreline hadn't moved from behind his desk. The solitary thin shelving unit by the door displayed a new sculpture by a mutual favorite artist—this one a wood-carved hibiscus flower, along with a koa wood Aikane canoe that could have belonged in a museum of island history. But it was the five-foot carved wooden surfboard that often captured her attention. The intricate details and attention to tradition in the symbology and technique made her throat tighten with emotion and she finally began to settle. Mano breathed the islands. Their heritage. Their ancestry. And he filled his office with everything that reminded him of those principles on a daily basis.

He'd refrained from adding too much holiday decor here. She knew why. The season had never been particularly joyous for them growing up and when he'd been married, he'd asked his wife to take care of all that. Mano had his head so far in the business and running the Hibiscus Bay, she'd bet he barely looked at a calendar unless instructed to do so.

From the outer office, the definitive sound of Kai wailing sounded. "Seems like my nephew's not happy," Mano murmured without glancing up. "Alaua's got her hands full."

"Your assistant was generous to offer to watch him." Tehani sat on the edge of her chair and tried to keep her hands steady. "Kai in a temper might have her quitting on you," she teased.

"Alaua's dealt with me in a temper," Mano said blithely. "Trust me, Kai's no competition."

"Maybe that's a contest you don't want to win."

Mano glanced up and arched a brow, but refrained from saying anything before he started reading again.

Her brother had always been the strong, silent type. Emphasis on the silent. Oh, he was talkative enough with people he was close to, but you could count the number of those people on two hands with fingers left over. He was a firm believer in there being more to be learned by listening. She often wondered if that had been one of the lessons he'd learned from their father, who hadn't taken kindly to a young Mano speaking when he wasn't spoken to or, heaven forbid, offering his opinion on something. More often than not, those offenses earned him some form of punishment.

Mano glanced at her. "So these projections on attendance—"

"Are a little less than what is on record for last year. Lowered expectations," she added at her brother's doubtful expression. "If we meet them, great. If we exceed them, even better. I think it's unrealistic to think the event won't take a hit moving it at this late date. It pulls a lot from locals and Kona is significantly larger than Nalani."

"But we're closer to Hilo," Mano countered. "Nalani's a lot easier and faster for people to get to than Kona. And we might be underestimating how many in Kona will still want to attend. That all works in our favor, no?"

"Absolutely." She was glad to see him looking on the positive side. "As long as we get the marketing together and word gets out. Three weeks isn't much time."

"Marella's already got the ball rolling on that front. Online advertising on social media to start with." Mano typed into his laptop and leaned forward. "Everyone else pretty much has their engines revving. We're just waiting for the starting flag."

At least she finally had the distraction she'd been wishing for. "The council's approval is just a formality, right?"

"Off the record, they're all on board. This positive projection will lock it in," Mano said. "It's still a great way to bring more attention and business to Nalani. Never anything wrong with that."

That had always been Remy's take on things. Tehani winced. She was doing it again. Circling back around to Remy.

"I was thinking about the Kona businesses who expressed interest in remaining sponsors. What do you think about hiring out a tour bus to take interested parties to Kona a few times a day? Maybe Hori would be willing to drive? If we don't have any tours booked through Ohana, we've got our tour van we can use, too."

Mano nodded. "I like that idea. Check with Aimita and I'll have a talk with Hori." There was little their local cabbie liked better than shuttling people around the island. "If I can work out a deal with the bus rental company, we can offer discounted tickets to encourage attendees to come a day or two early so they can take that day trip."

"Okay." She added that option into the notes section on her tablet.

"I've spoken with my partners in the Hibiscus Bay," Mano said. "They've agreed to take on the main sponsorship role once the town council approves the event. Sydney's looking to do the same thing with Ohana. We can open it up to other local businesses once we've got that locked in."

Tehani nodded. Once Mano and Sydney were solidly on board as sponsors, the rest of Nalani would fall in like neatly placed dominoes. "Depending on how this year goes, I think we should make a place for anyone on the Big Island who wants to participate as a sponsor in the future. SportsFlex apparently wanted the number of sponsors limited so there wasn't very much advertising dilution."

"Probably wanted to come across as a savior sponsor," Mano muttered. "Karma. Could explain why they're going belly-up."

Tehani wasn't going to argue with that logic. "Aimita's getting in touch with all the people who volunteered for the actual event. I'm not worried about food or the special events thanks to Keane, and Wyatt made a great deal with SurfsUp for most of the promotional items."

"Did he?" Mano quirked his head.

"The only major issue I see right now is lodging. How many rooms—"

"Still working on that side of things." Mano nodded and typed something else into his laptop. "I've got backup plans if we can't find enough here at the resort. For the participants at least. We might be okay on guest reservations."

Hearing his confidence even in the face of an obstacle made her feel a bit better. "I bet we can pull this off, Mano." It was daunting to be certain, but the more she worked on it, the more she thought everything out, the more optimistic she became. Especially now that she felt like she could breathe. "And I'm not just talking about this year. I think we can really make a go of something special with this event."

"Agreed." He paused. "I've been pretty buried with work here at the resort, so I haven't had a real chance to check in with you lately. How are you doing?"

She shrugged. "Fine."

"Would you tell me if you weren't?"

"Probably not." She forced a laugh and flipped her hair behind her shoulder, a nervous habit she could never quite control. "I'll admit that some things are difficult. Of course they are." How could they not be when she was raising her son alone? Except… "I miss him." It hurt to admit out loud, but it also stitched part of her back together. "I'll miss him for the rest of my life. But I have you and I have Sydney, and Wyatt is there every time I turn around. He always seems to know I need something even before I do."

"Yes," Mano murmured. "I have noticed Wyatt hanging around quite a bit. Is there something…?"

"He's a friend." Even to her own ears, her protest sounded a bit defensive. "A good friend." A good friend she kept kissing! She really needed to stop doing that. She ducked her head before Mano noticed her suddenly hot-pink cheeks.

"Nothing wrong with friendship turning into something more, T." Mano glanced at the picture sitting on the sideboard—the framed photograph of him and Remy, arms linked around one another's shoulders, the rushing surf behind them as they laughed into the camera. "I'm certainly not going to be the one to break our family's cycle of unsuccessful relationships. And Remy wouldn't want you to be alone. If you find someone to make you happy, don't push them away."

"I don't think Remy would want me dating one of his best friends." Her eyes went wide. "*If* I was dating—" She took a deep breath and quickly centered herself. "Remy hasn't even been gone a year. It's too soon to be thinking of anyone in that way, let alone Wyatt Jenkins."

"Wyatt is one of the best men I know," Mano said in a way that surprised even Tehani. Her brother wasn't one for compliments, especially if he didn't mean them. But it was his faith in his friends that fed his heart and soul. "No one is going to judge you for moving on. You've known each other a very long time. It would make sense—a lot of sense, actually—if the two of you connected in that way."

She would blame herself. Guilt had taken up residence where her love for Remy had lived. She couldn't, for the life of her, figure out how to replace either of them. "It's too soon."

"So your plan is to wait an appropriate amount of time to pass before you allow yourself to feel something again? To be happy?" Sometimes her brother had the annoying talent of hitting the proverbial nail on the head. "How long is enough? A year? Two years? Ten?"

Twenty? "I know your concern is coming from a caring place," Tehani said with meaning. "But as you said, considering how things ended between you and Emilia, do you really think you're the right person to give me advice on personal relationships?" She gestured to the photograph of Mano and his former wife. They'd always been an inspiration for her despite the difficulties Emilia experienced marrying a workaholic with tunnel vision. That he kept a photograph spoke of the impact she'd had on his life. And maybe the longing he still felt for her.

Tehani and Emilia had been very close for a long while. Her former sister-in-law was smart, sweet, headstrong—she'd have to be to have married Mano—and determined. It had broken Tehani's heart almost as badly as Mano's when she hadn't returned from the mainland after a visit home. Instead, Emilia had sent divorce papers. Tehani missed her friend. More than she had ever admitted to Mano. Emilia had written her a beautiful card and had a bird-of-paradise plant delivered in Remy's memory when he passed. The gesture had brought a smile to her face.

"Remy's death was a gut punch for all of us," her brother said without looking at her. "But in my case, it shone a spotlight on the mistakes I've made. None of us ever knows how much time we have. I wasted most of mine with Emilia trying to make a home for us that ended up empty. I know how much it hurt for you to lose him, T. But I don't think he'd like the idea of you spending the rest of your life alone because you were pining for him. Or worse—because you think you should."

"I'm not pining." Mano had always thought the sun rose and set on Remy's shoulders. And it had for the most part. But her relationship with Remy had been far from perfect. *Remy* had been far from perfect. She knew his reputation got shinier with each passing day, but tarnishing that image felt like throwing added dirt on his nonexistent grave. The truth was the truth. She knew it. That was all that mattered. "I've only got room in my life for one man at a time and right now, that spot is reserved for my son."

"Your son needs to see you taking care of your heart as much as you care for his. Wyatt cares about you and Kai. It's painted all over his face whenever he's around you."

She didn't want to hear this. She didn't want to know this. She just wanted things to stay as they were. Perfect and unblemished. Friends only. Now and forever. "Do you really think telling me all this is going to help the situation?"

"Can it hurt?" Mano challenged.

Yes, she thought. *It could hurt a lot.* "I was going to ask Marella or Daphne to watch Kai a couple of nights over the next few weeks. I'm expecting this event will require some overtime. Maybe I should add you into the rotation." She fluttered her lashes at him like she used to do when they were kids, when she was both teasing and testing the waters of a new idea.

"Ah, I don't think that would be a good idea." He made a wide gesture toward their surroundings. "I'm not exactly set up for babies."

"Might I suggest you get set up?" She smirked. "A playpen right there." She pointed to the corner behind his desk. "Come the new year, I think it would be a good thing for Kai to spend more time with his uncle Mano. To help you make up for past mistakes," she added, just to make certain he knew she'd been listening. She stood up. "Consider yourself warned."

CHAPTER SEVEN

WYATT SAT ON the edge of the porch railing of the beachside cottage, watching and listening to the ocean. Something he didn't give himself nearly enough time to do these days. Finishing the new shelves at The Hawaiian Snuggler hadn't taken him very long. He could have finished last week if the parts he'd needed had been in stock. He may have even set a Guinness World Record on the last of the installation process, but Shani was thrilled with the end result and he had the rest of the afternoon to meet with Sydney and Keane on a special project they'd come up with.

Since they asked to meet at the second of two vacation cottages owned by Ohana Odysseys, he knew something of what was about to land in his lap. Once upon a time, this work in progress had been on the top of his list. But work had screeched to a halt when Remy passed.

The cottage, like its sister dwelling just down

the beach, was somewhat isolated, wedged into a thicket of palm trees that, from the road, made the building completely disappear. Privacy was definitely one of its selling points. With its location only feet away from the tide, there really weren't many more perfect places in Nalani. Or in all the islands, to his thinking.

One of the best parts about living in Hawai'i was that this sort of peace was literally steps away from wherever you were. It wasn't peace that he needed right now, necessarily. Clarity, perhaps. A resettling of mind and spirit. In fact, maybe he did need peace.

Kissing Tehani had tilted a few things off balance for him. True she'd instigated two of those kisses, but he'd done his best to make the most of the third. He couldn't quite let himself believe that something was possibly, maybe growing between them. He'd buried his feelings for her for so long that he was afraid to let them out. Except…

He took a deep breath, willed his pulse to calm.

It had been difficult—crushing on his best friend's girl for years. And he had considered it a crush. Except crushes weren't meant to last forever. Probably why his grandfather had remarked on more than one occasion how much he liked "that Tehani girl."

Crushes came and went with the frantic and frenetic emotions that were typically attributed to growing up and overactive hormone activity. No. What he felt, what he *had* felt, for Tehani went beyond a crush. It would take time to come to terms with the feelings he'd denied. Feelings that even now battered against his heart, demanding to be set free.

"Sorry we're late." Sydney and Keane trudged through the ankle-deep sand as they made their way down the beach toward the large cottage. "Mano called. The town council approved Nalani hosting the Surfing Santa competition so it's all official."

"Yeah?" Wyatt's spine straightened as he stood up.

"Yeah." Sydney dragged a hand through her loose long blond hair, stopped for a moment at the foot of the stairs and gazed out at the water. Keane did the same, only with his hands planted on his hips, he looked like the surfing megastar he was with that twinkle in his eyes. "We've got a lot of work to do in a very short amount of time."

"Ready for it." Wyatt smiled and gestured to the cabin. "So, what's the plan? Why'd you want to meet here?"

"Because this place is about to become our secret lodging weapon." Sydney gestured to the cottage and dug a key out of her pocket. "Come on in. I know you did some upgrades to it a while back—"

"Some," Wyatt said as he followed her inside. Upon her brother's death, Sydney had inherited all of Remy's properties, including the two vacation cottages. The one Theo and Keane had both once stayed in had been refurbished and set up as a rental shortly before Remy died, but this one, the larger one, had been all but forgotten in the void of his loss.

The bones of this two-bedroom, two-bath beach cottage were impeccable, but the second you stepped through the door, it was like walking through a time portal. And not into one of the more decor-forward decades. Wyatt stepped in behind them and wandered around, his flip-flops slapping against the stained and scarred wood floor. "Remy wanted to finish the smaller cottage first so he could start to rent it out, but then I stopped work in here."

"Well, I'd like to start it back up again." Sydney stood in the middle of the large living area, to the left of which was a long galley kitchen with outdated cabinets that looked as if they needed a serious facelift. "What do you think, Keane?"

Their friend nodded and kept walking as he assessed the place. "I think it would work. Tight quarters for sure, but yeah." He nodded again, stopped at the window overlooking both the wraparound porch and the ocean. "It'll definitely do."

"Work for what?" Wyatt asked.

"Mano's going to struggle to find enough rooms at the resort to cover the reservations from Kona as well as the actual competitors," Sydney said to Wyatt. "Keane suggested putting at least some of the tournament participants up here. Hopefully maybe half? Say...fifteen?"

"Fifteen surfers. Here?" Wyatt wasn't normally one to sound defeatist, but... "Syd, that'll take a lot of work to get it livable by the time the tournament starts, and where would everybody sleep?"

"It'll have to be ready before the competition starts," Keane interjected. "The participants will start showing up a few days ahead of attendance goers. They like to get a feel for the waves and most of them won't have surfed this area before."

"Right." That made complete sense.

"How do you feel, Wyatt? Can we pull off getting this place into shape in less than three weeks?" Sydney asked.

Never one to rain on anyone's parade, Wyatt shrugged. "I'd need to hire some help." He knew of several contractors he could rely on, but they wouldn't come cheap.

"I'm happy to volunteer," Keane said. "I'm not exactly useless at construction."

"Okay, that's one," Wyatt agreed.

"Theo isn't bad with a paint roller," Sydney added. "And I bet we can wrangle a few others along with whoever else you'll need. Even if it'll take most of Nalani, I bet we can cover it."

"Doable?" Keane asked. "Realistically, Wyatt."

Wyatt couldn't hide his frown. "I mean." His mind spun. "The demo is almost done." He crouched to touch his fingers to the wood floor. "This is salvageable but it'll need proper sanding and finishing. The walls have to be painted and…" He waved behind him. "There are no appliances. Then there's the lighting. The electrical needs upgrading and I'm not sure what condition the plumbing's in." That said, getting this done would be one less thing Tehani would obsess over. "Provided I can find everything we need and that nothing major like the plumbing needs refitting…" Supplies were what worried him the most. Home design projects on the islands were always tricky given unreliable supply chains and shipping issues. Still, he liked a challenge. And if he had to scrounge and barter for what was required, all the better. Social media marketplaces tended to be a gold mine for projects like this. "I suppose so." It would mean really early mornings and very late nights because he wasn't going to abandon Tehani when she needed him.

"Wonderful. Let's talk numbers," Sydney said. "How many surfers do you think we could put in here comfortably, Keane?"

"Surfers are pretty amenable to their lodgings," Keane said. "As long as there's some place to sleep and food to eat and it's close to the water, they'll be happy."

"Explains why Jordan's lived in a fitted-out van for most of last year," Sydney said.

"And why she kept getting tickets for illegal parking. Of course, our sheriff got a serious kick out of it." Wyatt laughed as he walked past them into the farthest bedroom. It was particularly large. "Bunk beds. One set there… there…" He pointed to two of the walls, then the third. "Another set can go between those windows. If we go up, we get more space. Same with the other rooms. So…twelve people, for sure. Fifteen, maybe, if we add in additional bunks in the screened deck area. Also, a couple of hammocks on the porch?" He winced. "Close quarters."

"For a cottage located steps away from the ocean?" Keane dismissed his concern. "Heck, I've been known to sleep on the beach when lodgings were out of my price range. I say it's totally doable."

"And we might have some dropouts once the official announcement is made about the change of venue," Sydney said.

"The waves are stellar this time of year," Keane said. "Die-hard surfers will put that above anything else. The fact this entire event is for charity works in our favor, too. I've already posted to a few online message boards and the event's social media account trying to drum up excitement."

Wyatt's mind was already pinging with ideas. "We still want to do this in a way that makes renting out the cottage feasible for the rest of the year," he said. "It doesn't make any sense to do this for only one event."

"Agreed." Sydney nodded. "Do they make disposable bunk beds?"

"Not disposable ones, no. But they do make them for camping." Wyatt made a mental note. "I'll start looking into options."

"Is that your way of officially saying you'll do it?" Sydney asked.

"Yeah," Wyatt said with false bravado. "Consider it done."

CHAPTER EIGHT

"Oh, my gosh, look at him grin."

Tehani blinked out of her reverie as Kai offered a toothless, drooling smile to the camera poised over his head. Pride and joy filled her heart. She'd thought she knew what love was, but she'd been wrong. Kai had opened her heart in unexpected and miraculous ways.

It felt so good, after the chaotic last few days, to be doing something mostly unrelated to the surfing tournament. Just to be away from the computer for a good while was refreshing.

"Your son is a natural model." Delaney Evans shifted positions and kept snapping. "This outfit looks amazing on him!"

"Give him a little while and he'll add his dinner to the front," Tehani teased. "You're welcome to use him anytime you want," she added.

"I am definitely going to take you up on that. Luau Lullabies couldn't have a cuter representative." With a keen eye and curly brown hair frizzing around her face, Delaney stepped down off the stool and looked at her camera screen. "These are fab. You want a few to print out?"

"Sure." Tehani wasn't about to turn down free photographs.

"Cool. I'll e-mail them to you." She walked to the counter on the other side of the small storefront located near the Pulelehua main drag. Shelves and racks were stuffed to the gills with Delaney's unique offerings. Most of her income came from online orders, but she definitely got a run on sales in her shop when a baby shower or toddler's birthday came around.

Tehani picked Kai up from where he'd been lying on a changing table and cuddled him close as she followed Delaney to the register. "So. Did you hear about the Surfing Santa Championship coming to Nalani?"

"Hard not to." Delaney nodded. She plugged her camera into her laptop and started uploading the images. "Word gets around pretty quick."

"I imagine so." Tehani pinched her lips. "You also probably heard I'm kind of in charge of the whole weekend event."

Delaney turned wide brown eyes on her. "That I had not heard. Seriously?"

"Seriously." Now that it was official, the nerves had begun to set in. There was a lot riding on the success of the event, not the least of which was Remy's legacy here in Nalani. She had faith in her town and their ability to put on a great show, but that didn't mean she wasn't going to worry things to death. "And I wanted to talk to you about something. We need T-shirts made. A lot of them," she added. "Would you be interested in taking that on? We can offer you free advertising during the event, and of course we'd pay your costs, plus a little extra. I need to take a closer look at the budget, of course, and the time frame is tight—"

"What kind of T-shirts?" Delaney sounded a bit doubtful. "And how many is a lot?"

"Various colors with different logos and lettering. All together? About three hundred." Tehani winced. "The original printing company is already cutting us a deal on other items and since you're so good with this kind of thing…" She turned to look at the myriad of rompers, onesies, dresses and jumpsuits hanging from little hangers all around the brightly colored store. "I know it's a big ask. Especially since we need them in less than three weeks."

"Three—" Delaney eyed her and Tehani could swear she saw the gears turning in her brain. "Three weeks." She blew out a breath. "Okay. Can I create the design?"

"Do you want to?" Tehani had almost hated

to ask. Personally, she didn't want a single SportsFlex idea anywhere near the event.

"I'd prefer to." Her admission had Tehani breathing easier. "I've got a couple of contacts in the wholesale clothing business," Delaney mused. "Do you have a list of what you need?"

"I do." Because she'd been feeling optimistic, she'd printed off the details. She dug into her bag and pulled the sheet out, then handed it over. Now for the tricky part. "This might be pushing it, but would you be able to do them for only fifteen percent above cost?" She was pushing it, but she also knew the quality work that Delaney produced.

"No," Delaney murmured as she scanned the list. "I can do it for ten."

"Yeah?" A bubble of tension popped in Tehani's chest.

"Yeah." Delaney nodded. "A, it's for charity. I can use that to negotiate for the price of the shirts, so that's a no-brainer. B, it's for you. Again, no-brainer. I made rent thanks to your baby shower."

Tehani chuckled at that.

"And C," Delaney continued, "it's great advertising for the business. It's a worthy investment for the future of Luau Lullabies. Nalani's been so supportive since I opened this store. I've been waiting for a chance to give back."

"Then here it is. You are the best." One thing

about her Ohana in Nalani, they rarely, if ever, let her down.

"Yeah, I'm sure I can deliver this order." Delaney nodded. "It'll take extra hours, but my mom and sister can help with production. What does the free advertising include?"

"Off the top of my head..." Tehani's mind whirled. "Your name and logo on programs and flyers. Maybe we put together posters for storefronts with the main sponsors on them. We can add your store to the HOEF website. I can have Marella talk to you about specifics. She's handling all the promotional aspects."

"I'd love to work with Marella," Delaney said, a bit wide-eyed. "Maybe she'd even have more marketing ideas to suggest for me and the store."

Tehani would make sure Marella did. "So, we can put you down as a yes?"

"Absolutely yes." Delaney beamed. "Happy to be part of it. Thanks for thinking of me."

Tehani practically floated out of the store, pushing Kai into the late afternoon breeze. Things were falling into place and at a pace that made her feel so much lighter.

She'd earned a bit of a break and Kai always loved taking walks through town. The moment they hit Pulelehua Road, she was once again struck by the wonder of the exponentially increasing holiday decorations. Just ahead, she spotted a pair of maintenance workers setting potted red poinsettias and brilliant yellow and green pineapples in an alternating pattern beneath the base of a palm tree. Judging by the other palm trees lining the main road of Nalani, they'd be adding thick, long evergreen ropes up and around the tree trunk, ropes that would then be used to anchor the glowing multicolored LED lights.

She glanced over her shoulder, stopping when she saw the familiar electric golf cart *put-put-putting* its way down the street. Tehani grinned as Benji Taupu pulled over and parked beside her. The hard plastic canopy had been lined with frenetic, twinkling colored lights, between which hung small plastic flamingos wearing giant Santa hats. At the back of the single-bench vehicle, two life-size flamingos stood beak to beak with cloth Santa hats fluttering in the breeze.

"Aloha, Tehani!" Benji's tanned, wrinkled face stretched into a wide, generous smile. The old man had been making his daily treks around Nalani since before Tehani was born. "What do you think?"

"I think—" Tehani rested a hand on the stroller handle, shaking her head in amusement

"—there can't possibly be a flamingo left in all of Nalani."

Benji cackled. "That was the goal! Love me those pink birds. And so does Kahlua. Right, girl?" He reached out to scratch the pig sitting beside him. As usual, pig and owner wore matching Hawaiian shirts and today they even matched the cart with neon-pink flamingos covering their torsos.

Kahlua oinked and, if Tehani wasn't mistaken, sighed in acceptance.

"Heard you're spearheading this Santa surfing thing happenin' down the road," Benji said, waving to someone across the street when they called out to him. "Don't suppose you'll be needing a mascot?" He leaned over, put his face next to Kahlua's and raised hopeful dark eyes in her direction. "She comes with her own surfboard."

That she did. Kahlua the Pig had been featured in multiple online videos now that she had her own YouTube channel, and the most popular newscast program on Oahu had come out to do a feature story. "How do you feel about photo ops?" she asked on impulse. While the main idea behind bringing the event here was to save it, she wasn't going to miss any opportunity to showcase everything their town had to offer. And one of their best offerings was sitting right in front of her. "We can set up a booth on the beach, let people take pictures with you and Kahlua, say it's for a donation to the HOEF."

Benji sat up straight, eyes wide with surprise. "You mean it?"

"Absolutely. Does Kahlua have a Santa hat? We'd want her to blend in with the other surfers."

"Got one at home somewhere." Benji was practically vibrating with excitement. "Hot dog! Our own photo booth! Did you hear that, Kahlua? Today, Nalani, tomorrow…the world!"

"We'll be in touch about the details!" she called after him as he pulled back onto the road, lights twinkling, flamingos shimmying. "We'll just keep that to ourselves for the time being, won't we, Kai?" She dipped down the sidewalk ramp and headed across the street.

Pulelehua Road stretched close to being a mile long and boasted dozens of locally owned shops, businesses and services. Need your taxes done? Second floor over the real estate office. Family portraits need updating? Try Island Focus Photography. Is your neighbor's dog barking at all hours? Check in with Sheriff Alec Aheona Malloy and if you don't find him at the station, check the beach where he is probably watching his girlfriend, Jordan Adair, try to tame the island waves.

Everything anyone could need could be found somewhere along this stretch of road that had changed and grown so much over the years. But it had always, always stayed true to the heart of the island's spirit. Days like this, when the sun shone down from a cloudless sky, she wondered what had come over her to ever consider leaving.

She paused in front of Sky & Earth Jewelry, where a new display of holiday-inspired creations glittered in the window. Moving on, she spotted a couple of familiar faces seated in the window of Seas & Breeze, the local shave ice and frozen treat shop. Cammie and Noah Townsend, Daphne's seven- and ten-year-old step-kids, waved enthusiastically at her.

The impulse to head inside was cut short by the memory of the last time she'd been there, when Remy had needed to quench his craving for a coconut and lime shave ice. He'd given himself a headache, the delicious concoction was so cold, but the treat had definitely lightened his mood.

She very nearly moved on but irritation fluttered through her and she paused. "Not this time." She wasn't going to surrender to the sad memories any longer.

Swiftly, she turned around, then backed in through the open doorway and swung Kai's stroller toward the front table. "Hey, Noah. Hey, Cammie."

"Tehani!" Cammie, wearing what could only be described as an exploded rainbow of fabrics, had her long hair tied up in a ponytail worn so high it looked like a whale spout. She jumped out of her chair and, dripping shave ice cone in one hand, dove in for a hug. "We haven't seen you in forever!"

Tehani gave Cammie a quick squeeze, then reached out and ruffled Noah's shaggy hair. "How are you guys? What's going on?" She reached for a small black iron-back chair and set it at their table.

"Oh, my gosh, so much!" Cammie retook her seat as Noah nodded in agreement. "We get our Christmas tree today! Our first one in our new house! We're going to bake cookies and decorate."

"Awesome, that sounds like fun."

"And you know what else?" Cammie slurped at her cone. "Noah and I both got roles in the school holiday pagcant. They don't call it a Christmas pageant like they do back in Seattle. Because of Maka… Maka…" She huffed a sigh and glared at her brother. "I forgot what it's called again."

"*Makahiki.*" Daphne's gentle voice echoed from behind Tehani.

"Right," Cammie boasted. "That. What Mama D said. It's kinda like Christmas, only it's not, right?"

"Pretty much," Daphne said. "*Makahiki* predates the popular version of Christmas here in the islands, but with its focus on resting, resetting and celebrating all that the earth gives us, we've made it a kind of combination holiday. And then of course there's the eating." She toasted Tehani with the large paper cup in her hand. "Have you tried these new smoothies they've got back there?" She gestured to the far counter with at least half a dozen people waiting in line for the icy, fruity drinks. "It's a miracle any of my clothes still fit."

"Might have to do that," Tehani mused. Normally she'd get a shave ice—tamarind and passion fruit were her favorite flavors—but she was determined to start some new traditions and break out of the routines that kept her trapped in the past. "Will you keep an eye on Kai for me?"

"Yes!" Cammie dropped out of her chair once more and crouched in front of the baby. "Hi, Kai!"

"Mama D?" Tehani murmured to Daphne as she passed. Her friend merely shrugged, but there was no mistaking the pride and affection in her friend's bright green eyes. She touched

Daphne's shoulder and gave her a gentle, encouraging squeeze.

Daphne's recent marriage to Griffin Townsend, her high school sweetheart, had come after a bumpy reunion with the man a few months ago. Tehani knew Daphne had been determined to stay unattached but now found herself the heartbeat of a family she'd never even dreamed of. A family who adored her beyond words. It was that kind of happily-ever-after that kept a thread of hope winding through Tehani's heart.

The new smoothie menu felt a bit overwhelming, but by the time she got to the front of the line, she was ready to order. When she stepped up to the counter, she recognized that the owner was behind the register. "Aloha, Ema."

"Tehani." Ema gasped and darted around the counter, arms open for a hug. Ema had a petite frame but she was strong enough to have run this Nalani institution for decades. The familiar squeeze of welcome and comfort brought tears to Tehani's eyes. "It's been too long since you were here." She set Tehani back and stared up at her. Touching a hand to Tehani's cheek, she tilted her head in that all too familiar and sympathetic way. *"Pehea kou naau?"* How is your heart?

"Ho'ōla." Healing. "Mostly," she added with a sad smile.

Ema nodded, then patted her cheek. "Remy's with you always," she murmured. "And the little one? How are you finding motherhood?"

"Challenging," Tehani admitted. "Exhausting. Intoxicating." Even as she said it her heart once again filled with hope. Kai was the reason she was healing. "He's right over there if you'd like to—"

"Dougie!" Ema called out and a young man with tight black curls poked his head out from around the corner. "Counter, please!" She flexed both hands in a way that reminded Tehani of how Sydney often did when she wanted to hold Kai. "Let me see that glorious baby boy of yours."

Tehani laughed and ordered her smoothie, deciding on the pineapple, coconut and carrot concoction that, according to the chalk menu on the wall, was their current bestseller. She took her time returning to the table, reacquainting herself with the photographic history of Nalani that hung on the far wall of the treat shop.

Dozens of pictures going back to the early days of the town hung in frames in a collage-like style. The original owners of the store, Ema's parents, stood on the beach with a surfboard between them, the waves washing up behind. A few short years after this picture was taken, they fulfilled their dream of establishing one of Nalani's favorite businesses. Shave ice was an island tradition. The snowy, soft ice doused in flavored syrups provided countless variations of a sweet, cold treat.

Cammie's squeal and laughter had Tehani turning in time to see her placing a bit of ice on Kai's tongue, much to the delight and encouragement of Ema, who held the baby in her arms. Kai's eyes went wide as he tasted, frowned, then tasted again before dropping his head onto Ema's shoulder.

"Oh, I remember when your daddy came in for his first shave ice," Ema said to Kai as Tehani returned to the table. "He always loved—"

"Pineapple and lychee," Tehani finished, waiting for that pang of pain to strike. But when it struck, she found it wasn't with its usual ferocity.

"You're going to be a swimmer just like him, aren't you, Kai?" Ema swayed back and forth as she held him in the crook of her arm and shot Tehani a knowing look.

"I'm not helping you win the pool," Tehani warned.

"Mmm." Ema narrowed her eyes. "We'll talk. I heard about this Santa surfing thing you've gotten us into. Tell me about it."

"Ah." Tehani glanced around. "Don't you have—"

"I've got a kitchen full of employees who know how to do their jobs. Besides." She looked down at the baby. "I'm not done cuddling with this one yet. Sit. Tell." She jutted her chin to the empty chair beside Daphne.

As Tehani gave Ema the rundown on the almost finished plans, the older woman was nodding and numerous people had gathered around to listen. It bolstered Tehani's confidence in being able to pull off the event, but didn't diminish her trepidation about the amount of work it was going to take.

"In essence, Nalani is going to be hosting one out-of-this-world charity party in just a few weeks. We're hoping to offer various sponsorship opportunities to local businesses," Tehani concluded. "We just need to work out the details as to what they'll all be." She had to get the team together now that they'd been given the go-ahead.

"What you should do is hold a town meeting," Ema said. "No need to bother the town council about it," she added at Tehani's frown. "A general open meeting where you can get everyone together and have them sign up for what they can support. Charlie Francis will have some... Charlie? You still here?"

"Here!" a strong male voice from the back of the gathered crowd called out. He stood up and waved, then moved forward. The middle-aged, rotund man was the head custodian for both the elementary school and the community center. "We've got bingo tonight," he said. "But we can have such a gathering tomorrow, if that works for you, Tehani?"

"Oh, and we can talk it up at bingo," Ema confirmed. "We'll get the word out. Gives you a little time to get everything together."

"That would be great," Tehani said. "How's seven tomorrow night? After dinner for everyone?" She looked to Charlie, who was pulling out his cell phone.

"Calling my boss right now," Charlie assured her as he stepped to a quiet corner.

Tehani took a long drink of her smoothie and instantly wished she'd gotten a larger one. The flavor combination was both unexpected and refreshing. But she needed to get going if she was to be anywhere near ready to handle a town meeting tomorrow night.

Ema returned Kai to his stroller, then touched a hand to the baby's forehead. "He's a beautiful boy, Tehani. You're doing well with him." She grabbed Tehani's hand and squeezed. "And for him."

"Mahalo, Ema," Tehani murmured in gratitude.

"Okay, guys, we need to stop at Ohana before

we head home. And you've got homework to do," Daphne reminded a groaning Noah. "After that and dinner, we can start decorating the tree."

"Awesome." Noah gave an energetic fist pump and gobbled down the rest of his shave ice. "Come on, Cammie."

"What's happened to Taco?" Tehani asked Daphne as the kids raced out the door.

"Taco has a special place of honor on Cammie's bed, full-time," Daphne said. "Thank goodness, because I'm not sure that big stuffed fish was going to survive another trip through the washing machine." She followed Tehani as she wheeled the stroller outside.

"She outgrew her comfort animal, then?"

"Happened a couple of weeks ago," Daphne said. "About the same time she started calling me Mama D." Her smile was quick. "Griff said she felt guilty calling me Mom since she still sees her mom from time to time. He suggested she make up something else."

"Change comes so easy to them," Tehani said. "Or easier, at least."

"Sometimes. What is it that people say? The only constant in life is that it's always changing."

"Something like that." They made their way up the hill toward Ohana Odysseys, where

Marella and Sydney had been keeping the business running while also helping with the event. She had enough new information to take the time to check in with them. Besides, getting out and walking around felt better than sitting behind a computer lamenting all the ways things could go wrong with the tournament.

"Oh, my gosh, look at the lights!" Cammie was jumping up and down at the foot of the stairs leading into the Ohana office. "They're amazing!"

Tehani had to agree. The entire building looked as if it had been outlined by a team of Santa's top elves. "I bet at night you can see this from space," she joked with Daphne as her friend lifted the front of Kai's stroller so they could carry it up the stairs.

When the overhead bell dinged and announced their arrival, Tehani found Sydney and Marella with their heads together at the round conference table by the back window.

"We have news," Daphne announced. "Cammie, Noah, be careful, please." The kids had dove forward to go through the plastic bins filled with ornaments and lights for the yet-to-be decorated tree propped up in the corner.

Namaka lifted his head from where he was curled up and sleeping on Tehani's office chair. He gave a feline-forward appraising look at the newcomers, then huffed out a sigh and went back to sleep.

"What's all this?" Tehani wheeled Kai's stroller over to the table that was piled high with papers and sticky notes. "Sydney, shouldn't you be concentrating on wedding details?"

Sydney waved off her comment. "It's nice to focus on something different for a change. Besides, Theo and I have done all we can do at this point. This is more important."

Tehani begged to differ, but she kept that to herself. "So what are you working on?"

"We've just about locked down a list of sponsorship tier ideas," Marella said. She stretched her arms above her head, then relaxed. "We used what was already in place in Kona to get started." She flipped her laptop around as Tehani leaned her hands on the table. "We didn't want to take a chance and lose the businesses that had already committed to staying on board so we've got this level here." She tapped the screen. "Starts at five hundred. Called the Tidal Wave Tier, which gives them logo placement and social media mentions as well as—"

Darn it! She'd completely forgotten about that. "I need to talk to Aimita about the social media accounts."

"I called her," Marella said. "You've got

enough to juggle. I can manage this side of things."

"What's this?" Tehani peered closer. "Two complimentary tickets to the VIP area? Do we have a VIP area?"

"That's my idea," Sydney said. "It doesn't have to be extravagant. At least not this year. We can set aside a designated seating area with the best view of the competition—provide comfortable seating, a canopy for shade. Add in a bit of light catering, a swag bag and some networking opportunities and it'll give an elevated experience." She eyed Tehani. "Something we can expand on in the future."

"I could speak to Wyatt about maybe building a temporary elevated area," Tehani mused. "Something we can dismantle and use again?" Sydney cringed. "What?"

"He'll be pretty busy," Sydney said. "I kind of asked Wyatt to finish upgrading the second cabin Ohana owns. We're thinking it would make a great place for the competitors to stay."

"Oh." Tehani nodded. "No, you're right. That makes a lot of sense. Okay. Maybe this year we just use some beach tents and cabanas. They could work well enough. Walk me through the rest of these tiers."

Tehani couldn't help but be impressed by the amount of detail her friends had managed to incorporate into the sponsorships. Ranging from the lowest five-hundred-dollar level all the way up to the highest for five thousand. They'd even noted how many sponsorships would be available so as not to strain their resources.

"We're just building up from the basic tier," Sydney said, "offering promotional opportunities such as having them participate in various ways throughout the weekend, like maybe having one of the Aloha Ambassador Tier hosting the award ceremony or even a short speaking slot during the opening or closing ceremony. It would be a good way to pull from the community and not have you or Mano tied to emcee duties."

"We're thinking we keep the number of sponsorships kinda low this year," Marella said. "We don't have enough time to go all out on the logo placements other than flyers and signage. We're thinking ten tier ones—that would bring in five thousand—then six of the Hono Haven level. We're estimating that could bring in close to thirty thousand. Maybe enough to cover most of our costs."

Tehani did the math, then shook her head. "We need to adjust. We're going to have to use one of these—" she pointed to the Kokua Kahuna Tier "—for SurfsUp Swag. They're cutting us a deal on our branded items in exchange for event promo."

"Okay." Marella scribbled on one of her notepads. "Anyone else?"

"Yeah. A Hono Haven needs to go to Delaney at Luau Lullabies. She's going to do the T-shirts."

"You've been busy," Sydney said.

"Those were Wyatt's ideas," Tehani said, wanting to give credit where it was due. "If we manage to book the rest of the sponsorships, we'd be north of twenty." Which was far beyond what she'd imagined they could bring in. Truth be told, she would have felt lucky to have broken even. But she was getting ahead of herself.

"Even with our expenses, that could put us on track for reaching a record amount for the HOEF," Marella said. "We made a list of the businesses in Kona that are still on board." She handed Tehani a printout. "Given what they've paid already, we've assigned them their tiers. It still leaves us with a good number left to offer to Nalani businesses. And they'll have a choice, too."

"Only thing we need is to communicate this as widely as possible. And fast," Sydney said.

Tehani skimmed through the numbers. "Ema suggested a town meeting. Tomorrow night at the community center." She tried to focus on the conversation at hand, but she found herself a bit detached, due to the shock of seeing all of this coming together. "This is super, guys. Can you get all this together in a kind of presentation? For tomorrow? Then we can have people sign up at the meeting."

"Of course." Marella flipped her laptop back around. "I'll run the final details by you before we finish."

Tehani sank into the chair beside Sydney. "This is going to happen. I think we're really going to pull this off."

"Still a lot to do yet," Sydney reminded her as she glanced at the clock on the wall.

"I should start calling the Kona businesses," Tehani said even as she smothered a yawn. "Let them know they've got a slot if they want it."

"I can do that." Daphne walked up behind her. "I need to contribute," she added at Tehani's surprise. "Give me the contact info. I'll start as soon as I get home. Kids'll have their homework and I'll have mine."

"Okay." Marella clicked her mouse. "I'll forward it to you. Let them know we need an answer by tomorrow, end of day, along with their logos so we can get everything together for all the printing."

"Hey." Sydney rested a hand on Tehani's. "You look wiped out. Why don't you head home and get some sleep?" She glanced at her nephew. "I bet you and Kai could both use a nap."

Tehani had to admit that sounded like a terrific idea, but she didn't think she could wind down enough to actually sleep. "Maybe. If my brain stops spinning."

"Then how about a little ocean therapy? Go take a swim. Let us deal with all this for now. There'll be plenty for you to do, Tehani," Sydney urged. "Take the time while you can. Before the chaos starts."

Smiling sleepily, Tehani nodded. "Hmm, some time by the ocean does sound kind of wonderful. I've got a suit in my locker. Keep an eye on him for me?"

"You never have to ask. Hey there, Kai." Sydney leaned over and scooped Kai out of the carrier portion of his stroller. "Whatcha been doing since I saw you last?"

Tehani felt a nervous kind of energy circling inside of her as she withdrew into the bathroom to change. During her pregnancy she'd made it a point to go swimming in the ocean at least once a day. Being in the water meant as much to her as the air she breathed, not only for her own peace of mind, but hopefully to pass along that affection to her son. Since Kai was born, however, she'd found herself making excuses not to swim or even spend time at the shore.

Maybe because he looked so much like his father that it hurt her heart to take him there. She couldn't be sure. What she did know, now, at least, was that it was the right moment to step toward change and put the daily ritual she loved back in place.

The bright yellow two-piece fit a bit more snugly than it had pre-pregnancy, but slipping it on felt right. As if she were regaining a piece of her past. She shrugged her shorts back on, slathered on her sunblock and, after tugging her shirt over her head, squeezed additional sun-screen onto her fingers for Kai.

"Oh, here you go, *keiki*." Sydney walked around the room with Kai in her arms. "Mama's going to get you all protected from the sun." She continued to hold him while Tehani quickly swiped the cream over her son's face and arms and chubby little legs. He squealed and giggled and earned a snuggle from both his mother and auntie before they were done.

"You going to head back into town?" Sydney asked as she settled him back into his carrier.

"Ah, no, actually." Tehani kept her voice low. "Is, um…" She took a deep breath. "Is Wyatt working on the cottage now?"

Sydney's brows went up. "As far as I know. He wanted to get a jump on things—finish with the demo before bringing in more help."

Tehani pinched her lips together, tried to push aside what Mano had said about her and Wyatt's *friendship*. But the truth was, she'd kept herself busy so she didn't have to think too hard on her brother's words. How could one kiss—okay, *three* kisses—have thrown her so far off balance that she was spinning like a tropical cyclone headed for the nearest island?

Across the room, Cammie and Noah were digging through the plastic bins of tree ornaments, deciding which ones they liked best.

Sydney touched her arm and drew her away from where Daphne and Marella commiserated over the sponsorship list. "What's going on, T?"

Tehani shook her head. "I don't know." Or maybe she did and Sydney wasn't the right person to talk to. Not about this. "Everything feels all tangled up in my head. And my heart."

Sydney's blond hair dropped over her shoulder when she inclined her head. "What's got you tangled up? Wyatt? Did something happen?"

"Something?" She almost croaked the word.

Sydney inclined her head and shot her that look that was just shy of an eye roll.

"It was...nothing." Even now, she could feel her cheeks warm with embarrassment. "I kissed him. The other night. After dinner."

If she expected judgment or disapproval, neither manifested on her friend's face. "Was it a bad kiss?" Tehani's cheeks went hotter and Sydney grinned. "I'm just teasing you, T." She rubbed Tehani's arm and her amusement shifted to concern. "Hey, a kiss shouldn't make you miserable."

"Well, it shouldn't have me feeling..." What on earth was she feeling? She felt like a dinghy out at sea, being tossed on the waves like a toy. She groaned, then covered her face. "I'm so embarrassed."

"About kissing Wyatt?" Sydney sounded genuinely baffled. "Nothing to be embarrassed about."

"There isn't?" It annoyed her that she wanted validation.

"Of course not," Sydney insisted. "If anything, I'm wondering what took you so long. The guy's crazy about you. Anyone who sees the two of you together for two seconds can see that."

An unfamiliar pang chimed in her stomach. Tehani pressed a hand to her tummy. "He is? But..." How was that possible? "But he was Remy's best friend. How...can he? How can I even think...?"

"Ah." The glint in Sydney's eyes eased. "There's nothing to feel guilty about, Tehani. I think my brother of all people would want you to move on. He'd want the same thing for you that the rest of us do. For you to be happy."

Guilt of an entirely different sort wound through Tehani as she was reminded yet again that no one was aware of the difficulties she and Remy had been having those last months. Since his death, she'd decided that guilt was like the ocean with its unseen and, at times, unfathomable layers. She no sooner peeled back the reality of one only to be faced with evidence of another. It was like needing to learn to swim all over again.

"I don't know how to do this," Tehani whispered. "With Remy it just…fell into place. One day he was my brother's best friend and the next…" And the next, she was a besotted seventeen-year-old who couldn't see anything or anyone other than Remy Calvert. "I'm only just finding my footing without him, Syd. I'm learning how to be a mother and how to get through the day on my own. I…" She straightened. She didn't want to go back to living in someone else's shadow. Something broke apart, or maybe free, inside of her the instant she said it. "You're right. Wyatt is a great guy and he's a good friend. I don't want to lose that."

"Nothing says you have to," Sydney argued. "The best relationships are based on friendship."

"But I don't want anything more than that."
Even as she said it, her heart ached a bit. "At
least not now." But maybe one day, in the future. When she didn't feel so...emotionally
wobbly.

"I can understand that." Sydney nodded in
the way only a good friend could. "You might
want to consider I'm not the one you should be
having this conversation with."

Yeah. Tehani sighed. She knew that was coming. "You're right. I need to talk to him." Exactly how did she even begin that conversation?
Did she say, *Look, Wyatt, you're a great kisser
and you nearly blew my toes off my feet, but
I think we should just be friends*? That didn't
particularly come across as endearing. "I'll go
do that." She pointed to the door and grabbed
the stroller's handle. "Right now."

"Okay," Sydney agreed. "Just remember that
sometimes your heart can have a will of its
own." She squeezed Tehani's arm. "Don't be
surprised if it keeps trying to overrule your
head."

CHAPTER NINE

WYATT SWEPT THE last of the demo debris toward the garbage can by the front door of the beach cottage. His body ached from an almost full day's work, but he felt good about the direction the project was headed. The old had been cleared out. Time to start thinking about the new.

He already had a paint color in mind—one that would complement the sister cottage that had served as a short-term residence first for Theo Fairfax and then for Keane. After the surfing competition concluded, Ohana Odysseys could add cottage rentals to their list of offerings for visiting tourists.

He'd keep with the natural color scheme: a soft, subtle blue for the water that lay just feet away and green hues representing the beautiful fauna the islands were known for. He'd leave the pops of color for the decor elements he assumed Sydney would want a hand in choosing. Remy had struck a deal with a number of the town businesses to display various handmade items in the other cabin. Chances are they'd want to do that again as it was a great way to drum up business. He recalled that after a few days, Theo had made a significant purchase from The Hawaiian Snuggler after appreciating the handcrafted quilt that had been placed over the back of the small sofa.

Instead of removing the cabinetry in the bathroom and kitchen, like he'd originally planned, he'd decided to leave them in place and refinish them. Replacement could come later, when he had more time and if Sydney wasn't pleased with the work he did. It would make finding the right-fitting appliances a bit trickier, but that wouldn't take nearly as much time as waiting on cabinets to be shipped.

Wyatt stood in the doorway, looking out at the ocean as the tide tumbled onto the shore. The water called to him, almost as loudly as the sunset that would soon begin. Satisfied with his accomplishments, he gave in to impulse, stripped his shirt over his head, toed off his shoes, pulled his wallet, cell phone and keys out of the pockets of his board shorts, then headed straight down the shore and dove in.

Losing himself in the white noise, he emptied his mind of thoughts and his heart of fear. Of desires. He'd learned a long time ago to keep his feelings and emotions tightly under control, secret even. The last person to accuse him of wearing his heart on his sleeve had been his mother and she'd been gone for so long.

His heart had locked itself up when she'd died and at times it felt as if it had stopped beating altogether. It was only after he came to Nalani that he felt as if he could breathe again. Live again. His grandparents had given him everything he ever needed from the day he'd arrived. Caring about anyone felt like an impossible risk to take before, but between their love and understanding and meeting Remy at school, he'd risen out of the grief.

And then he'd met her.

All he could remember of that day was feeling as if he'd been hit by a bolt of lightning. Lightning that emblazoned the image of her silky, long black hair and equally dark eyes that were constantly alight with humor, kindness and appreciation. She'd always seen him, always seen everyone, despite the towering force that was Remy Calvert spiraling around them. Her soft voice had brushed against his ears and tortured his heart. But he'd smiled through it if only to remain in her presence. Even as he watched her fall deeper and deeper in love with his best friend.

How many nights had he lain awake, wondering how Tehani might react if she ever discovered how he truly felt about her? He'd been determined to take that secret to his grave, promised himself to cling to her friendship rather than risk ruining anything between them. Friendship was safe and it was enough to keep him in her orbit. He could be happy with that.

Or at least he thought he could be. Until she'd kissed him.

He surfaced, slicked his hair back and blinked the salt water out of his eyes. Gulping air, he treaded water as he tried to push away the surging feelings that had broken free upon holding her in his arms.

It had been a lifetime of dreaming that led him to that moment. He'd keep it close, locked in his heart, and he promised himself, promised her, it would never happen again.

He dove once more, his lungs straining, only to surge back up and break free. He swam hard and slowed farther out, bobbing in the waves before he turned and headed back to shore.

His muscles flexed and pumped even as the water eased the ache of his physical labor. His internal clock began clicking in his head. He could feel the sunset coming on, like a radiating wave of promise as his feet hit the sand and he trudged out of the water.

He looked over his shoulder, ran his hands

through his soaked hair and did his best to leave his worry over Tehani out where it could vanish into the depths. When he turned, he found her standing at the base of the stairs, hands resting gently on Kai's stroller. Watching him.

Impulse nearly had him looking behind him, just to confirm he was the focus of her attention. She didn't move. She simply remained where she was with the evening breeze lifting her hair gently off her face beneath the soft glow of the porch light.

Heart hammering, he made his way toward her, unable to decipher the gleam in her eyes. "Hey." It dawned on him that he hadn't grabbed a towel out of his truck, so he kept his distance and shook himself off. "I was just about to head home. Everything okay?" He glanced at the stroller where Kai's eyes drooped. "It's almost dinnertime for him, isn't it?"

"I needed to talk to you," she said, an unfamiliar, almost uncertain tone in her voice. "I could have waited until…" She gestured to the setting sun. "About the other night."

He held up both hands. "Say no more." As uncomfortable as she clearly was, he didn't want their brief moments of intimacy to ruin the friendship he needed.

"No, I want to say this. I need to. I just…" She glanced away, then back at him. "I'm just finding myself, Wyatt. I'm finally learning who I am separate from Remy. I can't—"

He couldn't bear to see her so torn. "You don't have to say anything more." He remained where he was, steps away, even as his hands ached to reach for her. "I understand."

"I don't see how," she mumbled. "I barely understand it myself."

"It's enough that we're friends." It was a lie, but a necessary one. One he'd been telling himself for years. He could survive not being loved by her; he wasn't sure he could get by without her in his life. Period. "But if you ever change your mind—"

She stepped toward him, lifted her hands to his wet chest and flattened her cool palms against his chilly skin. He shivered, tightened his hands at his sides as she lifted her mouth to his. He remained still, refusing to touch her again, allowing her to take whatever it was that she needed. Every ounce of his being committed the feel of her, the taste of her, to memory.

Tehani pulled away with a soft sigh, confusion filling her gaze. "All the way over here, I rehearsed what I was going to say." Her hands rested against him. "I kept telling myself that I was doing the right thing—stopping this, whatever this is, before it gets started. But now..."

But now? He so desperately wanted to ask.

"This… Wyatt, I don't know what to do with—"

He couldn't take any more. He reached out, clasped her hips with his hands, drew her in and dipped his head. He captured her mouth and kissed her. Kissed her as he'd spent the last decade of his life dreaming about kissing her. The kind of kiss that, if he was very lucky, would sear itself into both their minds as a defining moment of their lives.

He'd never forget this. He knew that even as he felt her move closer to him. He felt the hitch in her breath when she gasped, felt the potency in her touch as she lifted her arms up and around his neck. He released her then but withdrew only enough to settle his forehead against hers.

"I don't know how to do this," she whispered, and he could hear the tears in her voice. "With Remy—"

"I'm not Remy." It didn't come out harsh or combative, but rather a gentle statement of fact. "I never will be."

"I know that." She leaned back to meet his gaze. She lifted a hand to his face and when she touched him, it was like being branded by the sun. "I do know that, Wyatt. But where do we…? How do we even…?"

"Begin?" He kissed the tip of her nose. "I think we already have."

Tears filled her eyes. "I couldn't bear to lose you as a friend."

"You never will." He meant it. He'd spent so long promising whatever powers that be that if he was just given a chance, he wouldn't waste it. That he would put absolutely everything he had into making her happy. Into giving her everything she needed and wanted. Into showing her he could be her future. Even now, he felt himself teetering on the precipice of that possibility and it was all he could do not to pitch forward and let himself fall. "Whatever happens, I promise that I will always be here for you." And Wyatt didn't make promises he didn't intend to keep.

"What if—"

He kissed her again, stopped the fear from escaping her lips. When he felt her hesitancy, he broke contact. "Let's say we make Sydney and Theo's wedding our first official date." He gazed down at her and stroked her cheek.

"The wedding?" Her eyes went wide. "But that's…weeks away."

The idea that she seemed disappointed felt like a positive sign. "You've got your hands full with the tournament and I'm going to be busy getting this place in shape. There won't be a lot of spare time and I would much prefer to put all my attention on you. Also, it means I get a New Year's Eve date so—" he shrugged "—bonus planning."

The tension he'd felt in her seemed to ease. "Okay. The wedding." She nodded and a slow smile lit her eyes. Or maybe that was the sun shimmering. "That'll give us the chance to come to terms with this…shift in our relationship."

"Just promise not to overthink it," he urged.

She nodded. "I'm scared, Wyatt."

"So am I." His admission seemed to perk her up and he grinned. "How about we be scared together, yeah?"

She nodded—a quick gesture that filled his heart instantly. "Okay. Together."

Kai let out a squeal that either meant he approved or he needed changing. Wyatt looked at him. "We should probably get him home and fed."

"Nope." She stepped back and pulled her tank top over her head, revealing the bright yellow bikini top that had featured prominently in his dreams. "There's formula in my bag and I'm feeling like a swim of my own." She shimmied out of her shorts, then kicked off her sandals. "Will you watch him for me?"

"Of course," he said as she raced down to the tide. "Always."

TEHANI AWOKE TO the sound of Kai's "I'm wet" cries shortly after six the next morning. Groaning, she threw an arm over her face and silently willed her son to go back to sleep. When it became quite clear he was going to ignore her telepathic pleas, she shoved out of bed and walked the few steps to her son's nursery.

"Okay, *mae-mae*, I hear you. I'm here." She stood over the baby and rested a gentle hand on his chest, a gesture that calmed him almost immediately. Her long hair fell over one shoulder and Kai immediately brightened, flexing a chubby fist toward the tresses. "You slept in this morning for a change." She should count her blessings for the extra two hours of sleep.

Not that the night had been particularly restful. She'd tossed and turned most of the time, trying to reconcile with how her mind was set on one thing while, as Sydney had warned, her heart had other ideas. She'd had every intention of letting Wyatt know she wasn't in any place to start something romantic but after seeing him walking out of the water like that—with the setting sun glowing behind him and that sweet smile so perfectly on display—all of her good intentions had drained right out of her and into the sand.

That was another great aspect to Wyatt, though. He truly had become someone that she knew she could turn to without hesitation and who would be there for her and Kai. No questions asked.

There really wasn't anything more appealing in her opinion, when it came to dipping her toe into the relationship pool once more.

"Looks like your mama is getting herself into some trouble." Even as she said it, she found herself smiling. But not quite yet. She'd need time to get used to the idea of dating Wyatt. Dating. A date.

Frowning, she tried to recall the last time Remy had taken her out on a date. They'd had their routine: Monday dinners at Hula Chicken and Thursday morning breakfasts on the beach after he'd raced the sunrise tide. Every few weeks they'd splurge on a dinner at the Blue Moon Bar & Grill, but other than that...

She slammed on the mental brakes. She was doing it again. Bringing memories of Remy into every current situation. Irritated, she bent down, kissed Kai's forehead and brought herself back to the moment, back to the gratitude she tried to start each day with. "We aren't going to do that today, are we, Kai?" She made quick work of changing him, then carried him out to the living room where she put him in his playpen and heated a bottle of formula.

When the bottle was warm and her coffee

was brewed, she picked him back up and settled then in the corner of the sofa for their morning routine. It was sacred time. Time she'd promised she'd give herself every day for as long as she could. She wanted Kai to know, to understand, to *feel*, how loved he was. And not just by her, but by her Ohana as well.

Her Ohana. Her support system. A system that featured Wyatt front and center. For a moment, the fear surged afresh if a relationship didn't work out for them, but she pushed it aside. She'd have a chance to fret later if the need really arose. But for now, things would remain as they were with Wyatt as they navigated the next frantic weeks of this holiday season.

She must have dozed off because when she brought her head up, she found a squirming Kai flexing his fingers for the bottle that had slipped out of her hold. "Sorry, *mae-mae*." She repositioned and kept widening her eyes to stay awake until he finished eating. Burping him turned into a very productive affair and she even managed to catch most of what he spit up on the shoulder rag.

Convinced he was satisfied, she got up to place him in the playpen. Only then did she see the paper that had been slid under her front door. She picked it up, pulled open the door and checked the driveway next door. Wyatt's truck was gone, but on her front porch sat a small pink bakery box.

Smiling, she brought it into the house. Two pineapple malasadas sat inside. She took a bite of one before flipping open the paper, smiling so wide her back teeth caught a breeze.

> *Can't wait for New Year's Eve. In the meantime, keep your strength up. See you at sunset. Wyatt.*

She covered her mouth but the giggle still escaped. Giddy. The note made her feel positively giddy and she actually squealed. Kai squealed back and she laughed. Now, that was the perfect start to the day.

CHAPTER TEN

"SORRY I'M LATE." Mano slid into the chair beside Tehani as the town hall crowd began to disperse. "My own meeting ran over. I didn't mean to miss your presentation about the event weekend. How did it go?"

"Really well, thanks." Tehani glanced up from the stack of sign-up sheets Jordan Adair had slipped in front of her a few minutes before. "Heartening for sure. The last time we had a crowd this size at a town meeting we were prepping for a hurricane." She scanned through the completed sheets, emotion clogging her throat. "We've almost tapped out of openings for volunteer positions." She flipped through more pages. The past day had flown by in the blink of an eye. Between getting the various opportunities organized and presented and keeping Kai on his schedule, she'd barely had time to eat. "And we've got ten RVs being offered for housing along with…" She did the math in her head. "Twenty-two other guest rooms available. And that's just from those who attended the town hall. I'm calling them host homes." She was hoping once word started flying around town, they'd end up with even more people offering their guest rooms for use.

She skimmed the thinning crowd, picking out all the familiar faces milling about, chatting, laughing and gesticulating as they admired the hall that was decked out for the season.

The air was filled with the aroma emanating from the half dozen slow cookers containing Pua's famous pear-and-pineapple spiced cider, minus the rum. Tehani's stomach rumbled at the promise of one of her favorite drinks of the season, but right now sugar was the last thing she needed.

"How about the sponsorships?" Mano eased the stack of papers out of her grasp to take a look for himself.

"We're in pretty good shape," she told him. "We're currently at about seventy-five percent, which still leaves room for latecomers." But they needed to sign up fast if they wanted in on the great advertising opportunities on offer. "I think we're going to be able to call this tournament a success." And honestly, that was all she wanted for this year. To be successful enough to build off of for next year.

"Looks great to me." Mano inclined his chin toward the sight of Benji and Kahlua making their way through the crowd. "Aloha, Benji." Her brother's smile was warm and amused, a normal reaction when it came to the old man and his pet pig. Kahlua's rope leash had some sparkly tinsel wrapped around it. "You just get here?"

"Was sitting in the back." Benji braced his toothpick-thin legs apart and leaned his hands on the table. "I want to volunteer."

"Okay." Options spun through Tehani's head. "What do you have in mind?"

"I want to be a spotter. Help with the surfing contest," Benji added with a tone of pride. "I was pretty good on the waves once upon a time. Be nice to be involved with the competition side of things again."

"Ah." Tehani was instantly worried since the job meant spending long hours in the sun and, well, honestly, at nearing ninety that was too big a risk to take with Benji as far as she was concerned. "Well, I suppose we could move you over to that position. But it'd be a shame to lose your and Kahlua's photo booth, though. I was banking on that bringing in some serious cash."

"You really think that'll be enough, in terms of contributing?" Benji didn't look convinced.

"I love this place. Gotta make sure this event is the best it can be."

"Of course." Tehani folded her hands on the table. "And Kahlua is, after all, Nalani's unofficial mascot. She's been featured on the news, been on the social media platforms loads of times. In fact, she's even got her own social media following." Of course a fashion-forward, Hawaiian-shirt-wearing surfing pig was an online star. "I planned to give you your own tent where people could get pictures with you and Kahlua in exchange for a donation to the HOEF, like we'd talked about. But if you'd rather—"

"No!" Benji stood up straight and held up both hands. "No, you're right. That is a better use of our talents, eh, Kahlua?"

Tehani leaned forward just as the pig snorted and gave a shake of her head. As usual, owner and pet had worn matching shirts, this one a bright green with flower-accented Christmas lights. The animal almost came up to Benji's knobby knees.

"I'm putting together the schedule of events and all the activities that will be available," she told Benji, who seemed a bit puffed up with pride now. "It would help if you could let me know what hours work for you. That way we can feature the two of you right from the start.

I bet we get people lining up around the beach for the chance."

"I can do that," Benji assured her. "You hear that, Kahlua? People around the beach! I should start thinking about our outfits." He looked Tehani in the eye, his gratitude and sympathy shining bright. "You're making Remy proud, Tehani. You were right before when you were talking. He never would have let this event die without doing everything he could to save it." He reached across the table to pat her folded hands. "You're keeping his legacy intact for you and your boy." His trembling smile brought tears to her eyes. "Miss that guy. But he's out there somewhere, maybe everywhere, watching over all of us."

Tehani swallowed hard. "I believe you're right," she managed before he walked away.

"You okay?" Mano's quiet question had her blinking back tears.

"Yeah, of course." What Benji had said, what she had said, was true. This did feel a bit like another legacy Remy had left behind. And it was her responsibility to make certain it remained one.

"Did you really have a photo booth in mind for him and Kahlua?" Mano asked.

"I did. It came to me the other day, out of the blue," Tehani admitted. "I couldn't imagine him not wanting to take part in this. I didn't expect him to want to be a spotter, though." The job was one of the more taxing ones for a surfing competition. Spotters acted as lookouts for the surfers while they competed, watching not just the surfers, but also for their safety. Like higher than expected waves and other surprise occurrences. "The idea of him being in the direct sun that long bothers me and besides—"

"He hasn't gotten his new prescription for glasses filled yet." Mano finished the thought for her. "I'd heard that, too. If you still need spotters, add me to the list. Unless you have different plans for me."

"Other than being our major sponsor, I was planning to use you as a fill-in. Spotter works for me." She scribbled his name on the sheet. "Sure you don't want to enter the competition yourself?" Her teasing grin could only be described as little-sisterly.

"I am positive," Mano said emphatically. "My surfing competition days are far behind me. We can leave that part of things to Keane. Speaking of our resident surf instructor, is he here?"

"I saw him earlier." Tehani craned her neck to search the crowd. "Are you good to finish things up here? I'd like to head over to Daphne's and pick up Kai."

"Daphne's watching Kai?" Mano's brows shot up. "I thought Wyatt was going to—"

"He's working late on the beach cottage," Tehani said. "He didn't want to chance Kai getting spattered with paint. Daphne volunteered. I think maybe she's trying to get Cammie and Noah used to having a baby around the house."

"Wouldn't surprise me. Oh, hey, there's Griff." Mano waved Daphne's husband over. "Howzit, Griff?" They exchanged handshakes after Griff set his camera on the table.

"Going pretty okay," Griffin Townsend, a freelance photojournalist, had wholeheartedly embraced island life since marrying Daphne a few months prior. "Marella suggested I get a jump on documenting the event from the early stages. I thought a feature on how the town is coming together to save the charity tournament and the HOEF itself was a good place to start."

"That's why you all are the A-Team. Always thinking beyond the ordinary." Tehani gathered up her papers and had just stuck them into her folder when Jordan appeared with another stack.

"That's the last of them," Jordan confirmed as she handed over the names of those wanting to host a food tent or truck. "What else can I do to help?"

"Um." Tehani referred to her endless list of

things to do. "Tomorrow morning could you put together info about companies that offer bulk rentals on pop-up tents? I should have a final count in a couple of days for what we'll need. We're looking for reasonable fees. And if you could pay attention to the delivery charges? Maybe stress the fact this is all for charity?"

"Consider it done." Jordan nodded and sent her bead-enhanced curls to bouncing around her shoulders. She reached down to rest her hand on the top of Namaka's feline head, which had poked out of the top of the bag Jordan carried. "I was wondering about local distilleries," she said. "Maybe one of them would be interested in taking on a sponsorship?"

"Excellent idea," Griff said. "There's that new one between here and Hilo. Lava Coast? I've tried a few of their brews and small operations like that are usually eager for new tasting audiences and promotional opportunities."

"A tasting tent," Tehani murmured as she made a mental note. "You want to make a run with that?" she asked Jordan, who seemed surprised but was nonetheless enthusiastic about taking on the task. "Approach Lava Coast about it and any others you think might work. When you have a chance," Tehani added. She might be a master of multitasking, but she didn't want to burn Jordan out.

"Of course," Jordan confirmed. "That one'll be easy. I just have to ask… Speak of the devil. Hello, Sheriff."

A tall, dark-haired man in khakis with a badge on his shirt pocket slid in behind Jordan and tugged her close. "Miss Adair." He bent his head and brushed his lips across hers. "Thought I'd stop by and see how things went. Any problems?" Their sheriff was one of the most easygoing people Tehani had ever known. He had a remarkably calm way of dealing with any disturbances or problems that arose, from wayward, misbehaving teens to keeping a caring eye on Haki, Nalani's resident *Menehune* hunter.

"Everything went great," Tehani assured him. "I did want to talk to you about security, though. Would you be up to finding and training some volunteers for the extent of the competition weekend? We already have the names of those who have offered to help you out. Oh, and we'll need a manned tent for kids who get lost and folks who might need first aid." And she needed to put the word out asking for lifeguards and Sea-Doo Jet Ski operators to patrol the waters. "A kind of general help spot."

Alec nodded. "I can make that happen, sure. And I've got a list of standby deputies back at the office. I'll start calling tomorrow and get back to you."

"Awesome." Another task marked off her own personal to-do list. "Okay. I need to get out of here before I micromanage locking the door." She slid her stuffed folders into her bag. "And I am grabbing a cider on the way out." Temptation had finally won. "I'll give you a call when I've got all of this organized into some kind of system." She brushed a kiss on her brother's cheek. "Night."

It took her fifteen minutes to get from the cider table to the exit as she found herself stopped frequently by people wanting to thank her or chat or present additional ideas that, for the most part, made really good sense. When she finally pushed her back against the bar on the door, her cider cup was empty and she was making a mental note to approach a few artists to paint seascapes during the competition that would then be auctioned off at the closing ceremony. "Always looking for new ways to raise money."

She wasn't two steps outside when she spotted Wyatt across from the community center, leaning against a railing. The butterflies inside her took flight. "Hey." Her smile came easily, if not a bit nervously. The pressure was more or less off them since they'd decided to wait for their first official date, but she was now reminded that every moment until New Year's

Eve had the propensity to be a bit…awkward. "I didn't see you inside."

"Just got here a few minutes ago." He reached for the bag on her shoulder and lifted it free. "I'll take that for you."

"Thanks." She smiled as he fell into step beside her. The sun had set already and as they walked through the increasing darkness, she felt a bit of loss at the fact they hadn't watched it together. Still, with the twinkling lights and warm December air, there was no doubt the holidays had definitely taken over Nalani. "This is a nice surprise."

"I finished painting sooner than I expected." Even as he spoke, she could see tiny speckles of paint in his hair and on his face. "Tomorrow I'm starting on the floors. Exciting times."

She laughed at his tamped down enthusiasm.

"You should have seen me the first time I used a floor sander. I think the thing was heavier than I was." His smile shone brilliantly in the growing darkness. "Reminded me of when Keane tried to teach me to surf on one of those fancy boards. I had no control. Got caught up with the cord and nearly pitched myself into the dock."

Tehani chuckled. "How old were you when you did that?"

"Ah, seventeen." He chuckled along with her.

"Before I started building up my muscles." He flexed an arm and Tehani tripped over her own feet. He reached out, caught her arm and tugged her back. "You okay?"

"Fine." Just incredibly susceptible to the man's muscle flexing apparently. "Ah, Daphne's place is that way." She pointed up the slight hill, the opposite direction of where they were headed. "I have to pick Kai up on my way home."

"I know. I thought we might take a little detour."

"Oh?" Her stomach jumped and she folded her arms over her chest. Her bare skin erupted with goose bumps and not because of the weather. The evening was a bit balmy even for December. "Where are we going?"

"It's a surprise." He held up a handled bag she hadn't noticed before. "Trust me."

"Always." The response was immediate and honest. She couldn't think of anyone she trusted more unless it was her brother.

Most of the shops along Pulelehua were closed at this time of night. Seas & Breeze boasted a late-night clientele, but even there, Ema was bringing in their specials sign. She gave them a wave as they wandered down toward the marina. Tehani wasn't entirely sure what Wyatt had in mind, but she was enjoying looking at all the holiday decorations in full nighttime glory.

She knew from years of experience that as Christmas drew nearer the amount of poinsettias would continue to multiply exponentially. They exploded in population this time of year and in a variety of colors. In addition, she loved how the different shops displayed themed trees. Shani had filled The Hawaiian Snuggler's window with a myriad of hand-quilted and stuffed ornaments arranged behind a light dusting of spray-can snow. The ornaments were a popular item for holiday tourists especially—easy to pack, beautifully made and affordable ones.

Luanda's pair of large windows were outlined in heavy string lights featuring extra-large bulbs. They blinked off and on, the colors changing with each step Tehani and Wyatt took. Across the street, the dim rumbling of the late dinner crowd from the Blue Moon Bar & Grill lilted gently out into the night, accompanied by the barely there lapping of the water against the boats and dock.

When Wyatt turned toward that marina, she grew anxious. She'd wanted to stop here the other evening after her meeting with Mano, but she hadn't been able to bring herself to. The memories of Remy had driven her away.

Memories that threatened to surge even now.

"Wyatt, I don't think—"

"I know." He reached out, took hold of her hand and squeezed. "I remember what you said the other night about how everything in this town is somehow tied to Remy. It got me to thinking."

"Thinking about what?" Where on earth was this going? Her footsteps slowed. She wanted to be home. She didn't want the cavalcade of ghostly sounds of her past chiming through her head. It wasn't that they were bad memories. Just…bittersweet. And she really didn't want anything bitter these days.

"I've been thinking how maybe you need to make some new memories. With me." He led her through the maze of puzzled-together gangways leading to dozens of slips filled with boats of all sizes. Round bulbs casting bright white light wound around the waist-high railings. "I thought maybe if you could do this just once to get you over the hurdle of that grief, that you'd be able to see things, see this place, in a different light. Even without me."

Her eyes misted. The bench toward the far end of the marina had always been one of her favorite places even before the countless evenings she'd spent cuddling there with Remy. Sitting here, she could watch the boats heading in and out of the marina or, if she looked in the other direction, a rocky outlined beach provided a beautiful, endless seascape to gaze upon. Still, she realized she had tightened her hold on Wyatt's hand.

"Just a couple of minutes, okay?" Wyatt sat on the bench, tugged her down beside him and set her bag on the ground between them. "It'd be a shame to miss the view this year." Opening the paper bag, he reached in and pulled out a cellophane-wrapped, pineapple-shaped cookie.

She tilted her head and couldn't help but smile as she accepted the treat. "You remembered."

"Your favorite shortbread? Decked out for the holidays of course." He pulled one out for himself, held it up to get a better look at the tiny, piped colored lights strung around the sweet, vanilla and tropically flavored baked dough. "I remember the one year you almost made yourself sick you ate so many."

"Never thought I'd eat another one." She slipped open the plastic now, bit into the cookie and felt her mood soar. "Oh, my gosh." She sighed and sat back, the trepidation melting away. "I forgot how good these are. Little Owl Bakery?"

"They make the best on the island," Wyatt announced as he broke off a chunk of his own cookie. "And there may be some Hawaiian snowballs in here, too. If you want them," he said dismissively. "Totally up to you. No pressure."

"No. Right." It touched her that he'd remembered two of her most favorite holiday treats. She'd forgotten what it was like to take pleasure in the smaller things—the little moments of life. Like sharing cookies on the marina overlooking the water. "Thank you." She looked at him, determined to create a new memory for this space that for so long had been special to her. "I didn't realize how much I needed this."

"That's what you have me for," Wyatt said easily. "I've decided I'm on a mission. To give you new memories to walk through town with. To that end, I've made a list."

"Oh, you have, have you?" She wondered if their lists would resemble one another's. "And what exactly is on your list?"

"Nope." He shook his head and ate more cookie as she did the same. "It's going to be a surprise. I do have one question, however. Have you gotten over your fear of heights?"

"It's not a fear," she countered grumpily. "Just a healthy distrust of anything too far off the ground. Why? Would that change your plans?"

"No." He shrugged. "Just creates a new level of challenge. If you're up for it."

She'd always enjoyed her sunset time spent with Wyatt, but she couldn't help but think she'd never noticed how cute and entertaining he could be. That easygoing manner of his was so well suited to the islands, so well suited to their way of life here. How lucky was she that he chose to gift her with these surprising reminders of everything that life had to offer. He felt like both her safe port in a storm and the storm itself, tossing her into the raging waters of the unknown. "I'm feeling just reckless enough this evening to say yes. At least, I think I am." She looked down to where his hand had settled over hers. She turned her hand over to entwine her fingers with his. "This is nice, Wyatt." The sound of the waves and the faint ding of the safety buoy clanging in the distance brought a familiar and almost forgotten sense of calm. "Thank you. For thinking of this." *For thinking of me.*

Now when she walked past this place, or she needed to take a few moments, she'd remember sitting with him in the moonlight, eating her favorite holiday treat. The shadow of Remy would still be there, but it was almost as if he was making room for more. Enough for her to scrunch through to the future.

That bubble of anxiety that had been building as they'd walked had popped in the last few minutes, leaving behind a desire to move closer to him, to lose herself in his warmth. She could smell the faint hint of citrus with the salty air and found it was a scent that was uniquely Wyatt. A scent she'd always equate with him.

She relaxed, sagging a bit into the bench as she crossed her legs and rested her head on his shoulder. He tensed for a moment, as if she'd surprised him, then he did what she hadn't realized she wanted him to do. He released her hand and slipped his arm around her shoulders.

"This might be better than a sunset," she murmured, more to herself than to him.

"Depends on what I've got planned for our next sunset," he countered. "You've got your hands full for several weeks. Lots to do. I aim to keep surprising you. To keep a smile on your face even as you work long hours and juggle everything you do so masterfully."

She rolled her eyes. "You don't take those rose-colored glasses of yours off often enough. I'm nothing special, Wyatt."

"You're entitled to your opinion," he argued easily. Nothing ever seemed to rile or ruffle him. "Even when your opinion is wrong. I know what I see, Tehani. I see the strongest person I've ever known."

"Not possible," she countered. "Unless you've stopped looking in the mirror."

His body vibrated as he laughed. "So we've created a mutual appreciation society it seems.

We're not paying any attention to one another's flaws at the moment."

"At the moment? No," she agreed. "We are not." Because the moment was perfect. This night was perfect. And she had no intention of ruining even a second of it. Even as she began to run out of time. "I hate to say this—" her watch chimed and she held up her wrist "—but I've got to pick Kai up from Daphne's. I promised I'd be there by ten." As it was nine forty-five, she had a little bit of leeway. Good thing Kai could sleep pretty much anywhere. "Want to walk me over, then home?"

"Yes, please." He gave her a quick squeeze, but before he released her, he bent his head and kissed her. Just a light kiss. A barely there brush of lips. An action that seemed so natural that she felt the foundation of her entire emotional well-being shift off balance. But in a good way. Island earthquakes were one thing. Wyatt's kisses? They offered their own kind of challenge.

One she was more than inclined to take on.

CHAPTER ELEVEN

WYATT STARTLED AWAKE AT… He glanced at his bedside clock. Two in the morning.

He groaned, threw an arm over his eyes and tried to get back to sleep. The night was loud with silence, pulsing against his exhausted ears.

It had been a harsh couple of days since his evening stroll with Tehani. Whatever peace and happiness he'd felt that night had quickly dissipated under the stress of traveling multiple times between Hilo, Kona and Nalani to pick up the items he'd managed to track down for the beach cottage. Twice he'd taken a break long enough to come home, not for a shower or to eat, but to watch the sunset with Tehani and Kai.

Last night, after she'd taken a fussy Kai into the house, he'd returned to the beach cottage. Since the few cabins in the area were currently unoccupied, he'd smoothed the final coat of varnish on the heavily sanded wood floors. The more time he could allow that to cure, the better. And given the way every muscle in his body continued to ache, he wasn't in any rush to get the repainted cabinets put back in place. He was very close to asking Keane to help with the rest of the job.

The image of Tehani nibbling on her pineapple cookie on the bench at the marina kept him awake, too. But he didn't necessarily mind that. There were sleepless nights, and then there were sleepless nights. Far be it from him to try to stop a very pleasant and smile-inducing vision from recurring.

An earsplitting wail had him shooting up in bed. Still a bit disoriented, it took him longer than it should have to realize the sound was familiar. He grabbed a pair of shorts, tugged them on and a shirt as he hurried, barefoot, out the front door. The screen door banged shut behind him as he raced down his walkway to Tehani's place.

Her living room lights were ablaze and he could hear her voice. He knocked once on her screen door and had just unlatched it when she pulled the door open. She looked frazzled, apologetic and more than a little scared. She had a seriously red-faced Kai in one arm and her cell phone tucked between her chin and shoulder. Her mussed long hair lay in tangled knots down her back.

"I'm sorry," she whispered and stepped back to let him inside. "Yes, I'm still here."

Wyatt didn't hesitate. "Give him here." He scooped Kai out of her hold and cradled him gently against his chest. The baby was as hot as lava rock. His hold tightened and the same concern he saw shining in Tehani's eyes rocketed through him. He lowered his head, pressed his lips against Kai's forehead and tried to will him to feel better. Kai whimpered, but his crying eased. A little.

"Yeah, okay." Tehani shoved a hand through her hair and squeezed her eyes shut. "Uh-huh. Eight thirty. We'll be there. Thanks." She hung up with a sigh and looked at Wyatt with such exhausted relief that he ached for her. "The advice nurse thinks it's an ear infection. Should have realized. He's been fussy the last day or so. Tugging on his ear." She started toward Wyatt, hands out as if wanting to take Kai back, then noticed the baby wasn't fussing nearly as much and she backed away. "Okay, tag, you're it for a little while. Coffee?"

"Sure." He followed her into the kitchen. Normally, she drank what was left from the morning before if Kai awoke, but this time the pot was empty. "How much have you had?"

"Enough that you shouldn't feel safe asking me that question." She set the pot to brewing and turned, then braced herself against the counter. "I'm so sorry. He woke you up, didn't he?"

"It's okay. I had to be up in a few hours anyway." He refrained from telling her he'd only just dropped into bed shortly before midnight. "How long has he been crying?"

"What year is it?" She tugged the hem of her tank top down over her bare stomach. "He's been fussy ever since yesterday. I brought him into bed with me around nine and I thought that worked. Then it didn't. I should have known something was wrong." She clasped her hands against her heart. "How did I not—"

"You're a mom, not a diagnostician." Wyatt tried to ease her guilt. "Babies get ear infections, Tehani. The only thing we can do is just ride it out. You've got an appointment in the morning, right?"

"Thankfully, yes. She gave me the option of driving him to the emergency room in Hilo or taking an early appointment at the clinic." She looked suddenly doubtful. "Did I—"

"You made the right call," Wyatt assured her. "And if you change your mind, I'll drive the two of you into Hilo. It's okay, Tehani. You've got this. And I've got you."

Tears filled her eyes and she covered her mouth. "Sorry." She tried to laugh, but it sounded as if she choked instead. "It's so hard. He's in so much pain and I just want—"

"You just want to take it from him. I know." He stretched out his hand and waited for her to grab hold. When she did, he tugged her close and tucked her into his side, still holding Kai against his chest. "I do, too. And we will. As soon as we see the doctor, he'll give Kai some antibiotics and we'll get him all fixed up."

"Yeah?" She sounded sleepy now and he took a little pride in thinking she felt safe enough in his arms to give in to the exhaustion.

"Yeah." He kissed the top of her head and gave her a good squeeze. "Did the nurse suggest anything else?"

"Uh, a humidifier in his room. I've got one in the closet somewhere. Don't usually go looking for extra humidity on the islands."

"True." She was back to finding the humor in situations, he realized. Looking around her usually very tidy home, he saw evidence of a panicked, overwhelmed Tehani. The living room appeared as if it had been tossed by a burglar with pillows and blankets on the floor and baby toys scattered about.

Her workspace was piled with unorganized stacks of paper and file folders. And there were not one, not two, but three coffee mugs buried among the clutter.

"Let's sit down. Come on." He moved her toward the sofa and he snagged one of the hand-quilted blankets from the back, then draped it over her bare legs in one toss.

"I should try to feed him again," she murmured. "He didn't eat much yesterday. The nurse doesn't want him getting dehydrated."

"Noted." He started to sit next to her, but the second he started to, Kai began fussing once more. He quickly stood back up, keeping his hold as steady as he could, and resumed his gentle rocking motion. Kai settled again.

"Looks like you're stuck," Tehani told him with a tight smile.

"There are far worse sentences." He was grateful to give her a break. She really did look knackered. "Why don't you curl up? Get some sleep. Kai and I will be fine."

"But—"

"I can take his temperature." He nodded toward the thermometer she'd left on the kitchen counter. "If it spikes or I think something else is going on, I'll wake you up and we'll go in, okay?" He nodded toward her legs and urged her to kick them up onto the sofa. "Take an hour. Just an hour, Tehani. Reboot. Recharge. I'm not going to go anywhere. I've got him. I've got you both."

"You promise?" She was half-asleep when she said it. "You won't leave me, too?"

"I won't leave you, Tehani." He longed to bend down and kiss her again, but Kai's comfort had to come first. "Sleep. I'll wake you up after an hour."

She snuggled into the sofa, tucked a cushion under her ear and within seconds was sound asleep.

"You're really putting your mama through it, little guy." Wyatt pulled his gaze away from Tehani. She didn't need him lurking over her while she slept. He kept his eyes on the sweet face of her son, grateful some of the redness had left his face. "Let's say we give her a break."

The aroma of the brewing coffee wafted out of the kitchen and into the living room. He walked—transfixed, like a cartoon cat being lured by an open can of tuna—to pour himself a mug.

He spent the hour Tehani slept walking around her house. Rocking Kai at a slow and careful pace. He still shimmied and squirmed a bit, still lifted a tiny, fisted hand to his ear and grimaced in his sleep, but the crying had abated.

Her house had always been on the charming side—and reflected the vision of an island woman who was beyond proud of her family and culture. Her walls were lined with framed photos of her with friends or, most often, with her brother. He found himself chuckling at the goofy picture of the two of them at Tehani's high school graduation. Mano didn't often show that side of himself, but when it came to Tehani, she tended to be his emotional kryptonite. She could make anyone smile and laugh.

The promised hour passed, as did a second one. Tehani slept on. She hadn't moved an inch.

Kai's crying didn't return, at least not to the point of waking up his mother. Wyatt sat him up a bit straighter in the crook of his arm and offered him a warmed bottle. The infant didn't gobble it down as quickly as usual, but he did drink some of it, for which Wyatt gave silent thanks. The baby needed something in his belly to help give him the strength to fight off the infection.

His arms ached, and he was still a bit anxious of the heat radiating off Kai's small body. Wyatt detoured away from memory lane and retrieved the thermometer. Convinced Kai wasn't doing any worse thanks to the digital record, he resumed his walk, this time going to the framed photograph of Remy Calvert that sat on the top edge of her fireplace mantel.

A solitary handmade candle, one he recognized from the Coconut Cove Candle Company a few doors down from Luanda's, lent a soft scent of the tropics to the room, even without the wick being lit.

Remy's tanned face beamed at Wyatt, that always-there glint of mischief sparking in his eyes. Across the frame, Tehani had strung Remy's favorite blue-dyed kukui nut necklace—the same necklace Remy wore in the picture.

Wyatt remembered when this picture was taken. He and Mano and Remy had started the day as they often did, riding the waves. He remembered that Tehani often waited for them onshore, but never seemed to want to interfere in what they were doing. *Always on the sidelines*, Wyatt thought now with some regret. "Always in Remy's shadow." The quiet comment came out without much thought, but the idea of it scorched Wyatt's heart. He'd always seen her, always noticed her, but in his haze of unrequited affection, he'd never seen the truth of what she'd been feeling. The smile that always lit her face at times didn't come close to reaching her eyes. In hindsight, he thought that quite sad. Maybe he hadn't seen her as clearly as he'd believed. But he saw her now. He loved her now.

More than he ever had before.

Deciding to gamble a bit, Wyatt gently lowered Kai into his carrier that was perched on the kitchen counter. He made certain the baby was sitting up as high as possible. When he eased his hand out from under Kai's head, the baby's face scrunched and twisted as if he were about to ring the alarm for the entire island to hear, but he snuggled back with a sigh, touched his fist to his ear and dropped off to sleep.

With a sigh of relief Wyatt shook and stretched the soreness out of his arms. The coffee was going to need another brewing, but he suspected putting yet another pot on would wake his fellow caffeine addict. Instead, he started the laborious process of cleaning up.

More time passed until mother and son awoke within seconds of each other. Kai's squeal a little before seven had Tehani finally stirring. Wyatt went to Kai first, took his temperature and felt some of his worry ease. The baby still had a fever, but it was less than the last time he'd checked.

"You lied." Tehani's accusation sounded filled with sleep.

"About?" Wyatt didn't turn away from Kai since he was seeing if the baby needed changing.

"You let me sleep more than an hour."

"You needed it." He did, too, but he could grab a couple of hours before he headed to the cottage. "Feeling better?"

"Mmm." She pushed herself up, tucked the blanket around her shoulders and inched to the edge of the sofa. "Oh, my gosh." She stared at the room, blinking in shock. "The place looks amazing. Thank you so much."

"Wasn't a problem." Wyatt touched his hand to Kai's stomach and gently coaxed the baby back to sleep.

"How is he?" Her voice broke a bit.

"His fever's a little lower. But he's still trying to pull on his ear." Even now, he caught the tiny hand in his and gave it a reassuring squeeze. "Sleep's nature's cure. My mother always said that."

He turned toward Tehani and noticed her smile. "You never talk about her very much."

He shrugged. "I think she used it because she slept so much toward the end of her illness," Wyatt said softly. He'd never spoken about his mother with anyone, not even his grandparents. But with Tehani… "She was trying to reassure me that the sleep would help her get better."

"I'm sorry it didn't." It wasn't pity he saw on her face, but compassion. Understanding. Two of her superpowers on full display. "What was her name? I don't think you've ever said."

"Julietta."

"That's a beautiful name."

"She was a beautiful person." His mother had been everything his father never had been: caring, thoughtful, gentle, but with a spine of steel that—when activated—transformed her into a quiet, fierce warrior. "I wish you could have known her."

"Me, too. She didn't leave any doubt in your mind that she loved you."

"No," Wyatt agreed and considered that a small blessing. "She didn't." He paused, considered. "You have doubts about yours?"

Tehani shrugged. "Enough that I make darn certain Kai will never question my love for him." The vehemence in her voice reminded him of his mother. "My parents' marriage wasn't a good thing for either of them. They brought out the worst in one another and neither really had anything left for us. At least Mano and I had each other."

"I remember when your dad took off. You were what? Fifteen?"

She nodded. "My mom didn't last long after that. She wasn't strong enough to be alone."

"Despite having you and Mano?"

"We learned pretty early on we couldn't count on her. She was like this shadow who lived in our house. The only time she came to life was when he gambled away the rent or he couldn't work enough hours to get it in the first place." She shook her head. "When she died, it was almost like smoke disappearing into the wind." There wasn't anything other than wistful acceptance in her voice. "I'd much rather think about your mom. You're a testament to her."

"I'd be a bit of a bafflement, I think," he laughed. "She wanted me to be a doctor or a lawyer or—"

"She didn't want you to work with your father?"

Wyatt rolled his eyes and pulled over one of the stools from the breakfast bar to sit and still keep a hand on Kai's gently rising stomach. "She knew the kind of man she'd married. But she thought she could change him, and when she realized she was wrong, she was stuck. Apathy is a difficult companion in a marriage."

"Sometimes it seems like a miracle that the two of us are as well-grounded as we are," she observed. "I'm so grateful you had your grandparents."

"Yeah, me, too. But I also have Mano and Remy to thank. And the Calverts." He met her gaze. "You."

"That's sweet." It was evident by the expression on her face she didn't believe him.

"I mean it. You all gave me stability that I'd never really had before. You all accepted me as I was. No expectations. Only respect. That built confidence and self-worth inside of me I didn't realize I needed. I felt safe here. That no matter what life threw at me, I'd be able to handle it. Because I wouldn't be alone."

"We did that, huh?" She sat up, a bit more proudly. "Well, go us."

"It's why I've never even thought about leaving," he added. "Where else could I possibly go where I'd have such good friends? Houses, jobs, circumstances—they may all change but that core? It holds. And it holds fast."

"Wyatt Jenkins," Tehani mused softly. "Proving yet again he's a true romantic at heart."

Only for some people, Wyatt thought. Definitely when it came to Tehani.

She stood up, blanket still around her shoulders, to check on her son. "He really seems to have settled down a bit. Maybe long enough for me to grab a shower?"

"Go ahead. You want breakfast?" He pointed to the refrigerator. "I can put something together."

She looked at the clock on the wall, did the same math he'd done a little while ago. "If you want to give it a shot, sure. But I want to be there when the clinic opens." She stopped in front of him and lifted a hand to his face. A shiver raced down his spine. A shiver of promise, of affection. Of hope. "I am so glad you came into our orbit, Wyatt." She brushed her mouth across his. "I don't know what I'd do without you."

He smiled and watched her retreat into her room. "Hopefully you'll never have to find out."

DESPITE HER CONCERNS that Wyatt had a lot of work left to do on the beach cottage, he still made time to drive her and Kai to the doctor and then went in with them to hear the diagnosis and treatment instructions for what did turn out to be an ear infection. Ear drops and some antibiotics should kick in and get Kai back to his playful, giggly, rambunctious self in a few days. Days that seemed to be creeping up on her when it came to the surfing competition.

She'd turned her cell phone off before bed last night and had resisted the urge to turn it back on. Kai had to be her focus. Everything else could be caught up with or addressed later. She'd made a promise to herself the second she'd learned she was pregnant. Kai would always come first. No matter what.

She stood at her living room window, cradling Kai in her arms, and watched Wyatt head out in his truck. He'd taken less than a half hour to shower and change and as he opened his truck door, he glanced over the top of the cab and smiled and waved at her.

It was as if her emotions tumbled over one another. His care and concern felt like such a normal, everyday occurrence. A utopia kind of event that didn't seem real. She glanced over her shoulder at the framed photo of Remy, her favorite picture. The one she'd taken shortly after she'd graduated from college. Before the reality of life and relationships had descended.

She still missed him. Especially now, with Kai going through his first illness. He was missing everything that he should have been here to see. There was anger about that, but not so much that he'd left her alone. Because she wasn't. The support system surrounding her was nothing short of perfection. And that's where the doubt crept in.

Remy would have made a wonderful father; he and Sydney had had a fabulous one. The Calverts had all but adopted Remy's friends. Their home had been their refuge more times than she could count and when the Calverts had died in an accident, it was as if she'd lost her own family. Wyatt had been there for her then as well. Always such a sturdy shoulder, always dependable and…steady.

She bounced gently, curving her head over Kai's as she hummed softly to him.

Doubt circled like a sand shark, skimming the surface of her feelings. The temptation to move forward with Wyatt, to explore and test what might be possible, bordered on over-whelming. She'd been so determined to do as much as she could on her own, but last night with Kai had shown her how important Wyatt's place was in her life. In their life.

By shifting Wyatt into a different role, into a romantic role, was she risking what they had already for something that might not work out?

"But it could work out," she reminded herself as Wyatt's truck drove off. "You're not looking at the entire picture," she muttered. But what if she was? What if she was making a mistake in letting her heart lead her somewhere that could risk everything great that she already had?

"Your mama is letting her thoughts get away from her," Tehani whispered to Kai, whose fever had finally begun to break. She hadn't known she could ache so much, but his being sick shifted everything into perspective. "Let's say we try to get a little bit of work done." She'd made a mess of her tasks these last few days.

The charity event was falling into place easily enough, but she wasn't as focused or organized as she'd have liked to be. First things first, she had to turn her phone back on. While her text messages loaded and beeped at her, she held Kai in one arm and prepared to tackle the mess she'd left on the table.

Except there wasn't any mess. Her coffee cups had been removed, washed and put away. All her papers had been sorted, stacked and set neatly to the side of her laptop. Even her file folders, now far more full than they had been before she'd fallen asleep, were arranged by color and fanned out for easy access.

Hope I didn't mess up your system. Just wanted to help you ease back into the work. Thinking of you. Wyatt.

Tehani lowered herself slowly into the cushioned chair, her throat tightening as tears burned the backs of her eyes. "Darn it, Wyatt." She tried to shake her head, to get the tears to clear, but then she couldn't swallow. *Thinking of you.* "The man should use that as his life's mantra." He was always thinking of her. Even when he probably shouldn't have been. How on earth could she see that and still think the risk was too great to take? Her love for Remy had been all-consuming, to the point she didn't know who she was without him. But with Wyatt...

"He always puts me in the sunshine." And honestly, how could she ever want or need anything else?

"OKAY, THERE!" Wyatt twisted his head and wedged himself into an unnatural angle beneath the upper kitchen cabinet so as to screw the last two bolts into place. "Do not. Move."

His order to Keane was met with a grunt of irritation followed by a relieved gasping laugh. "Okay." The whir of the drill stopped and he set the tool down on the edge of another cabinet with a dull clank. "And that's done." He stepped back, admiring first the paint job he'd done on refinishing the cabinetry, and then his expert placement. Rearranging the layout had opened up the space significantly and would allow for a larger communal area that could be used for dining or whatever else their wave-riding guests would require.

"Dude." Keane planted his hands on his thighs and bent forward. "This is an unexpected workout. That was tougher than surfing Oahu's North Shore!"

"Seriously?" Wyatt snorted in disbelief, thinking of the over-fifty-foot waves that part of the ocean produced at times. "Then you might be out of shape, man. Hang on." He frowned, stepped forward, then double-checked. "I think that one's crooked. We might need to—" The pained expression on Keane's whiskered face stopped the joke cold. "I'm kidding!" His laughter echoed in the nearly empty cottage and earned him a not-so-subtle glare from his friend. "I swear, just kidding. Come on." He jerked his head for Keane to follow him outside where he kept a cooler filled with iced drinks. "Take a break. You earned it."

Keane grabbed a beer while Wyatt chose an energy drink. He'd earned a beer, too, but he wouldn't indulge until he was done for the day. And only once he was home.

"I can't believe you're almost finished here." The admiration in Keane's voice boosted Wyatt's confidence. "The colors you chose are perfect. It's like you've brought the ocean inside."

"That was the idea." The compliment pleased him. He enjoyed the ego boost of a job well done. And it didn't do his referral portfolio any harm, either. "I don't want to jinx things, but we might be ahead of schedule. Just need to head into Kona tomorrow and pick up the washer and dryer I found online for a serious steal. Nothing fancy," he added at Keane's arched brow. "But they'll handle whatever the guests throw at it. For a while at least."

"Sydney will be glad to hear it." Even as Keane said her name, a familiar helicopter with a bright hibiscus flower painted on the side buzzed overhead, tilting a bit in their direction as if saying hello. Keane looked up, shielding his eyes. "She makes it look so easy up there."

"Remy got the water, his sister got the air." Wyatt took a long drink. "Thanks again for your help today."

"Not a problem. Marella's been on a cleaning kick when she isn't working on the charity event. Gave me an excuse to get out of the house. A productive excuse," he added. "In case she asks."

"All ready for your first big family Christmas?" Wyatt had to admit he was a bit curious about his friend's new familial situation. Like Wyatt, Keane Harper had what could only be called less than an ideal childhood and it had left him leery of close connections. But that was before Marella, who had taken away all the darkness he'd been carrying with him. "When are Marella's parents coming in?"

"Next week." Keane's brows knitted. "Her brother and sister and her husband arrive a couple of days later. Then there's Tag of course. But he's already here."

"Of course." Wyatt had yet to really get to know Marella's younger brother who had immersed himself in the island culinary world. Tag had spent a few months in Maui after the Lahaina fire working food trucks and feeding relief workers. Since his return, he'd been making his way up the food chain in the kitchen of the Southern Seas restaurant. Rumor had it he had his eye on the head chef position once Hema retired. What Wyatt knew of Tag he liked. But he also recognized a young man who was desperate to prove himself—and prove the naysayers wrong who still weren't convinced he planned to stick it out for a career in the food arts. "How about Pippy?"

"Ah, Pippy. Marella really hit the grandma jackpot with her." Keane laughed and leaned back against the railing. "Pippy called last night to say she's flying in early and not because she misses Marella or even me. She misses her boy-friend." His look had Wyatt joining in on the smiling. "Watching her and Benji together is going to be my favorite Christmas entertainment for sure."

"Think she'll like the flamingos on his golf cart?" Wyatt teased.

"Man, those birds were her idea. She and Benji Zoom once a week apparently." Keane finished his beer. "We're getting the pool house ready for her so she can have all the freedom she wants with us still being close by. So. You and Tehani..." He slipped it in so well and under the radar that it took Wyatt a moment to realize what he'd said. "Making a go of things?"

Wyatt grimaced and kept his attention and his gaze on the ocean view. "Don't you see those great waves to catch out there?"

"Nah." Keane stretched out his legs. "I got my fix this morning. If you don't want to talk about it, that's fine. Marella wanted me to ask."

No doubt Keane was happy to stick his nose

in. That said, his inquiry did give Wyatt the chance to do some questioning himself. "Are you the only one who's noticed?"

Keane snort laughed. "Do you forget where we live? Even by small-town standards, Nalani is tiny. No, I'm not the only one who's noticed. But I did hear about it at Vibe a few days back when I was getting my caffeine hit." He paused and examined his bottle very closely. "You've waited a long time for this, haven't you?"

"I don't know what—"

"Wyatt." Keane's tone had Wyatt swallowing the rest of his words. "I was around back in those days, with you and Mano on the beach. On the water. You were besotted with her even back then."

"Besotted?" Wyatt's brows went up. "Does anyone ever use that word anymore?"

"Yes. I did. Just now. Remy didn't know, in case you were wondering."

Wyatt couldn't take another drink, not with the way his stomach was churning. "Well, you did apparently." He couldn't quite process the idea that any of his friends had seen him struggling against what was so completely inappropriate. Being in love with his best friend's girl? That went against every bro code he'd ever been taught.

"I'm more observant than Remy was," Keane

said easily. "I loved him like a brother, but the man had the ability to make himself the center of everyone's attention. Intentional or not. Just the way it was. But he wasn't perfect, Wyatt. Not by a long shot. And I imagine it's been hard having to pretend he was, given how everyone in this town puts him on a pedestal."

"That's not what's been hard." Even now, he felt the need to defend his friend. "Remy was who he was. He gave everything he had to this town. To his friends. He was always fighting to make sure people got what they needed or deserved."

"There's no arguing that," Keane agreed. "But I imagine that couldn't have been easy for Tehani. Being relegated to coming after everyone else. She deserves someone who puts her first. And you always have. And I'm betting you did for years and she's never realized it."

"Returning to Nalani gave you new insight into our teenage years, did it?"

"Coming back," Keane said. "Seeing things through different eyes. Remy made room for us—for me, for Sydney, for Daphne and even Silas—to become part of Ohana Odysseys and I'm grateful for that. But it certainly hasn't escaped my notice that Tehani wasn't anywhere in those plans." The spark in Keane's eye surprised Wyatt. He'd never heard Keane speak so blatantly when it came to Remy. "She should have been top of the list to get in as a partner."

"I'm sure he figured once they were married—"

"That's Tehani talking," Keane cut him off. "Do you think that was his plan?"

He didn't, in fact. But Remy would have had his reasons. "He's gone, Keane. There's no use in kicking at his memory."

"And there's no reason you should feel guilty for going after who you've wanted. Just saying," Keane added at Wyatt's open mouth. "I've always seen it when you look at her and I see it now. But I also see the doubt, the trepidation, the wondering if you have the right to love her. I'm going to tell you because you need to hear it. You have every right. And I say that as an honorary big brother—to her and to you. If you two have even the tiniest shot at what Marella and I have, then don't you dare walk away from it, Wyatt. If you even try to, I'll have to stop thinking you're one of the best men I know and neither one of us wants that."

"I'm not Remy," Wyatt said.

"No, you're not. Remy will always hold a special place in everyone's heart, but none of us can live our lives based on what he may or may not have done. Or even what he might have thought. He'd want you to be happy. He'd want Tehani to be. Their son needs a father. Take it from someone who grew up with one who completely failed in that department—Kai is not going to find better than you. And with that—" he stood up and grabbed another beer "—I declare this heart-to-heart over. You need help with anything else?"

"No. I'm good with the rest of it." He gestured to the cottage's front door. "Thanks."

"Anytime." Keane stopped at the bottom of the porch steps and glanced over his shoulder. "Sunset will be here before you know it. Best not waste it."

No, Wyatt thought as he watched Keane head off down the beach. He didn't intend to.

CHAPTER TWELVE

INCHING CLOSER TO CHRISTMAS—and the tournament—meant they were nearing an even bigger event: Sydney and Theo's wedding. Being in final countdown mode to the surfing championship wasn't going to stop them from celebrating Sydney's bridal shower.

"Another passion fruit mimosa?" Marella held up the glass pitcher filled with bright orange liquid and poured before Tehani could answer. Daphne followed behind with the bottle of prosecco and topped Tehani's flute glass off with the bubbly. All of them were dressed in colorful, flowery sundresses reminiscent of the bridesmaid dresses they'd be wearing on Sydney and Theo's special day. "Careful, though." Marella's smile brightened her always sparkling dark eyes. "Last time you had a girls' night out you kissed Wyatt and tilted the world off its axis."

"Ha ha." Tehani did her best to control the

blush, shooting her friend a warning look before she sipped. The drink was refreshing, tropical, and tingled all the way down to her stomach. She sighed, content. After the long workdays and dealing with Kai's ear infection, it felt so good to be somewhere other than her house or in the office. "Aren't you supposed to be making note of all of Sydney's bridal shower presents?" Tehani prodded Marella as she motioned to where Sydney sat in the center of the living room surrounded by voluminous gift bags and wrapped boxes, along with all their island friends and Ohana. She looked a bit like a queen holding court, just as she should.

Marella had volunteered her home for the special event and—aided by Daphne, since the two of them really had become a Nalani dynamic duo when it came to celebrations—she'd decorated the recently remodeled space in Sydney's upcoming wedding colors of turquoise, cream and bright green. Adding peachy-pink coral finished off the look perfectly. The vibe was festive and, much like the bride, laid-back. Sydney wasn't the kind of person who liked being made a fuss over but Tehani was on Daphne and Marella's side: some women—and events—deserved a major celebration.

"We were hoping you were going to bring Kai today," Daphne said, glancing over her shoulder to where her stepdaughter, Cammie, had put herself in charge of collecting the wrapping paper, tissue paper and bows as Sydney unwrapped her presents. "I know it's a females-only thing, but we'd have given him a pass."

"I bet you needed the break," Marella countered. "Poor little guy was probably miserable with that ear infection."

"That's one word for it." Tehani was so tired she was amazed she could stand upright and blink. "I didn't realize how easy a baby he was until this week. My boy has lungs that could be used as an industrial alarm warning. And his timing usually had him screaming at the top of his lungs somewhere around two a.m."

"But he's better now, yeah?" Daphne asked.

"Much." Thankfully, he was back to mostly sleeping through the night with only a modicum of crankiness.

"Wyatt looking after him for you while you're here?"

"Ah, no. Wyatt's finishing up with the beach cottage today. I asked Mano to come over and watch him." Tehani smirked behind her glass. "I thought it was time he fully embraced his uncle-y responsibilities."

Daphne and Marella exchanged skeptical looks.

"He'll be fine," Tehani insisted as she kept

the doubt in check. "Especially since I bet my brother he couldn't make it four hours before crying...well, uncle."

"Tell me you have hidden cameras set up around your house," Daphne pleaded. "What I wouldn't give to witness that feat of babysitting trauma."

"Poor Mano." Marella lifted her glass in a toast. "He may never be the same."

Tehani laughed, thankful yet again for these women who had become more like sisters than friends. The three of them stood in front of one of the giant windows overlooking Marella's increasingly spectacular backyard. Part of the renovation—done by Wyatt of course—had turned the large, screened-in patio into a sun-room that was more glass than walls. Marella had agreed to the change only after Daphne— a professional botanist—had assured her that she and Cammie would tend to and keep an eye on the plants that turned the space almost into a greenhouse. The oxygen rush one felt just walking in was almost as big a hit as standing in front of the ocean tide.

"Smile!" Pua, Daphne's neighbor who spent a good part of her time chasing down her cat named Tuxedo, aimed her cell phone at them and snapped a few pictures once the three of them leaned in closer together. "Excellent. Beautiful," Pua murmured. "Just beautiful."

"Brunch was delicious, Pua," Daphne gushed when Pua beamed at them. "You and Akahi outdid yourselves."

"We both wanted to contribute to Sydney's big day," Pua responded. "I was so glad when Marella suggested we work together." She cast her gaze to the older woman sitting in a plump chair, a pair of canes poised on either side. "It's hard for her to do everything she used to, but she can cook up a mean buffet, yeah?"

"Definitely," Tehani agreed, thinking of the beautiful selection of traditional Hawaiian food that had been put on the tables for all to enjoy. The cake, a two-tiered creation reminiscent of the one Theo and Sydney had ordered for the wedding, was just waiting to be cut into, with beautifully piped tropical flowers in Sydney's chosen color scheme. Tehani wondered if the tiny indentations and missing icing she'd spotted a few minutes before had something to do with Cammie's enthusiasm and inability to wait for dessert.

"You and Akahi are going to have a booth at the surfing competition, I hear," Daphne said. "What are you going to offer?"

"Lots of grab-and-go snacks." Pua shifted in

a way that made her colorful muumuu flow a bit. "Musubi of course."

"Of course." Despite being stuffed from brunch, her stomach rumbled at the promise of Akahi's famous Spam and rice concoction.

"We've consulted with Vivi at Hula Chicken to make sure we don't duplicate anything," Pua said. "So we're going to keep it simple with the musubi, haupia squares and a tropical popcorn snack mix."

"Keep me away from the haupia," Marella grumbled. "I can't get enough of that coconut pudding since I moved here. I think that's why I've gone up a dress size."

"I don't think that's why," Daphne murmured behind her glass as Pua drifted away to take more pictures. Marella elbowed Daphne and Tehani noticed. It took her a moment to put the pieces together.

"Marella?" Tehani said as a bubble of excitement rose in her chest. "Is there something you'd like to share with the class?"

"Not really," Marella practically sang. "Not yet anyway." But she touched a hand to her stomach in a way that was familiar to Tehani. "I don't want to get in the way of Sydney's big day." She beamed at the bride-to-be as Sydney joined the group.

The smile in Marella's eyes confirmed the

secret that soon would be too big to keep, no doubt. "I haven't told anyone, not even Keane." Marella reached for Tehani's hand and squeezed. "He's still getting used to the whole idea of maybe having a baby."

"Hmm, he'd better get used to it," Sydney laughed as Daphne sniffed back tears. "I'm so happy for you guys!" She hugged Marella tight and Tehani noted the happiness in her friend's eyes. "Looks like Kai's going to be the big cousin pretty soon."

"Looks like," Tehani confirmed. "And, Daphne? Didn't you say…"

Daphne rolled her eyes. "We're trying." She shrugged, as if trying to dismiss the idea. "Cammie and Noah are excited at the prospect of a new sibling. Even after babysitting Kai the other night. The fact he ended up with an ear infection shortly thereafter might not have been the best result."

"Babies get ear infections." Tehani echoed Wyatt's sentiment from the other night. His calm presence had left her feeling encouraged rather than defeated. "We can't keep them in a bubble all their lives."

"No matter how much we might want to," Daphne added. "Griff took Noah for surfing lessons this morning. That kid." The unadulterated affection she had for her stepson was as bright and intense as the Hawaiian sun. "Keane thinks he might be ready for a juniors' competition in another year or so. The idea both elates and terrifies me."

"Mama bear wanting to protect her cub." Marella nudged Daphne with her shoulder. "At least Cammie's a bit more…" The three of them looked over to where Cammie was crouched on the chair beside where Sydney had been sitting, looking a bit like a balancing acrobat the way she was leaning over to examine the yet to be opened gifts. "I was going to say reserved."

The four of them laughed and Tehani's heart felt lighter than it had in months. Sydney returned to her chair, shot them a playful look when she opened one of the last gifts—a rather small gift bag—and pulled out a very lacy silk nightie.

"That would fit one of my dolls!" Cammie cried as she snatched the gift bag before Sydney could try to stuff it back in.

"Out of the mouths of babes," Marella laughed as the rest of the room joined in. "If you and Wyatt aren't busy tomorrow evening, and if Kai's up to it, Pippy's getting in late in the afternoon. I was thinking about having a little welcome back to Nalani dinner for her here."

"Will Benji be invited?" Daphne teased.

"Yes, he will." Marella looked a bit pained at

the mention of her grandmother's very active social life. Or, she was worried about the possibility of Kahlua the Pig being a last-minute guest.

"Great. I'd be happy to come." Even now an idea began to percolate in her mind. "Can I bring something?"

"Anything you'd like. I've got plenty of wine. Tag's taking care of the menu, which is bumming Griff out because he really wants to try out our new grill."

"Is Sydney making her mom's macaroni salad?" Daphne asked.

"I should hope so," Tehani said. "It wouldn't be a party without that." Even after all these years, she had yet to pry that recipe out of Sydney's hands.

"Okay then. We'll see you about six?" Marella asked.

"I'll be here." Tehani smiled and joined the others clapping as Sydney finished opening her gifts.

WYATT PARKED HIS truck in his driveway a little after three. He hadn't been able to wipe the smile off his face since his phone had blown up with Mano's panicked pleas for help.

"This is what the town should be wagering on," he told himself as he circled around to

Tehani's house. "How long did it take to turn strong, tough Mano Iokepa into a clueless, helpless wreck of a babysitter?"

The door opened before Wyatt even reached the steps. Mano, wearing dark-colored board shorts and a now-stained T-shirt that exposed the tattoos on his arm and climbing up his neck, held a seriously teed off Kai against his chest.

"Took you long enough." Mano stepped back as Wyatt moved inside. "I called you—"

"Fourteen minutes ago." He'd timed it. "And, lucky for you, I just finished installing the new washer and dryer in the utility closet. Hey there, Kai." The wailing almost drowned out Wyatt's voice. "What's going on, little man?" Without waiting for Mano to hand him over, Wyatt took hold of Kai's waist and lifted him free, then tucked him into the crook of his arm as he had the night he'd been coping with that ear infection.

"Tehani said the infection had cleared up," Mano said helplessly. "I think he's in pain."

Wyatt could feel Mano's uncertainty and helplessness vibrating around the room. "Babies can sense fear. Hey, now, it's okay." He shifted Kai to his shoulder and wandered over to the cluttered kitchen counter to retrieve a cloth. "You're fine, Kai. Nothing to worry about. There you go." He patted Kai's back and waited for the telltale hiccup that preceded him calming down. The silence that resulted was sudden and loud. "See? He's okay."

"What did you do?" Mano approached, then stopped short. "Was there a switch you flipped or something? How did you—"

Kai turned his head, rested his damp, pudgy cheek on Wyatt's shirt and heaved a relieved sigh.

"There's no real way to tell, Mano. A lot of it is instinct," Wyatt assured his friend. "You okay?"

"I will be. Eventually." He began straightening up. "Tehani'll be ticked. I made a complete mess of this place."

"She'll understand." Wyatt refrained from telling Mano his sister had made an even worse mess the other night. "Organized is the last thing you are when you've got a screaming baby in your arms."

"He's so little," Mano said with a bit of wonder. "How does something so little make so much noise?"

"Practice?" Wyatt teased. He touched Kai's forehead that had been cool for the past few days. "Did you give him his medicine?"

"What do you think caused all that? He practically spit it all out at me."

Wyatt ducked his chin to hide his smile. Even

at only two months old, Kai was a master at spotting weakness. He patted Kai's bottom and nodded. "Did you even check if he needed changing?"

"I did, actually." Mano had the good sense to look sheepish. "That's when I called you."

Wyatt couldn't help it. He laughed. "Okay, come with me. Kai, we're going to teach your uncle Mano how to change your diaper. Mano?" He had to stop and look over his shoulder because Mano wasn't following.

"I'm good."

"You're not," Wyatt argued. "But you will be. Come on. You can't be part of his life without knowing the basics of taking care of him. Besides—" he headed down the hall to the nursery "—imagine how impressed Tehani will be when you can do this all by yourself."

"I sense mocking," Mano grumbled but joined him. With his significant height and bulk, Mano took up a lot of space in the small bedroom.

"Maybe a little," Wyatt admitted. "Okay, first off, grab a clean diaper." He pointed to the shelves next to the changing table.

"I'm no expert, but don't you have to take the old one off first?" Mano did as he was instructed, though. "Where do you want it?"

"Close by." He laid Kai on his back and earned a wide, bright-eyed smile from the baby as he carefully unsnapped his onesie and lifted it high on his chest.

"He likes you." Mano's observation could have sounded envious or even surprised. Instead, it came across as impressed. "Look at that." Kai flapped his arms up and down, trying to grab hold of Wyatt's hand.

"He's just used to me." But he had to admit, knowing Kai was comfortable around him did boost his confidence. "Okay, here's the trick to changing him."

"There's a trick?"

"For boys? You bet." Wyatt made quick work of detaching the diaper and sliding it free. The second he did, he grabbed the clean one and quickly covered Kai's belly and below. "Cover him up quick otherwise—"

"Otherwise, what?" Mano frowned over his shoulder.

"Otherwise he's going to imitate a lawn sprinkler and you'll have a huge mess to clean up." He popped open the container of cleaning cloths, keeping one hand on the diaper, and quickly tidied Kai up while quietly talking to the baby the entire time—like an adult because baby talk felt condescending in his opinion—before he quickly snapped everything in place and tossed the dirty diaper in the receptacle. "See? Nothing to it."

"Says you," Mano said.

"Next time, your turn."

"I won't be here next time. Right?" Mano said hopefully.

Kai let out a squeal of laughter that clearly stated his uncle was flat-out wrong.

"Okay, Kai. Back to your uncle." Wyatt didn't leave Mano any choice and handed the baby over. "I'll do a quick cleanup before I leave. Unless you want Tehani to know you completely lost the plot and called for help."

"I'm both amused and annoyed that you get me." This time when he held Kai high up on his shoulder, he seemed to have a bit more confidence about it. Instead of appearing as if he were holding a ticking bomb, it was more of a guarded if not reluctant acceptance. "We'll help."

Wyatt almost made a perfect getaway. He was just tossing the last few toys into the playpen when he spotted Tehani heading up the walkway.

"She's home." He swung on Mano, who had found Kai's favorite stuffed octopus and was waggling it in front of Kai's wide eyes. The trepidation and abject fear he'd seen earlier in his friend was gone. "Wall of silence, yeah?"

"Absolutely."

Tehani stepped inside and in the moment he

first saw her, Wyatt lost his breath. How was it possible that happened every time? Whether it had been a day or mere hours, she just broke his heart wide-open by walking into a room.

"Hey!" Wyatt tried not to sound overly cheerful. "How was the bridal shower?"

"Wonderful." Tehani set her little purse and keys on the table by the door. "Is everything okay? I thought you were working on the cottage this afternoon."

"I was," Wyatt said. "Finished early. Thought I'd stop by and see…"

"He rode to my rescue," Mano interrupted with the ease of someone who had planned it that way. "It's taking some getting used to, I think. But me and my nephew are getting there now." He looked at Wyatt with a knowing gleam in his dark eyes. "Thanks to Wyatt."

"Well, then, thank you to Wyatt." She touched a hand against his chest as she passed, holding out her arms for her son, who was babbling a bit. "Thank you for taking care of him for me."

"Of course. Anytime," Mano insisted. "I even got a diaper changing lesson out of the deal. If you're good, I'm going to head home. Was thinking about taking my board out, catching some waves." He cast his glance to the picture of Remy on the mantel. "It's been a while since I did that."

"It's a perfect afternoon for it." Tehani cuddled Kai close, cradled his head in her hand and pressed her lips to the crown of his head. "I missed you, *mae-mae*."

"Okay then." Mano grabbed his cell phone off the kitchen counter. "Have a good evening, you two." He completely avoided Wyatt's narrowed gaze as he headed out.

"Something wrong?" Tehani asked Wyatt as she shifted her arm to support Kai.

"Nope. Nothing." Other than being set up by his not as incompetent friend as he'd been led to believe.

"How's the cottage coming along?" Her long, shimmering black hair hung down her back and made his fingers itch to touch it.

"Almost done." Grateful for the distraction, he pointed to the door. "I'm going to be heading back over there. Have a few more of the beds to set up and then, tomorrow, Sydney can come by and let me know if she wants anything else tweaked or added." He was babbling. He never babbled. Why on earth was he—

"I'd love to see it. How about Kai and I come by later this evening? I'll bring food. We can honor its completion with dinner on the porch? A kind of unofficial christening."

"Ah, sure, yeah." Unexpected excitement

sparked inside of him. He glanced at his watch. "Give me three…three and a half hours?"

"Perfect. I need to finalize assigning tent space to our sponsors. We've got exactly six days before things get going." Instead of the anxiety he'd seen on her face in recent days, he saw the promise of completing a job well done. He couldn't blame her. He'd be glad when this event was behind them and they could focus on…other things. "Hula Chicken okay? Oh, I hear Vivi's dad has come up with a new guava-and-banana cake that's really popular."

"Sounds good." He made his way to the door. "I'll see you in a bit, then."

"Okay." She followed him, smiling as he returned to his truck.

Driving away, he glanced into the rearview mirror and found her standing on the porch, Kai in her arms, holding up her son's hand so they could both wave to him.

WITH KAI'S STROLLER filled not only with her son and his various belongings but with an extra-large paper bag filled with aromatic grilled and spicy huli-huli chicken, sides, and the promised guava and banana cakes, Tehani walked around the hill to the beach cottage.

She'd only been here once since Remy had bought the place two years ago—that night when she'd taken an evening dip in the ocean. Remy hadn't had a lot of time to figure out what he wanted to do with it since he'd kept his attention on Ohana Odysseys and getting the smaller cottage up and running. Truth be told, she'd practically forgotten about the second planned guest property until Sydney had mentioned it for possibly housing the surfers participating in the charity event.

Tehani liked its placement—right on the beach, set far enough back from the main road, wedged into a near forest of palm trees that made it almost invisible to passersby. Unless they happened to know it was there and only the locals did. The narrow sandy path leading around to the back of the house where the porch and main house entrance were would be easy on bare feet, something she had no doubt Wyatt had paid attention to. She could smell fresh paint mingling with the salty freshness of the ocean, which was so close it felt as if she could reach out and touch it.

Across the horizon, the sun beat down, bathing her skin with warmth, and a friendly breeze lifted her hair off her shoulders. There was a round metal table situated in the far corner of the porch, along with a trio of padded chairs. The lightweight cloth billowed a bit, but was held in place by a plain drinking glass contain-

248 A HAWAIIAN CHRISTMAS ROMANCE

ing a handful of the flowers that grew along the north side of the cottage.

She smiled. He really did have a caring, considerate heart.

She could hear Wyatt banging around inside, so she took a moment, sat down on the steps and, turning Kai so he could look at the same view, exhaled. Kai's quiet sigh had her grinning and when she turned her gaze on him, she found her son smiling up at her and stuffing a too-large fist into his mouth.

"You're early."

Wyatt's comment had her turning slightly. "I was antsy just sitting at home. Hope you don't mind."

"I never mind seeing you." He wiped his hands with a rag. "You get the tent assignments all done?"

"They are done and sent to Marella and Daphne. They're going to double-check it and then send it to attendees so they know where to find what and who."

"So far you haven't hit one hitch in this event, have you?"

"Shhhh!" She held a finger to her lips. "Don't jinx us!" She had to admit, despite all the hard work, she'd enjoyed the process of getting this event up and running. The actual event itself might prove to be anticlimactic by comparison. "Can I come in and see inside?"

"Sure, yeah. Of course. Hang on." He stepped off the porch, picked up the stroller and lifted it over the steps. "Don't want him catching a chill. No more ear infections for you, Kai."

Kai babbled a bit in response. "Let's leave him here by the open door, though. The paint and varnish fumes are still a bit strong. I need to air this place out for a few days."

Tehani barely heard him. She hardly recognized the place. The scarred floors, the dented, peeling walls, and the musty smell that clung to every wall had all been replaced by Wyatt's unwavering and scarily perfect workmanship. The hardwood looked brand-new with its smooth, high polish and glossy finish. He'd chosen a sea green with a faint blue tinge for the walls and a softer eggshell white for the cabinetry. There was no furniture yet, but the appliances he'd found fit in with the cozy, casual atmosphere the islands always tried to evoke.

"What do you think?" he asked.

She heard the nerves in his voice and wondered how he could ever doubt his talent. "It's beautiful, Wyatt." She went to survey the other rooms. Simple but sturdy-looking bunk beds had been set up around the perimeter. The walls were a darker shade than the main room, but the design flowed nicely.

The bathroom was larger than she remembered and had been scrubbed down to within an inch of its life. It practically sparkled.

"Sydney's going to have Rewa stock the place."

Rewa was known as the best housekeeper on this part of the island and did a lot of the cleaning and maintenance for Nalani's homes and shops, and she had been keeping the first cottage up and running in the months it had been open.

"Her two sons tour on the surfing circuit," Wyatt continued. "So she'll have a good idea of what might be needed here. Then we'll revisit the place once the event is over."

"This is going to be perfect, Wyatt. You did an amazing job."

"Yeah?"

Compliments, she suspected, had been few and far between when he was growing up. At least after his mother died. "Definitely yeah. Let's say we try out the kitchen and get dinner set up."

It didn't take much to unload the boxes of fragrant food she'd picked up at Hula Chicken. The mom-and-pop eatery boasted the most popular roasted spicy chicken on the Big Island—

at least as far as she'd been able to determine, and she'd eaten a lot of huli-huli chicken. After filling their paper plates, they headed outside to the table. Before she sat down, she tucked a light blanket around a snoozing Kai and, just to be safe, put a teeny crocheted beanie on his head, covering his ears.

By the time they'd finished eating and were enjoying the sunset, the opportunity to put the last of her plan for the evening into action presented itself. "So I've been thinking about our upcoming date on New Year's Eve." She finished her soft drink.

"I've been thinking about it, too." His admission came with a sheepish grin that warmed her heart.

Her own heart pounded with something akin to fear. She'd been determined to push herself through the doubt she hadn't been able to shake. Doubt about changing their relationship. Doubt that could probably be shattered by another of his kisses. But she'd prefer to make the breakthrough herself. "I would like to suggest we make that our second date."

His brows arched. "I'm listening." He reached over and rested his fingers on top of hers. Only then did she realize she'd been tapping them. The instant he'd touched her, she'd stopped.

Tehani cleared her throat. "Marella's throwing a welcome-back dinner party tomorrow night for Pippy."

"Is she?"

"She is." Why was she getting more nervous as this conversation went on? "And I think we should attend. Together. Daphne's gotten a sitter for Cammie and Noah. Maru's granddaughter said she'd watch them and that she'd be happy to add Kai to the group."

"Maru's granddaughter starting up a baby-sitting business?"

Tehani had fond memories of Lani, who normally spent every morning helping her grandmother fry up the malasadas they sold at their cart near the beach. Tehani had been Lani's babysitter once upon a time. The chance for Lani to do the same felt like an appropriate, full circle moment. "I don't know if it'll be a business, but she gets along great with Cammie and Noah and they liked having Kai around before. So, um, what do you say? Will you be my date for dinner tomorrow night?"

He stroked the back of her hand, then entwined their fingers before turning her hand over. "I would love to be your date for dinner tomorrow night. You do realize that'll probably be the big news around the island rather than Pippy and Benji reuniting?"

"I know." It was time for Nalani to see her as

more than Remy's grieving girlfriend. And it was time for her to take a very important step away from her past.

"You're okay with that?"

"I wouldn't have asked you if I wasn't." Still, the past pressed in on her. "I think…" She paused and reconsidered. "I think maybe there's something you need to know. About Remy. Or more importantly." She took a deep breath. "About me and Remy."

"I don't think there's anything—"

"That would surprise you?" Her smile was quick and sharp. "Hold that thought. Those last few months before he died, things weren't great between us. In fact, after our trip to Kona last New Year's they got pretty awful." The confession had sat silently inside her for so long that she wasn't exactly sure if the words would come.

"If this is about the two of you not eloping—"

Tehani gasped, sat back and pulled her hand free. "You knew about that?"

"I didn't know that was the plan before you two left. I found out when you got back." He winced. "Remy told me."

"I see." Her mind raced. All this time she thought it had been her secret alone.

"I wasn't surprised he changed his mind," Wyatt went on. "You know how he was. Impulsive, a bit reckless. Didn't tend to think things through, especially emotional decisions."

Confusion took over her surprise. "Wait. Hold on. Remy told you he changed his mind about getting married?"

Wyatt frowned, as if replaying the memory in his mind. "He said it wasn't the right time and that he'd made a mistake springing it on you. I guess I just assumed—"

"It wasn't Remy, Wyatt. It was me." She swallowed hard and finally said the words out loud. "I was the one who didn't want to get married."

"Oh." He sat back without breaking eye contact. "Okay."

Angry tears burned her throat as she recalled that day after the last round of surfing. The way Remy had run up to her on the beach, his eyes bright with victory and joy. He'd picked her up and swung her around and when she was back on her feet he… "He never asked me." The admission broke apart the fog in her brain. "All those years he never asked me to marry him and even that day it was just…assumed. I didn't even warrant a real proposal and that hurt." A tear broke free and dropped onto her cheek. "It just hurt."

"I'm so sorry."

"In that moment, it was like the world kind

of shifted and I could see things clearly." She swiped at her damp cheeks. "I couldn't see where I fit with him anymore. Everything was always about him, what he wanted, what he had planned, and I seemed to be simply along for the ride. I felt so invisible and when I said no—" she blinked and two more tears fell "—he didn't see it coming, Wyatt. I've never seen him look so hurt. Even now I hate that I did that to him but—"

"You don't have to explain, Tehani." The gentle understanding in his voice had her choking back a sob. "You did what was right for you. I'm not going to judge you for it. No one is. But you also don't owe anyone an explanation."

"Don't I?" She'd spent months trying to rationalize this in her mind, but to no avail. "You know how people think about Remy in this town, Wyatt. They practically worship him. Can you imagine how people would react if they knew I turned down the chance to marry him?"

"No, I can't, because it's none of their business. Tehani." He reached out, caught one of her hands and squeezed hard. "Everyone loves you. Just as much as they loved Remy. Relationships are complicated. Remy was complicated."

"But what if..." Now that the tears had started, she couldn't seem to stop them. "We were barely talking to each other when he died, Wyatt. What if…what if he died because I broke his heart?" The disbelief in Wyatt's gaze had her gnashing her teeth. "Don't look at me that way," she ordered. "People die of broken hearts."

"Of course they do, but Remy didn't. Remy…" He sat back, scrubbed a hand down his face. "I guess maybe tonight's the night for admissions. He wasn't angry with you, Tehani. He'd been struggling with something for a long time. Even before you went to Kona. He wouldn't tell me exactly what, but something was weighing on him."

"And it wasn't me?" That couldn't be right, could it?

"No. If anything—" he spoke more emphatically now "—he thought marrying you could fix whatever it was. When you two got back he admitted he'd made a huge mistake, springing the eloping idea on you. He didn't realize how important it would be for you to get married here, in Nalani, with your friends and Ohana. I think you turning him down finally made him see how selfish he'd been with you. And he wanted to fix that. It was just taking him some time figuring out how he could. And then he ran out of time."

"I loved him for almost half my life," she whispered. "I loved him to the point of losing who I was. I don't know that there was anything he could have done."

"And that would have been okay," Wyatt said. "You know better than anyone that love has so many different forms. You still love him. You always will, if only because of Kai. But that's nothing to feel guilty about, T. It's okay to move on. It's okay to stop punishing yourself because you're afraid of what other people are going to think. You aren't under any obligation to keep Remy Calvert's reputation intact. It's simply not necessary."

"That's not what I'm doing." Was it?

"That's good to hear." Wyatt smiled and wrapped his other hand around their joined ones. "Because I have a confession to make myself. I've been waiting a really long time to cross that friendship line with you." He squeezed, as if silently asking for acceptance. "That kiss you gave me the other night felt a little like a starting flag at Indy."

"Got your engine revving, have you?" The very idea had her laughing. She returned his gesture, squeezing his hands hard. He bowed his head for a moment.

"I take pride in keeping on an even keel and having my emotions under control." He lifted his chin and looked her straight in the eye. "And maybe I'm feeling reckless now because I don't know what else to do, but I love you, Tehani. I've been in love with you since the first day we met." The waves behind them almost drowned out the words. "But I also knew you weren't for me, so I was happy being your friend. I still want to be your friend, but I also want more." She could see his throat tighten when he swallowed. "I want you and Kai in my life. I want it all. Cards on the table. I want it all."

"Wyatt." His name was a whisper on her lips. She knew they'd taken steps in different directions but she had no idea how far he'd already gone. On his own. Alone. "I don't know what to say."

"How about yes?" There was the hint of desperation in his tone. "How about you're willing to give it a try?" He was deflecting with humor, like he always did when conversations got too complicated or intense. "I haven't planned any of this, Tehani. This feeling we've been experiencing. I've let you take the lead. I'd be lying if I said I hadn't thought or dreamed about it. But I didn't dare hope. Remy was my best friend. Flaws and all. And I loved him. To be honest, if he was still here, I don't know if I ever would have had the courage to…"

"Say what you've said to me?" Her attempt to tease fell flat. "It wasn't going to work with Remy, Wyatt. I knew that before Kona. I was just too scared to break things off. Too worried about what people would think. How could I even consider doing that? But I was going to. Then I found out about the baby and before I could decide how to tell him—"

"Remy was gone. I wish you'd told me."

"I couldn't tell anyone." She'd been too ashamed, and she felt ungrateful for not appreciating what she'd had for as long as she'd had it. "But I'm so tired of living in those secrets. Of hiding. I want…" She took a deep breath. "I want something different this time. Something that's open and honest and without doubts or questions." She shoved the last of her reservations aside. "I think maybe I'm ready to take that chance."

"Me saying I love you doesn't freak you out?"

"Oh, it definitely does." She laughed and earned a smile from him. "But in a good way. Remy was always excellent with the words but you?" She stretched out her hand to touch his face. "You show me every day that you care. And I see how much you love my son. It makes me ache to see you with him. I just… It's going to take some work on my part to catch up with you." The words wouldn't come. Her courage faltered at the edge of admitting she loved him. Because as soon as she said the words, there would be no going back.

"I'll wait." He lifted her hand to his lips, kissed her knuckles and sent a tingle racing down her spine. "I promise, however long it takes, I'll wait."

CHAPTER THIRTEEN

"I CAN'T SEE anything that needs changing." Sydney's voice echoed through the newly renovated beach cottage late the next afternoon. "You said those bunk beds break down?" She emerged from the bedroom as Wyatt shoved his hands into his front pockets and rocked back and forth on his bare feet.

"They do. I can store them in my backyard shed after or we can build some storage behind the house." He pointed out the back door. "There's more than enough space within the property line. Could make things more convenient."

"Perfect. We'll get to work on that after the holidays. If that's okay with you?" she added, blond brows raised.

"Sure." Nothing wrong with taking on a new job ahead of time. "I'll pencil you in."

"Good." She finished walking through the cottage and was texting on her phone when she rejoined him. "Mano's on his way. He'd like to see it before it fills up with surfers."

Wyatt chuckled. "Don't blame him. I've just got one more thing to pick up this afternoon. You know Ora, who works at the electric scooter rental kiosk? She and her boyfriend split and she's looking to get rid of the surfboard storage shed he put up at her place. She said I could have it if I haul it for her."

"Excellent," Sydney said approvingly. "How many will it hold?"

"At least a dozen. I stopped by this morning and took a look at it. It's pretty sturdy so it should hold up to storms. If it doesn't, I'll just build a new one." Or maybe he'd start building his own line of storage sheds—customizable for various-sized yards and properties. It was amazing what ideas came to you when your brain felt less congested than it had in years. "So, will you and Theo be at Marella's this evening?"

"For Pippy's welcome-back dinner? Wouldn't miss it." Sydney's smile came with a light laugh. "Are you coming?"

"Yes. With Tehani. We, ah, we have a date."

Sydney pulled her attention away from her cell and stared at him. "Yeah?"

"Yeah. I know we don't really owe anyone an explanation or need anyone's permission—"

"No, you do not." She pocketed her phone. "I've only got one thing to say about the two of you dating." She stepped forward, caught his arms in her hands and squeezed. "It's about time!"

He hadn't realized the anxiety he'd been carrying around until it was gone. "Really?"

She nodded. "Yeah, really."

"You don't think Remy—"

"Remy would want you both to be happy. I know I do. And besides, if you two finally make it official, I can start pushing her to accept that partnership she keeps rejecting."

"I'd give that another shot in a few weeks," Wyatt told her. "She's working through some things right now, but when she gets on the other side, I have a feeling her answer might be different."

Sydney smiled wide and bright. "Second best news I could have heard today. You'll take care of her, yeah?"

"As much as she'll let me." And that, he realized, really was going to be the trick.

"Spoken like a smart man."

"Who's a smart man? Wyatt?" Mano rounded the corner and stepped up onto the porch. He was back in his usual suit, his dark hair arranged into a short tail at the base of his neck.

Only the teeniest hint of his neck tattoos showed beneath the dark, buttoned-down collar.

"He and Tehani have a date tonight," Sydney announced. "So don't you go all big brother on him and warn him off."

"Oh, I don't think he's going to do that," Wyatt said slowly, recalling Mano's attempt at matchmaking. "Are you, Mano?"

"So long as you don't break her heart, I'm behind you all the way."

"You got here fast," Sydney said. "Want a tour of the place?"

"In a bit, Syd. I need to talk to you about Golden Vistas first. It seems they're back and making another play at buying the Hibiscus Bay."

Wyatt frowned. "Isn't that the company Theo used to work for as an accountant?" If his memory served, Theo's financial evaluation of Ohana Odysseys as a potential investment for Golden Vistas was why Theo had originally come out to Nalani.

Mano nodded. "One of my fellow shareholders was approached by someone from Golden Vistas a few days ago, asking if they were happy with how the resort was being run."

"The resort you're running," Sydney clarified.

"Yeah. Lucky for me, profits are up and everyone's happy with their portfolios at the moment, but if Golden Vistas came to one shareholder, they're going to approach others." He eyed Sydney. "You get any weird calls lately? Anyone strange booking tours?"

"Not that I'm aware of," Sydney said slowly. "But I'll check with Jordan, see what came through in the last week or so. Maybe Tehani could take a look. She has a good memory when it comes to names. She might see something I'd miss."

"You really think they're going to come at you guys again? Attempt a takeover or buyout?"

"They want a foothold in the islands," Mano said. "That much I know for sure. Maybe Theo could reach out to anyone he's still friendly with at Vistas?"

Sydney agreed. "I'll definitely talk to him about it."

"In the meantime, I'm going to give Silas another call. He still lives in San Francisco," Mano said. "He's riding a desk at the police department these days, but as a good officer he's got contacts and avenues of investigation we don't. He's been keeping an eye on Golden Vistas and doing some digging. He'll go deeper for us now that they've reactivated their interest."

"Did you mention to him that he never responded to my e-mails?" Sydney asked with the slightest edge in her voice.

"No, but he did." Mano turned, looked out at the ocean. "He's had his hands full the past few years. His wife took off and left him caring for their daughter, Freya, soon after the girl was born, and apparently she's a bit of a handful. One reason Silas took a desk job with the San Francisco Police Department. I'm guessing the idea of dealing with Remy's death and the offer of buying into Ohana Odysseys was a bit too much for him to handle."

"Right. Of course." Sydney winced. "I should give him some grace."

"We all will," Mano said. "I'm working on getting him out here for a visit. A reunion might be just what he and Freya need in the new year."

"Always thinking about your Ohana," Sydney jokingly accused. "Why don't you come in and see the magic Wyatt worked on this place? And, Wyatt, feel free to head on home and get ready for your date." Her grin was one of pure amusement.

Wyatt's cheeks went volcano hot, but he tossed her the keys to the cottage and realized he was looking forward to the evening more than he probably had a right to.

WITH HER NERVES jangling from head to toe, Tehani smoothed a hand along the front of her turquoise flowered dress before she pulled open the door. "Hi." Her heart tipped at the sight of him wearing pressed, dark pants and a white dress shirt with the button at the throat open. His hair curled in that messy way that made her fingers itch to dive in. But it was the potted plant in his hands that brought a smile to her face.

"Hi." He held out the pot and it was then that she saw his hands were shaking. "Daphne helped me pick it out. It's a bromeliad."

She accepted the gift and gazed down at the pinkish-red blossom sitting in a protective crown of leaves. "It's beautiful."

"She said if you have any problems with it to let her know, but she's pretty sure you can't kill it."

"How she underestimates me. Come on in." It was comforting to know his nerves were on the same frayed level as her own. She carried the plant into the kitchen and set it beside the sink so she wouldn't forget to water it. "So, um. How was your…?" She turned and found him standing directly behind her. "Day?" The last word came out as a bit of a croak and they both laughed. She pressed her palms against her warm cheeks. "This is so silly! Why are we nervous?"

"Because neither of us wants to blow it." He shoved his hands into the front pockets of his pants. "Where's Kai?"

"I already dropped him off at Daphne's. He's all settled and under the care not only of Lani, but Cammie as well. She's decided they're adopting him."

"Has she?" Wyatt's smile widened.

Frustrated, Tehani dropped her arms to her sides and sighed. "You know what? This is ridiculous. I'm just going to—" Impulse grabbed hold and forced her forward. She rose up on tiptoe and kissed him.

Whatever doubt she may have had about his response, it evaporated the instant his hands came to rest on her hips. He held on while he kissed her back, sending shivers and tingles shooting through just about every cell in her body. When she stopped the kiss and looked up at him, she had the overwhelming desire to call off tonight's date and spend the evening snuggling on the sofa.

"I thought maybe we should just get that end of night kiss out of the way," she managed and earned a nod of approval from him. "You look really nice, Wyatt." She smoothed her hands down his arms, unused to the long sleeves with cuffs. "Very grown-up."

"I'll take that as a compliment," Wyatt said. "You're as beautiful as you always are." He brushed a finger down her cheek.

She blew out a long breath. "Man, you always

say just the right thing." She kissed him again and took pleasure in the fog in his eyes. "Just remember, Pippy's going to be there so we'd best be ready for anything."

"Oh, I am," Wyatt said. She gathered her keys and purse along with the bottle of wine she'd put in a holiday gift bag. "Where Pippy's concerned, it's my default setting."

"LOOK AT THESE LIGHTS," Tehani whispered as they walked up the stairs to Marella and Keane's front door. The house was situated on a corner, a few blocks from the lane where Tehani and Wyatt lived. The holiday lights had been strung all around the roofline and windows, the largest of which was filled with an enormous Christmas tree decorated gorgeously. "And that tree." She sighed. "I still need to get mine." Just the thought of digging out the boxes of ornaments gave her a migraine.

The sounds of a ukulele playing holiday music could be heard as the front door popped open.

"Come on in." Marella stepped back and waved them inside. "Pippy's flight was delayed leaving New York so Keane is at the airport now to pick her up." Marella was wearing an elegant dark green dress that flared out at the knees and matching emerald earrings and bracelet. She wore her brown hair long down her back with a solitary hibiscus blossom tucked behind her left ear. "We've got the bar right over there—" she gestured to where Theo Fairfax stood holding two different bottles in his hands "—and appetizers in the living room. We're doing a buffet-style dinner so just make yourself at home and relax."

"Maybe you need to take your own advice," Tehani told her friend after giving her a hug. "You look stressed."

"Yes, well, my grandmother doubles as family entertainment. No telling what she's going to say or do when she gets here."

"I'm sure it'll be fine," Wyatt told her. "You look beautiful."

"Always the charmer," Marella teased. "Please, go on in. Can you maybe keep an eye on Benji for me?" she murmured to Tehani as she closed the door. "He's looking a little uncomfortable. I think he's a bit lost without Kahlua."

"Am I the only one surprised he didn't bring his pig?" Wyatt asked and earned a gentle elbow in the ribs from Tehani. It was, she realized almost immediately, the most natural reaction she'd ever had. Being with Wyatt, despite the nerves that were still jumping inside of her, felt right. "Benji!" Wyatt slid into the seat on the sofa beside the older man. "Looking sharp tonight. New bow tie?"

"Got it special for my Pippy." Benji's weathered face lit up at the mere mention of Marella's grandmother. He looked so cute, sitting there all nerves like a teenager waiting for his first date. "Took me some time to get it tied just right."

"It looks smashing," Tehani assured him, but she still leaned down and gave it a bit of a tweak. He'd donned a short-sleeved dress shirt with a sharp collar the color of Santa's hat. The stark black bow tie matched the black cargo shorts he wore, along with a pair of flip-flops. His almost bald head shimmered in the glow of the tree lights.

"Where's that boy of yours?" Benji asked. "Was hoping to get a peek at him again."

"He's spending the evening with Daphne's kids," Tehani told him.

Benji eyed her, then looked at Wyatt. Then back to Tehani. "You two come here together?"

Tehani's gaze jumped to Wyatt's. "We, ah, we did. It's our first official date."

"A date?" Benji's eyebrows shot up. "You two are dating?"

"Don't act so surprised," Sydney said from behind Marella. "What can I get you two to drink?" she asked them.

"Whatever's easy," Wyatt said.

"Same," Tehani choked out. Her stomach pitched. She couldn't tell what Benji was thinking as he continued to look between her and Wyatt.

Finally the old man narrowed his gaze at Wyatt and pointed a finger at him.

"You going to take good care of her? She's had her heart broken enough for one lifetime. I don't want that happening again."

"Tehani can take care of herself," Wyatt countered as Tehani sputtered in disbelief. "But I'm going to do everything I can to make her happy. Will that suffice?"

Benji glanced at Tehani, then eyed him again. "Yep. That'll do. But you'll answer to me if that goes off the rails."

"Understood," Wyatt said with a nod and accepted an open beer from a silently laughing Sydney. "You want some of these meatballs, Benji? They look delicious."

Tehani got to her feet and found a smiling Sydney holding out a glass of white wine. "Thanks."

"Benji's just adorable, waiting for Pippy." Sydney hugged Tehani's arm against her. "I'm glad to see you and Wyatt together. You look happy."

"I am." It didn't dawn on her to lie. "It just feels strange." She'd never dated anyone other than Remy. How did she even *do* this?

"Just enjoy yourself—that's all that matters." Sydney tightened her hold on Tehani before releasing her. "I know it's going to be a tough Christmas for you. Your first without Remy. But it's also your first with Kai and that is cause for celebration. We all miss him, too. We'll be here for you. Always."

"Thank you." Tehani glanced away for fear that Sydney would see the guilt in her eyes. The guilt she still hadn't quite managed to rid herself of despite Wyatt's reassurance last night. Was there any point in admitting the truth to Remy's sister? Or anyone else for that matter? Or was her indecision and uncertainty an avenue of self-sabotage because she didn't think she deserved the happiness Sydney encouraged her to embrace?

Wyatt's laughter broke her out of her self-conscious reverie. There was no way not to smile at the sight of him and Benji enjoying their conversation as they plowed their way through the substantial pile of sweet and sour meatballs that always included lush chunks of fresh pineapple. Sydney and Theo—along with Marella, Daphne and Griff—chatted in the alcove between the dining room and kitchen. Tehani made her way around them, looking into the kitchen, where she found Marella's brother Tag Benoit bopping between the prep area and the stove as he oversaw multiple dishes in various stages of creation.

Tag caught sight of her, his bright blue eyes twinkling as he waved her over. "Hey, Tehani. Merry almost Christmas."

"Merry almost Christmas, Tag." She accepted the small plate he handed to her after he spooned out a luscious-looking teriyaki beef. She tasted and nearly swooned. "Oh, my gosh, that's soooo good! And a little spicy."

"I added a kick," Tag boasted. "I like to put spins on traditional recipes."

"Well, you've spun this one just right. How are things over at the kitchen in Southern Seas?"

"Busy. I was lucky to get tonight off." He cleaned up one of his workstations before turning his chef's knife on a plump red tomato. "Hope you've brought your appetite. I'm looking for feedback on some of my recipes tonight."

"Happy to oblige. What's on the menu?"

He rattled off some familiar and other not-so-familiar offerings, but won her heart with a promised pineapple cheesecake with passion fruit sauce.

"I'm glad I'm walking home." The mention of Southern Seas made her think back to her dinner with her friend Maylea. "Is Crystal coming for the holiday?"

Tag shook his head. "She'd planned to, but she and Chad got the opportunity to visit a new resort in New Zealand. It's on their bucket list so that won over coming here."

"Tough decision." One she was grateful Crystal had made. Now Tehani wouldn't feel obligated to mention Maylea's Maui wedding to her. As firm as she was about Maylea asking Crystal directly, she couldn't quite shake that people-pleasing tendency she possessed. Being a bridesmaid, however reluctantly, did bring the responsibility to do what she could to make the bride's day perfect.

They chatted until Marella poked her head in. "Pippy's here!" She waved them out. Tag stayed back, shaking his head and urging Tehani to join her friends.

"I'll see her later," Tag said of his grandmother. "She's going to be poking her nose into the pots soon enough."

Tehani joined her friends at the front door as Keane helped Pippy up the stairs. The older woman positively beamed when she caught sight of the welcoming committee.

"Well, I'll be. Look at you all. Pretty as pictures." She batted Keane's hands away when he held them out to steady her. "I'm not feeble yet, young man." Still, she grabbed hold of the doorknob and hauled herself inside. "Merry Christmas!" Her smile was as bright as the lit star on the top of the tree.

Tehani waited for Pippy to make her rounds to accept her hugs and declarations of welcome. Her birthday last month had been her eighty-fourth and while Tehani noticed she moved a little bit slower than she had back at Marella and Keane's surprise wedding, there was no dimming that spark in her eyes. She'd woven starry tinsel through her platinum-silver hair that had been piled on top of her head. Pippy was known for her collection of velour track-suits and this evening's was as red and bright as Rudolph's nose. Her gold, glittery sneakers sparkled with every step she took.

"There's my girl." Pippy hugged Marella so tight that Tehani could almost feel it. "My happy, happy girl."

Marella laughed and stepped back from her grandmother. "What?" she asked when Pippy's eyes narrowed.

Pippy reached out and placed a hand on her granddaughter's face.

"Is something wrong?" Marella looked guilty.

"Nope." If it were possible, Pippy's eyes bright-ened. "Nothing at all."

Pippy turned to Tehani and immediately grabbed hold of her hands.

"Aloha, Pippy." Tehani bent to kiss the woman's cheek. "We're so happy to have you back with us for the holiday."

"Aloha. Where's that boy of yours?" She quickly scanned the room. "I don't see him or hear him."

"He's with a babysitter tonight," Tehani told her. "He's been a bit under the weather and more than a little cranky."

"Know just how he feels," Pippy said and released a soft sigh. "You'll bring him by soon for me to see? I want to get my hands on that sweet guy. Love me a chubby little baby. And don't you worry none if he cries. Music to my ears."

"You say that now," Tehani warned as Wyatt came up beside her and slid his arm around her waist. "Pippy, I don't know if you met Wyatt on your last visit."

"I remember you." Pippy had to tilt her head back to meet Wyatt's gaze. Marella, Griff and Theo instantly moved behind her, ready to brace her if she should tip backward. "You were on that boat with us."

"Yes, ma'am." Wyatt offered his hand. "It's a pleasure to see you again."

Pippy's gaze shifted to where Wyatt's hand rested gently on Tehani's hip. "See there's been some changes around here, hmm?" She eyed Tchani with approval. "Nice to see you looking so happy, Tehani. Nothing like a good man to put a shine on your face. Speaking of good men." She turned and the group parted, giving her a clear shot to the sofa where Benji had been trying to stand up for the past few minutes. "Stay where you are, Ben-man. I'm a comin'." She sat on the sofa, her bamboo tote dropping onto the cushion beside her. "Told ya I'd be back." She planted a loud, smacking kiss on his cheek and tugged on his bow tie. "You look very handsome tonight. Did you doll yourself up for me?"

Benji's entire being lit from the inside and, like Wyatt, he slid his arm around Pippy's shoulder and held her close. "I missed you."

"I missed you, too." Pippy rested her head on his shoulder and closed her eyes, utter and complete bliss blanketing her face.

Tehani's eyes misted and she noticed the other women having similar reactions.

"It looks like everyone is exactly where they're meant to be," Wyatt murmured in Tehani's ear. She could only nod. Her throat was too tight for words. "Merry Christmas, Tehani."

"Merry Christmas, Wyatt," she finally choked out as Tag came out of the kitchen to announce dinner was ready.

Tehani stepped into the line as the people ahead of her began to fill their plates. The aroma wafting through Marella's house was absolutely intoxicating. The roasted pork sliders were each topped with a skewer of pineapple chunks. There was macadamia nut crusted mahi-mahi and pineapple fried rice with tiny chunks of Spam. She made sure to take one of the half avocados filled with ahi poke, spiced with ginger and red pepper flakes.

"Save room for dessert," she told Wyatt, who was right behind her. "I hear cheesecake is on the menu."

"Should have brought my second stomach," he said and gave a short laugh as they found seats together beside the decorated tree.

Pippy insisted on making her own plate and Benji, not one to be left behind, followed suit.

"I don't know about you," Wyatt said, "but I need to start my Christmas shopping."

She sampled the mango-and-jicama salad with citrus dressing and replied, "If that's your way of asking if I have," she told him, "remember—I'm the one who hasn't even gotten her tree yet." But she had ordered Kai a custom wooden puzzle featuring their names and various animals from a store in Maui. "Anything you're hoping Santa might bring you?"

"Santa can skip me this year. I already got what I wanted." The words seemed to come so easily and with such sincerity that tears blurred her eyes. "I'm really happy we're here together, Tehani."

"Yeah," she choked and nervously tucked her hair behind her ear. "So am I."

"Pippy! What are you doing?" Marella's voice drew everyone's attention as Pippy dumped a second spoonful of lomilomi salmon pasta onto her granddaughter's plate. "I've got plenty already."

"You're eating for two," Pippy declared. "Salmon's brain food for you and the baby."

Marella wilted on the spot. She dropped her plate on the buffet table with a dull *thunk*.

The room went silent.

"Marella?" Keane stood and stared at his wife.

Tehani gasped at the abject adoration and surprise on Keane Harper's face.

Marella's cheeks went red. "I, um." She let out a sound that was a cross between a groan and a laugh. "I was going to wait until Christmas morning to tell you, Keane." She shot her grandmother a dark glare before she looked back at her husband. She tried to laugh but soon sobered, then shrugged. "Surprise?"

Keane nodded and only started walking over to her when Mano gave him a gentle shove forward. "We're going to have a baby?"

Marella nodded, tears brimming in her dark eyes. "Uh-huh. You good with that?"

Keane kissed her soundly, wrapped his arms

around her and lifted her off the ground. "I'm great with that."

The cheers and applause that erupted had Tehani's own tears spilling over. Her heart was full. She was so happy for her friends.

"Pippy, how did you know?" Sydney called out from where she and Theo stood.

"Girl's got a look about her," Pippy announced.

"If you say I'm glowing, I'll… I'll leave right now," Marella threatened lovingly.

"You are glowing," Keane confirmed.

"You always take her side," Marella grumbled even as she snuggled into her husband's embrace.

"Didn't mean to ruin the surprise," Pippy said in an unusually contrite tone. "Just want to make sure you're taking care of yourself. That's my first great-grandchild in there." She pointed at Marella's still-flat stomach. "I aim to be the first to hold him or her when they're born."

"Second, maybe," Marella clarified for her grandmother. "Keane gets first dibs."

Tag poked his head out of the kitchen, his expression confused. "What's going on? Everyone too busy eating to talk I hope?"

"We are," Daphne confirmed. "But we're also celebrating. Congratulations, Tag, you're going to be an uncle!"

Tag dropped something in a clatter and confusion shifted to shock. "I am?" His gaze locked on his sister. "You're pregnant?"

"That's usually how it works," Keane teased and earned a nudge from Marella before she embraced her younger brother.

The conversation picked back up, a bit livelier and more excited than just a few moments before.

"You knew, didn't you?" Wyatt asked her as they resumed eating.

"She told us at Sydney's bridal shower," Tehani confirmed. "We knew something was up when she turned down a mimosa."

"Keane's going to be a dad." Wyatt shook his head, a soft smile curving his lips. "He really did get his happily-ever-after, didn't he?"

"He really did," Tehani agreed. "They both did." And maybe, if she played her cards right, she might get one of her own very soon.

"I WOULD SAY our first official date was a success." Wyatt looked up at the moon as it cast its usual glow on him and Tehani. They were heading home from Daphne's. Kai was wrapped up and fast asleep in his stroller. The warm December breeze swirled around them. Marella and Keane's announcement—or had it been Pippy's?—had added an extra layer of joy to the evening's festivities.

"Agreed." Tehani smothered a yawn before she looked over at him. "Sorry. Long day. Long couple of weeks, actually."

"And yet the frenzy is only about to start." According to Keane's latest update, at least half of the participating surfers were arriving tomorrow, well before the official festivities began late Friday afternoon. "Did Mano agree to offer the *Pule* at the kickoff luau?" The traditional Hawaiian blessing always began the festivities by honoring the land, the food and all those in attendance. Normally a *kaku*, or island spiritual leader, would lead the ceremony asking for the guests and feast to be blessed, but Mano had frequently stepped into the role when the town elder wasn't available.

"He did," Tehani confirmed. "I think he's happy to take on something that isn't quite so detail oriented. Besides, we all know how he loves to put on a show for luau guests."

Wyatt laughed, nodding. "He does take his island traditions very seriously."

"Our grandfather was the *kaku* in Nalani when my mother was growing up."

"I didn't know that." Even after all these years, Wyatt was still learning things about her and her family. "That's pretty cool. So Mano's carrying on the tradition. Maybe Kai will take it up after him."

"That's a lovely thought." She kept the stroller moving, but glanced at him again. "I will be so grateful when this whole tournament is behind us. You caught me out earlier. I haven't even had time to do my Christmas shopping yet. And I have to get our tree!"

"I've got yours and mine on hold down at the lot," Wyatt told her. "I can bring it by, get it all set up for you to decorate."

She stopped walking and faced him, an odd, determined light in her eyes. "For *us* to decorate." She rested a hand gently on his arm. "I'd like it if you decorated with me. Maybe start a new tradition for the three of us?"

His heart swelled, but he kept his cool. "I would love to." They began walking again but suddenly he stopped and frowned. "Are you asking because you need help hauling boxes down from your attic space?"

She blinked wide eyes at him, her face all innocent-looking. "I have no idea what you're talking about."

Laughing loudly, he wrapped his arm around her shoulders and they resumed their walk home. "Just tell me when you're ready."

"I will." Much like Pippy had with Benji earlier in the evening, Tehani rested her head on his shoulder. "I'm very much looking forward to our second date, Wyatt."

"Me, too." He pressed his lips against the top of her head, feeling—maybe for the first time in his entire life—that there was nothing left to want for or dream of. He had absolutely everything he could ever want. Right here. Right now.

CHAPTER FOURTEEN

"OKAY, THE HUT-HUT'S tent should be second down on the left. Right over there." From her own headquarters—a pop-up tent outside the Hibiscus Bay Resort—Tehani pointed in the general direction so the restaurant's employees could start setting up for their full day of food offerings beginning with breakfast.

"Tehani, where do you want these?" Griff Townsend carried a stack of director's chairs, some with longer legs than others.

"Uh, look for Oliwa down there." She rotated to try to spot the volunteer and pointed toward the beach. "Those are for the observation seating for the VIP section. There should be more—"

"Theo's helping unload the delivery truck as we speak," Griff called over his shoulder.

All around, locals pinged about like pinballs, bouncing back and forth across the street from shops and homes to the rows of sponsored tents,

and beyond to the shoreline where the participating surfing contestants continued to get a
feel for the waves.

Nalani residents had turned out in full force
for early events, cheering on the surfers, helping with tent setups and loading and unloading cargo and supplies. In a few hours, they'd
be ready when the *imu* was opened and the
kalua pig was removed from the underground
oven where it had been placed at sunrise, and
the party—and the weekend—could officially
begin.

Out of habit, Tehani reached back to touch
her hand to Kai's kicking leg. She'd wedged
his stroller between her chair and the empty
one at her side, keeping him out of the sun but
also part of the festivities as they began to happen. She wanted him to get used to noise and
crowds. It was important to her that he know
what it was like to be part of this community—
from his first memory and lasting his entire
life.

She was hunched over one of her spread-
sheets, marking off all the things that had been
completed—including setting up a check-in
desk for attendees who were staying in Nalani
residents' guest rooms—when a shave ice was
pushed in front of her nose. She sniffed, the
sugary syrup wafting through her senses to the

point of emptying her mind. Glancing up, she found Wyatt looking a bit haggard and rumpled, holding out the frosty treat.

"*Lilikoi* and strawberry," Wyatt said. "Not your usual, but I thought maybe you'd be up for a twist." He put it into her hand. "Come on. Take a break. Let's go for a walk."

"I can't take a—"

"Sure you can!" Sydney popped up behind Wyatt, slipped around him and gently nudged her out of her chair. "You've been going non-stop since nine this morning. You didn't even finish your lunch."

Tehani looked at the bento box of Spam musubi, fresh fruit and teriyaki chicken that Tag had delivered to her a few hours before.

"I've got Kai." Sydney settled herself and shooed Tehani away. "We've caught up with our tours at Ohana. Jordan and Daphne are around here somewhere finding something to help with, and Keane's playing tour guide and escort to our surfers. Seriously, go. We've got this, T."

Kai squealed and kicked his blanket free, exposing his custom-made Nalani Surfing Santa Charity Championship onesie that Delaney had personally delivered two nights ago. The T-shirts she'd created for their volunteers and participants, as well as business sponsors, had gone above and beyond anything Tehani had expected. And, according to Delaney, they had already earned her business a major contract with a clothing shop in Kona.

"See?" Sydney jerked a thumb at Kai. "My nephew might not have words, but he knows when we're right. Shoo. Hey, Shani." She turned her bright smile on their friend and Nalani's quilt store owner. "What's going on?"

"But—" Tehani's protest died as Wyatt gently took her arm and led her down Pulelehua toward the main walkway to the beach. "I really don't have time to relax, Wyatt."

"Make time. It'll do your brain some good. Hi, Maru!" He called toward the crowded malasada cart. The top of Maru's head was barely visible as she chatted with customers buying her fried treats by the box. "Haven't seen Nalani this busy in a long time."

Looking behind them, Tehani made note of the jam-packed streets, the lack of parking and the jingling bells of the decorated pedicabs shuttling people up and down the road.

"It's even busier than I thought it would be." Their little town wasn't so little at the moment. There was a long line weaving out the front door of Seas & Breeze. Luanda's had a special surfing sale rack out, and everywhere she looked she could see Christmas lights twinkling.

"You gave people a lot to see and do," Wyatt told her. "Come on. You have to experience this." He prompted her to head down the path to the beach. Pop-up tents and various chairs with cushions had been set up along the top of the shore. People stood or sat and cheered, drinking and eating the snacks from the tents that had made their offerings available earlier than expected. She saw families and groups of friends and even some of the elderly folks from the retirement center watching the surfers currently riding the Nalani waves. Ankle-deep in the tide, Keane stood with his arms crossed and a whistle in his mouth as he directed the surfers in and out of the water.

"No costumes yet," Wyatt said.

Tehani reached down to pull off her sandals, all the while munching on the freezing cone in her hand. The tropical mix of fruity flavors settled her anxious stomach and also gave her a jolt of energy.

"They're keeping those a surprise apparently." Wyatt grinned down at her. "Keane suggested a contest for wildest getup. Don't worry. He's added it to the schedule along with a prize. A feature in the next brochure from Ohana Odysseys."

"That sounds like more of a prize for us than

them," Tehani observed and earned a shrug of agreement from Wyatt.

"No such thing as bad publicity. An up-and-coming surfer being featured with Keane Harper? That'll earn them some cred."

They sat, the warm sand coming up and around her bare legs like a comforting blanket. She gave in and tried to relax, focusing on the impressive array of surfers riding the surprisingly active waves. "Namaka's being kind to our participants," she said as one surfer in particular caught a perfect crest.

"I assume you mean the ocean goddess and not Jordan's cat," Wyatt teased her.

She playfully pushed her cone toward his nose. He responded by catching her hand, bringing the cone closer and taking a healthy bite of flavored ice. "Hmm." He nodded, then drew a finger under his sticky lips. "I chose well with those flavors. Need to remember that one for next time."

Tehani stared, unable to blink. Barely able to breathe. He looked…absolutely perfect sitting here, on the beach, surrounded by a growing crowd, the ocean, and their family and friends. Their Ohana. The way he kept his hand touching hers, even if it was only fingertip to fingertip, settled something inside her she hadn't realized needed calming. He made everything, every day, better for her. For her son. For everyone she knew.

How could she ever doubt that she loved him?

"Earth to T." He squeezed her fingers. "You okay?" Those eyes of his bore into hers with the power of the ocean roaring around them.

"Fine." She glanced away, waiting for the panic. The doubt. The guilt to land. For the image of Remy to take over everything around her. But nothing materialized. Other than the absolute acceptance that Wyatt was one of the good ones. A special man. A man who had been willing to remain in the shadows. A man who had loved her far longer than she'd ever realized. And she…she loved him, too.

Fear created a new secret; one she didn't want to keep, but one she was too frightened of to set free just then. Instead, she remained where she was, holding hands with Wyatt, eating her shave ice and enjoying the perfection of the moment.

"COME ON, Swell Rider!"

Wyatt stood beside Tehani on the beach, the sun beginning to set after having spent the day pummeling the tournament attendees with its warm rays. After a chaotic, successful first day of the Surfing Santa Charity Championship, the top three contenders found themselves in a tie.

The resulting added round of unexpected surfing brought out not only the number of people from yesterday's pre-event activities, but an additional couple of hundred folks who had heard about the excitement and wanted to see how things would play out.

"No way Swell Rider gets it," Sydney said between giving encouraging shouts and applause. "Sandy Claus has him beat after that loop off the waves."

Wyatt sipped on his lukewarm coffee and touched a hand against the back of Kai's head. Kai was bundled securely against Wyatt's chest. The tiny sun hat's brim dug into Wyatt's skin, but kept the rays off the baby's face. "You're both wrong." He felt both of their glares as he kept his gaze on the surfers. "Beach Bum's gonna take it. Look at those cutbacks."

"What's a cut— Awww, man!" Noah Townsend shoved his sister's shoulder when his half-eaten malasada landed filling side down in the sand. "Cammie!"

"Sorry." Cammie rose up on tiptoe, trying to see over the crowd. "I was trying to see."

"I've got you." Mano came up and lifted the sweet girl over his shoulders. He folded his arms over his chest and stood statue-still while Cammie beamed, ate her snack and scanned the crowd. "My money's on Beach Bum," he said.

Tehani turned her glare on her brother. "Why? Because he's your friend?"

"Because." Mano pointed to the surfer in the neon Hawaiian shirt and bucket hat. "Look at the air he's catching. He's practically riding above the waves." He threw a grin at his sister. "Being my friend is just a bonus."

Sure enough, Swell Rider and Sandy Claus both wiped out within seconds while Beach Bum coasted almost effortlessly to shore. When he jumped off his board, he threw his hat into the air and held both arms up in triumph.

"Guess we've got our winner," Sydney grumbled. "Glad I didn't put money on it."

"Next year you can bet on me," Jordan shouted above the cheers of the crowd. "I've got a new goal. I'm gonna win this thing!" Without waiting for a response, she pushed through the crowd to where the surfers were gathering at the podium to congratulate the winner.

"Fun's over," Tehani announced. "We need to get to the platform for the award ceremony." She turned and, like Cammie, craned her head to scan the crowd around them. "Aimita said she was going to try to make it out today. Has anyone seen her?"

"She's at your tent," Sydney said and they made their way toward it. "She's trying to stay off her feet as much as she can."

Wyatt nudged Mano to follow, but Mano shook his head.

"I'm good, bro. Cammie, you okay up there?"

"Uh-huh." She nodded so hard she almost flipped off Mano's shoulders. "Thanks for the lift!"

"Anytime," Mano said with a laugh. "Let's go find your folks." Mano and Cammie headed off down the beach.

Wyatt caught up with the others. Kai squirmed in his Snuggie, but when Wyatt touched his hand to the baby's back, he settled down immediately. "T, it's almost time to feed him again."

"I've got his bottles in the cooler at the tent," she called over her shoulder. The loudspeakers screeched on and soon Keane's voice blasted out, inviting everyone to gather around the platform soon for the presentation near the garden entrance to the Hibiscus Bay Resort.

Wyatt couldn't, for the life of him, remember Nalani ever being as crowded as it had been the last two days. Whatever projections Tehani had made for attendance had been entirely surpassed. He'd been seeing familiar faces from all over the Big Island and, from what he'd heard, the resort's new RV and van parking lot had been filled to capacity for the first time since it had opened. The number of people on the beach were as many as the number of people he saw flooding in and out of stores, standing in line at the Seas & Breeze and wandering up and down Pulelehua, getting in some all-important Christmas shopping.

Sydney and Tehani quickly flanked the woman sitting in one of the chairs in the tent that had served as Tehani's office the past couple of days. A beaming Aimita held her hands against her heart.

"These numbers, Tehani," Wyatt heard Aimita gush. "They're amazing. Spectacular." She beamed. "We're so grateful. The amount you've brought in as of yesterday is going to be enough to keep the HOEF going for at least three years. Maybe more! We can expand our reach—hopefully to other islands." She grabbed hold of Tehani's hands and squeezed. "I'll never be able to thank you enough. And Remy." She looked up to the sky despite the tent overhead. "He's definitely had a guiding hand in all this."

Wyatt kept a close eye on Tehani and saw the slight dimming in her eyes.

"This is still your event," Tehani told Aimita. "And emceeing the closing ceremony and handing out the awards is all yours if you want it."

"Really?" Aimita looked over at a tall, lanky dark-haired man wearing board shorts and one of their I Brake For Waves event T-shirts. He stepped closer and caught hold of Aimita's hand. "This is my husband, Nohea. Tehani said I could give out the awards."

Nohea dropped a kiss on Aimita's lips and rested a hand on her shoulder. "If you feel up to it, I'll be right behind you." He shot a grateful smile toward Tehani. "Thank you for taking this on. It would have broken our hearts to have to shutter the charity."

"It was my pleasure," Tehani said. "How about we get you over to the podium, yeah?" She stopped in front of Wyatt and pressed a kiss to Kai's head. "You okay with him for a little while longer?"

"However long you need. Go," he insisted at the flash of doubt on her face. "Enjoy this moment. You've earned it. We'll be there in time to see the presentation."

Wyatt hung back and checked to see if Kai needed a diaper change before they gradually made their way with the crowd to where all of the participating surfers had lined up for the presentation. Wyatt had helped construct the wooden platform. Sydney soon joined them, alternating between watching the crowd and playing peekaboo with Kai. By the time Aimita and Tehani stepped up to the podium, Theo, Daphne, Griffin and Mano—who led Cammie and Noah over—also joined them.

"The band's back together," Theo joked as

they stood in a group a little away from the main crowd. "Feels like a reunion concert or something."

Wyatt's ears vibrated with the crowd noise. This was what Nalani was all about. Supporting one another, celebrating what the world had to offer and working together to protect that which couldn't protect itself. It had been a long few weeks of hard work, but there wasn't a second of it he would ever regret. Especially given the look of satisfaction and happiness on Tehani's face.

The crowd exploded into applause as Keane took the microphone first.

"Thank you, everyone!" He had to shout to get them to quiet down. He was wearing his bright yellow organizer T-shirt along with matching board shorts. "What a great turnout for this event. On behalf of everyone at Ohana Odysseys and the Hibiscus Bay Resort, as well as the Hawai'i Ocean Education Foundation, we'd like to say thank you for your support and attendance. And to our amazing athletes who put on a fantastic show for all of us. We couldn't have made this weekend a success without all of you."

"Look at Marella." Sydney elbowed Daphne. Wyatt looked at Keane's wife, who was standing just off to the side of the platform, hands clasped beneath her chin, eyes shining with pride and happiness. "They're still on cloud nine."

"By now I think it's more like cloud seventeen," Mano said. "It's going to be a good new year. Starting with your wedding," he said to Sydney.

Daphne reached out and grabbed her stepson—who had been doing a bit of a dance with a friend—hauled him in front of her, and rested her hands on his shoulders.

"And now, to present our awards for this weekend's event—" Keane spoke into the microphone again "—the president of the HOEF, Aimita Haoa. Aimita?" He stepped back and waved her forward. She walked a bit slowly, her very pregnant belly leading the way. The afternoon breeze kicked up and whipped her dark blue floral dress around her knees.

"Thank you, Keane. Aloha, Nalani!" Aimita held out both arms as if trying to embrace the crowd. When the cheers quieted, she cleared her throat. Even from a distance, Wyatt could see the genuine emotions on her face. "As a lot of you know, this weekend almost didn't happen. But because of the dedication and determination of one person, it did. Because of her, I'm able to stand here today, with all of you, announcing a record amount raised for the Hawai'i Ocean Education Foundation!" She turned to Tehani. "Tehani Iokepa picked up the torch when I had to drop it. She didn't hesitate. She didn't doubt. She pushed forward. We thank you, Tehani. From the bottom of our hearts. You are the best. We'd also like to recognize someone else, who probably provided the inspiration for many of you this weekend." Aimita directed her eyes skyward. "Before I give out our very well-earned awards, I'd like to mention this person."

Wyatt's stomach clenched. His gaze flew to Tehani just as the light faded from her eyes. It was happening again, wasn't it? Something of Tehani's that was about to be shifted onto Remy's memory. He wanted to say something—to will Aimita to rethink what she was about to say. But even as he saw Tehani duck her head, he knew there was no stopping what was coming.

"Remy Calvert was one of our earliest and staunchest supporters," Aimita said. "He was there for whatever we needed, whenever we called, just as Tehani was a few weeks ago. This organization would not exist if it wasn't for him. Because of that, and because of the rousing success of the tournament this year, it's my honor to announce that moving forward, this annual surfing competition will be named The Remy Calvert Memorial Championship."

Sydney gasped and covered her mouth but didn't quite catch the sob. Daphne grabbed her friend's hand and squeezed. Wyatt swallowed hard. Cheers and applause exploded once more as Tehani offered a shaky smile and nod of approval when Aimita looked to her.

"It is the HOEF's sincere hope," Aimita continued, "that Tehani will remain a part of this event and accept an honorary appointment to the board. Together we can work toward great change in our environmental education programs. We are certain with her support and inclusion that every year we hold this event it will become more successful than the last. Mahalo, Tehani. *Ia oe ko makou maau.*"

"You have our hearts," Mano murmured when Cammie turned confused eyes on him.

"I need to get Kai's bottle." Wyatt backed away, twisted and turned through the crowd to return to the tent as the winners were announced and received their awards. He sat in Tehani's chair and settled in to feed Kai, whose appetite had flared with a vengeance now that the antibiotics had kicked in.

He'd seen that look on Tehani's face before. The borderline desperation. The heartbreak. She'd put everything she'd had into this event and making it a success only to have Remy front and center in the spotlight that should have been hers.

"That can't be what you wanted for her," he accused his friend. "Why couldn't you see what you were doing to her?" Robbing her of her light. Pushing her into the shadows even if accidentally, when the only place Tehani Iokepa ever belonged was standing in the middle of sunshine.

Kai had long finished his bottle when the crowds finally dissipated. Their friends bid their farewells and headed home or back to the resort, ready to crash and recharge as the town moved from hosting the charity event to celebrating the holidays.

Wyatt sat with a sleeping Kai in his arms as volunteers took down the tents. Dismantled tables. Returned supplies and unsold items, food and drinks to their businesses or homes. When two young men came to pop down the tent that he'd been sitting under, he finally returned to the beach where he knew he'd find Tehani.

He waited, steps away, as she said goodbye to Aimita and her husband. When Tehani turned, there were only a few remaining people. She beelined for him, arms stretched out for Kai as she approached. She curled herself around her son, shoulders shaking as she cried. Wyatt slipped his arms around her and held on, wondering what she was thinking, even as he knew the truth.

"That had to hurt," he murmured as she rested her head on his chest. He rubbed her back, wishing he could take her pain away. "I could see it on your face."

"I didn't expect it," she whispered. "I suppose I should have. It was just a surprise."

"For everyone," Wyatt confirmed. "It's bittersweet, I know."

She took a deep breath, stepped back and shook her head. That familiar shock in her eyes had him resisting the urge to frown. "It's like I'm caught in this undertow I can't break free of." She lifted her hands in surrender. "How do I say no to that, Wyatt? How do I walk away? It's such important work and yet…" Her jaw tensed. "If I say yes, does that mean I'm going to be trapped forever? But how do I walk away from something that will mean so much to Kai?"

He hadn't wanted to be right. "I think only you can answer that question, T."

She blinked up at him. "You don't want me to take the board position, do you?"

"I want what I always want for you, Tehani." It physically hurt not to touch her, but he knew as soon as he held her, he wouldn't ever let her go. "I want you to be happy. You've worked so hard to step away from the past. This is a decision you need to make yourself."

"I don't know what to do."

"I love you, Tehani. But I'm never going to be someone who tells you what to do. I just have to have faith you'll make the right decision for you and for Kai." Every word he spoke felt as if it was the last breath from his lungs.

"Until now, I've found that an incredibly attractive quality about you." Her sad smile broke his heart. That wasn't what he wanted to see when he said those important words to her.

He didn't want to see regret or confusion or... pity. He wanted to hear that she loved him as well.

"I hope you don't let guilt pull you into something you've worked so hard to break free of. If you want to move beyond what was and into what is, you know where I am." He turned to leave and yet everything inside him told him to stay.

"You're leaving?" She began to follow him, then stopped. Kai squirmed and let out a howl before crying in earnest. "Like this? Right now?"

"I'm walking away to give you the chance to decide what you want to do, Tehani. With or without me." He knew she had to stand on her own two feet and not rely on him or anyone else to persuade her. That was her only chance to find her way back to him. "I'll be here. When you've decided what you really want."

Because he needed to, for her, for himself, he walked away.

CHAPTER FIFTEEN

BECAUSE SHE WANTED time to decompress from
the last few weeks, because she couldn't get
her head around what had been thrown at her
since and because she didn't want to be ques-
tioned by her well-intentioned friends, Tehani
took the next few days off from work. It wasn't
until the first sunset hit that she realized just
how much damage her relationship with Wyatt
had sustained. His truck was gone by the time
she got up in the mornings, only to return to
his driveway well after dark. Two days. Three.
Going on four.

The entire situation made her sick to her
stomach and her unease wasn't going unnoticed
by Kai. He seemed as irritable and untethered
as she felt. She felt so…alone without Wyatt.
It didn't help that Christmas was around the
corner and she still didn't have the enthusiasm
to decorate the tree he had set up in the corner
of her living room. So the tree just stood there,

much like she was at the moment, looking out of place and feeling oddly abandoned.

It didn't sit well that she felt the need to sulk and wallow. But it felt like something she had to do before she poked her head back out of the sand and returned to her life. Whatever she decided to do with it.

Frustrated, she spent a few hours straightening the house and boxing up all the accumulated paperwork from the charity tournament while Kai napped. She also went through Kai's clothes and set some aside to give to Marella for when the mom-to-be started to organize.

Kai was redefining cranky. He had been growing increasingly cross ever since she'd spoken to Wyatt that night on the beach. She never imagined her indecision would drive him away. She supposed he had a point. This was something she had to do on her own, but how did she choose between an obligation to the memory of her son's father and leaving it all behind? How did she simply ignore what had made her who she was?

She'd dusted everything in sight, mopped every floor, and nothing had stopped the circling thoughts in her brain. She'd eaten the last of her crisis cookies already and was about to start baking a brand-new batch when someone knocked on the door.

Hope exploded inside her as she hurried to answer it, only to deflate completely at the sight of Sydney, Daphne and Marella standing on the porch.

"Wow." Sydney shook her head. "It's worse than we thought."

"What is?" Tehani didn't have a second to invite them in. Sydney pushed the door open and stepped inside, Daphne and Marella right on her heels. The fact they each carried bags from various Nalani shops perked her up a little bit.

"Okay. First off, wineglasses." Sydney snapped her fingers and picked the correct kitchen cabinet on the second guess.

Daphne began unloading the reusable bags filled with fresh fruit, but also some serious junk food. "Wine, red. White." She set bottles on the counter. "Cider for the mama-to-be." She eyed Marella.

"Have you and Keane crashed down to earth yet about the baby?"

"I think we're still in orbit," Marella admitted. "But we're not here about me."

"No, you're here about me." Tehani sagged onto one of her bar stools.

"In case you were wondering, Wyatt looks as knocked out as you do," Daphne said. "And we got tired of waiting to hear what had happened. Time to fess up."

"I don't know. Honestly," she added at their looks of disbelief. "I thought we were fine. Then that whole renaming the tournament thing happened and Aimita hit me with joining the HOEF board. How was I supposed to react to that?"

"How *did* you react to that?" Sydney poured the wine and then dug into the second bag for bakery boxes with the Little Owl Bakery logo on them. "We only saw what you wanted us to see. So tell us." She popped open a pink box that contained one of Tehani's favorite cheesecakes. "What didn't you want us to see?"

"The truth." She'd already turned Wyatt against her. She might as well destroy whatever relationship she had with Sydney. She leaned her elbows on the counter and buried her face in her hands. Only when she felt their hands on her back offering gentle encouragement did she take a deep breath and look at her friends. "Things weren't good between me and Remy when he died. In fact—" She didn't want to see the shock on Sydney's face, but she forced herself to stay focused on her. "Things were pretty bad. The only reason I hadn't broken it off completely was because I found out I was pregnant."

Sydney pushed her wineglass away. "I see."

"I loved your brother, Syd. I loved him with

everything I had, but…" She still couldn't find the right way to explain it. "A lot happens in eleven years. You aren't…the same after all that time."

"I never told you why I left Nalani for college, did I?" Sydney's question was quiet and devoid of the anger Tehani expected to hear.

Tehani shook her head. "No."

"I left because Remy stayed." Sydney stepped around the island, reached out and grabbed hold of Tehani's hands. "Remy was my big brother and, like you, I loved him so much. But man, he was really hard to take. It was like he'd step into a room and suck all the attention away from everyone and everything else. And he didn't mean to, but he also never saw it. Everything he said, everything he did…it seemed perfect, and that's just really hard to live with. So I took off. Escaped. I needed to make a go of my own life. On my own terms. Especially after our parents died. I was afraid if I didn't leave, I'd suffocate."

Tehani sucked in a breath.

"Seems like that sounds familiar," Marella said gently. "Tehani, why didn't you tell us you were feeling guilty? We could have helped."

"I couldn't tell anyone. It was Remy," Tehani answered almost desperately. "Everyone always saw how good things were with us. I didn't want to, I don't know, tarnish their memories of him—"

"By reminding everyone he was a very human, sometimes very frustrating guy?" Sydney picked up her glass and toasted Tehani. "Boy, have I been there."

"But you came back," Tehani said. "And you stayed."

"I came back for Remy. I didn't stay for him," Sydney corrected. "I stayed because he believed in Nalani and so do I. He'd worked so hard to make this place something special. I didn't want that to go away. And I stayed because of you, T. You and that beautiful nephew of mine and because Theo looks adorable in flip-flops and those glasses of his. And I stayed for you, Daphne. Ohana. That's the only thing that matters. It was all that mattered to Remy, even though at times he might have messed up on that."

Hearing all this was like a key being turned in the lock of her self-imposed prison.

"Do you want to accept the position with the HOEF?" Daphne asked her.

"I don't know. I keep going back and forth on it. I like the work they do," Tehani admitted. "It's important. And I loved organizing the surfing event." She cringed as she glanced at Sydney. "But I love Ohana Odysseys, too."

Sydney waved off her concern. "Ohana Odysseys doesn't factor in right now. We're focusing on you."

How did that one statement feel like a salve on her bruised heart?

"So let's say we put all that in the pro column," Marella said. "Now tell us what's stopping you from jumping at this opportunity."

"I want this on my own merits. My own abilities. I don't want to be thought of as Remy's girlfriend first and everything else second."

"Fiancée," Sydney corrected as she glugged down another mouthful of wine.

"Huh?" Tehani blinked.

"His fiancée," Sydney said again. "You said girlfriend."

The time had arrived, only now the truth didn't feel quite so scary. "There was no official engagement. Remy never asked me to marry him. He just assumed I would because that was the logical next step." Once she started the confession, she couldn't stop. "One day he called me his fiancée and that was that." She met her friends' piercing gazes. "I never had the heart to correct him, probably because I assumed that's where we were headed as well. When he finally got serious and brought up the idea, it was to elope. Alone. Without any of our family or friends there. Just…do it like it wasn't anything special." She still couldn't believe how much that had hurt.

Daphne balked. "I had no idea."

"None of us did," Sydney added.

"I turned him down," Tehani said. "I finally understood that I couldn't go the rest of my life without being seen and I think...I think I broke his heart."

Sydney grabbed her hand again and squeezed.

"And then Aimita offers you that job in front of everyone, invoking Remy's name and... wow." Marella twisted the cap off the sparkling cider and took a long drink. "Not the way to top off a successful tournament."

"I can't break free," Tehani whispered as she clung to Sydney. "If I take the job, it's because I'm tied to Remy. If I don't, how do I explain that to Kai when he's old enough to understand? I hoped Wyatt would help me figure it out, but he said I had to make the decision on my own."

Daphne, Marella and Sydney remained silent. Something she did not expect.

"What?" What was she missing?

"Maybe Wyatt hoped you'd see the answer clearly without his help. Maybe..." Daphne paused and glanced at them. "He was hoping you'd choose him over all of it."

"But he wasn't part of the equation. He didn't factor—" Her stomach dropped clear down to her toes. "Oh." Every inch of her burned with regret. "I didn't see him. Nothing else should have mattered except him." She should have turned to him for support, not answers. They should have made the decision together, once it was clear that she wanted him by her side. As part of her life. Forever. Because she did want that. More than she'd wanted anything in a long time. "I've been so scared to tell him. To admit—"

"That you love him?" Marella suggested. "Sometimes those three little words are really hard to push out. It's like you're turning yourself into bait waiting to get gobbled up by a shark."

Daphne frowned at her. "Interesting metaphor."

"You know what I mean." Marella rolled her eyes and sorted through the fruit for a fresh orange. "Nothing's going to be the same after you say it. It either blows up in your face—"

"Or everything that's wrong in your life suddenly takes a turn for the better." Sydney watched Tehani closely. "Do you love him?"

How could she possibly deny it? She nodded, and suddenly she could breathe again. "So much. He's never not seen me. Never not been there for me. Even before I knew how he felt—"

"Then you were the only one," Daphne said with a gentle laugh. "Seriously, that betting pool should have been about you and Wyatt, not when Kai was going to hit the waves."

"On a board? I've already talked to Keane about taking Kai out on his birthday."

Marella tilted her head, a giant smile on her face. "I just won the pool."

They all laughed, but when they went silent, Tehani was still left with a lot of decisions to make. "I've got a ton of thinking to do."

"Well, I hate to add to your load, but now's the right time to throw this onto the pile." Sydney reached into her back pocket and pulled out a folded piece of paper. "Whatever you decide to do, I still want you as a partner. We all do. Consider it an investment for Kai's future or as a fallback if things don't work out with the HOEF."

"I haven't decided if I'm going to—"

"You will," Sydney cut her off. "Because it's the right thing to do. You were also right. You'd be great at it. You already have been. But there is a caveat to you taking that board job."

"Oh?" Tehani looked down at the contract to search for the small print. It appeared to be the same contract she'd witnessed when Keane and Daphne and Mano had all signed theirs.

"You can't move away," Sydney announced. "Ever. You're stuck here in Nalani. With all of us. With your Ohana."

Tehani met her friends' gazes, her heart overflowing. "Now, that's a deal I can accept." Grabbing a pen, she scribbled her name on the contract.

WYATT DREADED GOING HOME. He'd spent the past few days chastising himself for making such a mess of things with Tehani. For not sticking by her when she'd needed him. For walking away because her indecision had felt like a kick to the heart.

For as long as he'd loved her, he should have been less touchy, less selfish. Watching her up on that platform, seeing her sink right back into the weight of responsibility that Remy's memory demanded, had been like watching his future disappear like sand through his fingers.

He'd been wrong to expect her to be able to climb out of that on her own. He'd paid the price the last few days. Unable to sleep, he'd taken on every single job he could get, but his results had been far from stellar. He'd made mistakes and been distracted and even edgy with his customers. He needed to get his head on straight and the only way to do that was to apologize to Tehani and admit he'd made a mistake. That he was wrong.

His ego wasn't so small that he didn't dread the admission. No one liked to have to own up to their mistakes. Especially mistakes that could very well put an end if not to his friendship with Tehani, then certainly any romantic progress they'd been making.

He'd always promised never to be like his father. And yet he'd become the kind of man that had left Tehani alone just when she'd needed someone. So now, here he was, driving home, the sun setting, hoping that she'd accept his apology and let him back into her life.

He'd missed her these last few days. And he'd missed Kai, so much so that it hurt. This time of year was supposed to be celebratory and happy. It was time to get that back. For all of them.

His gaze automatically fell on her front porch as he turned onto their lane. He wasn't surprised not to find her there. She hadn't been the past few nights. Why would tonight be any different? But he did have a plan now. He'd grab a quick shower, change his clothes and take over the dinner he'd picked up at the Hut-Hut. Ask if she'd be up to talking to him. He needed her in his life as a friend if nothing else.

He'd settled for that before. If it meant being part of her and Kai's life, he could do so again.

Head down, he circled around his truck, dinner bag in hand. He made it to the bottom step of his front porch before he glanced up.

And found her sitting in one of the rocking chairs beside the door.

At first, he thought he was imagining things. With the angle of the setting sun, that glorious face of hers and that silky onyx hair were caught in its rays. She looked more apparition than real.

"Hi." That one word, along with her smile, had hope blossoming inside him.

"Hi." He climbed the stairs and noticed the baby monitor in her hand that was lighting up to the sound of Kai's soft snores. "Everything okay?"

"Not really, no." She crossed her legs, then motioned to the chair on the other side of the small table. "In fact, everything pretty much stinks."

Her matter-of-fact statement pulled a smile out of him as he joined her, setting the bag of food on the table. "Is there anything I can do to make things less…stinky?" He frowned, unsure that was the right word to use in this situation.

"There is. But there's something I need to do first." She turned to face him and, after leaning forward, held out both her hands for his. "Before I say anything else, it's important for you to know that I love you. So much. I love you so much, Wyatt, I can barely think straight and not having you around these past few days…" She squinted as if determined to keep the tears at bay. "I never should have expected you to fix what was wrong. You were right. I'm the only one who can make the decisions that need making and putting that on you, when you've done so much for me, was flat-out unfair. I'm sorry."

He shook his head, clinging to her as if she might vanish in a puff of smoke. "I'm the one who's sorry, Tehani. You needed me and I—"

She stood and tugged him up to meet her, to press her lips to his as if to capture his apology. Tehani slipped one hand free and brought it to the back of his neck, holding him in place as she kissed the worry out of him. The doubts. The regret that had been pressing in on him for days.

"I will always need you," she murmured against his mouth. She rested her forehead against his, gazed down and whispered, "I can't not have you in my life, Wyatt. I don't work properly without you. But I don't know if I can go back to being mere friends with you. I want your friendship, but I also want more."

His pulse hammered so hard that he almost couldn't hear her. Was it possible everything he'd ever dreamed of was coming true?

"I want everything you have to give," she said. "I want today. Tonight. Tomorrow. I want an entire lifetime with you. I want you to be a father to my son and I want you to come home every night and watch the sunset with me. I want to love you as much as I possibly can, even though I know it will never be equal to the love you've shown me these past years." She stepped back but still held his hand. "I signed the papers to become a partner in Ohana."

"You did?" That shouldn't have surprised him. It was where she belonged after all. Other than with him.

"I did. And I accepted the job with the HOEF. I'm going to work part-time for both and I'll take over the annual surfing event. It dawned on me I can do everything I want to do if I have you by my side. No more ghosts standing between us. Remy helped shape me into who I am, but I'm done letting his memory dictate who I should be. I want a life with you and with Kai. Please tell me it's not too late."

He smiled, lifted his hands and cradled her face between his palms. "It would never be too late, Tehani." He kissed her gently, carefully, because he was still a little bit afraid she was going to disappear. "There's never been anyone other than you. There never will be."

She sagged in relief, laughing even as those tears filled her eyes now. "You mean I get everything I want for Christmas?"

"You'll get everything you want for Christmas," he assured her as he drew her into his arms. "Always and forever."

She held on to him and he acknowledged how right it felt to be there with her, like this. "You know what I want to do right now?" she asked.

He chuckled as every ounce of doubt and fear drained out of him, replaced by the knowledge that Tehani loved him. "I can only imagine."

She leaned back, caught his teasing gaze with hers. "I really, really want to go home and decorate the Christmas tree. Our first tree. Together. As a family." As if on cue, Kai's wails erupted over the baby monitor. "He does have perfect timing." She beamed as she squeezed his hands. "Shall we? Our first official Christmas together as a family?"

Wyatt lifted their joined hands and kissed her knuckles. "I can't think of anything I want more."

CHAPTER SIXTEEN

"Wow."

Tehani smiled at Wyatt, thrilled with his re-action. He blinked up at her as if he was look-ing at the brightest star in the sky.

"You look amazing."

He stood, abandoning the various shell and starfish decorations he was putting on Kai's stroller—since the baby would be accompany-ing Wyatt and Tehani down the aisle at Sydney and Theo's wedding. Kai, wearing one of the custom onesies Delaney had designed for her new fancy babywear line, kicked and fussed from where he sat in his carrier.

"Sydney did us all a favor with this color scheme," Tchani said as she did a little twirl. She loved the tropical turquoise dress that was elegant enough for a wedding, yet was flowy and comfortable—and most importantly, easy to dance in. Thc beach ceremony promised to be as Nalani casual as the couple getting married.

"You don't have a tie to straighten." She walked toward him, lifted her hands to his chest and smiled wider. How he stared at her, how she felt when he focused on only her, had long erased any doubts or misgivings she'd had about moving forward with him. He was the answer to everything.

Wyatt grinned. "I do appreciate that Theo went with these boho shirts rather than tuxedos." The crisp white with turquoise embroidery and accents matched the bridesmaids' dresses perfectly.

"Oh, I don't know." She sighed happily. "I would rather enjoy seeing you in a tux." She pressed her lips to his, only to smile when Kai's squeals demanded attention. "We should get going." But she didn't move. Not quite yet.

She had to take a moment to absorb everything that had happened—everything around her: the man in her arms, her son by his side and the six-foot decorated tree in the corner by the fireplace. She had never before felt such appreciation and gratitude. And love. So much love.

Wyatt was the one who stepped away first, retrieving Kai and depositing him in the stroller. "Comfy, little guy?"

Kai giggled and kicked and in pure Kai fashion, spit up his dinner.

"You have got to be kidding me." Tehani watched as Kai giggled and more milk dribbled down his front.

"I've got it," Wyatt said and laughed, but she nudged him away.

"You're wearing white," she said firmly as she scooped Kai up. "It's bad enough he has to change. But you don't have a backup outfit."

"Here, wait." He snatched a towel off the kitchen counter and draped it over her as she held Kai against her chest. "Just in case."

"My hero." She kissed him again and carried the baby into the nursery, calling out, "Back in five!"

It was closer to ten, but they still made it to the ceremony with plenty of time to spare. Wyatt kept Kai with him—the boys, he reminded her, needed to stick together—while Tehani joined her fellow bridesmaids and Sydney in one of the bridal suites at the Hibiscus Bay Resort. The honeymoon suite, located down the hall, had been booked for Sydney and Theo for the next three days as a gift from Mano for their wedding.

"We were getting worried," Daphne said when Tehani finally arrived.

"Sorry. Kai's digestive system has been a bit off today." Her smile faltered as she caught sight of Sydney standing by the bay window. "Oh, my goodness." She pressed a hand to her chest as she took in the sight of the bride, gorgeous in her white spaghetti-strap dress accented with lace and floral appliqués reminiscent of the island's traditions.

Sydney's hair was loose, but with far more curls than Tehani had ever seen. Her face was alight with happiness and her eyes filled with the faintest hint of nerves.

"What do you think?" Sydney stuck a leg out, which exposed the knee-high slit in the dress. Her sequin-studded flip-flops were utterly and completely Sydney.

"I think you look amazing."

"Mama D, it's six o'clock. You said to tell you when it was six o'clock." Cammie, wearing a smock dress in the same turquoise fabric as the attendants, ran over and grabbed hold of Daphne's hand.

"I guess it's time, then." Marella passed each of them their bouquets comprised of vibrant pink hibiscus, lavender orchids and sprays of white plumeria. Turquoise ribbons that matched their dresses held the flowers together, the ends cascaded down. Cammie clutched her white basket filled with rose petals and bounced up and down in her sandals as Marella retrieved Sydney's special bouquet.

"They did a beautiful job," Sydney whispered

as she accepted the flowers that matched her attendants', save for the pair of orange birds-of-paradise in the center. Tears filled her eyes when she looked at Tehani. "I wish Remy was here."

Tehani nodded. "I know." She embraced the woman who had, in all ways, become her sister. "So do I. Mano was honored that you asked him to give you away."

Sydney dabbed at her eyes. "I was honored he said yes…" She took a deep breath. "Shall we do this?"

"Yes!" Cammie yelled before flinging open the hotel room door. "Here we come!"

WYATT STOOD TO the side, watching the wedding reception luau play out as if it were some kind of dream. The day had been perfect. As perfect as a wedding day could be, he imagined. The bride and groom were utterly besotted with one another as they visited the guests at dozens of tables that had been set up on the beach. Theo's family—his parents, sister, sister-in-law and their eight-month-old son—mingled with the Ohana crew as if they'd always been part of Nalani. The music, provided by a local band, alternated between romantic ballads and familiar island songs.

Sydney and Theo's happiness was infectious,

as was their laughter as they celebrated with pretty much the entire town.

Mano stood clustered with Daphne, Griff, Keane and Marella, toasting with champagne just as Noah and Cammie tempted fate by taking swipes out of the bottom layer of the flower-adorned wedding cake.

The sun had long ago set, bringing with it the promise of a new year. A new beginning. A new life.

"It's almost midnight," Tehani whispered in his ear. He kept one hand on Kai's stroller as he slipped his arm around her waist. Being with her here, being with her at all, felt utterly and completely natural. "I want to dance with you."

"You sure?" he teased. "It's not my forte."

"Nor mine." She signaled to Daphne, who joined them. "Would you mind watching Kai for a little while?"

"I'd love to." Daphne gave a loving look to Kai, who was peacefully sleeping, unbothered by the party sounds all around him.

Wyatt started toward the portable dance floor where Pippy and Benji were putting on quite a show, but Tehani tugged him back, shook her head and led him away from the party.

"Are we making a break for it?" The music could still be heard, however faintly.

"No." She stepped into his arms, fitting as

perfectly as if they'd been made for one another. "I just want you to myself for a little while." They swayed to the music as voices became increasingly louder and midnight crept closer. She rested her arms around his neck and gazed at him. Even in the darkness, she lit up everything around him. Inside of him.

As the countdown was shouted and celebrated, he glanced up into the star-filled sky. He hoped, truly, that Remy would be looking down on them, approving.

Fireworks exploded overhead as everyone welcomed the new year. He and Tehani stood there, in each other's arms, watching the colors and pyrotechnics light up the sky.

"Happy New Year, Wyatt," Tehani murmured as she snuggled into his embrace.

"Happy New Year, Tehani. I love you. More every day."

"I know." She smiled. "You show me every day. I can't wait to see what the new year brings us."

He'd be happy to simply live in this moment. "Whatever comes, we'll figure it out together." He pressed a kiss to the top of her head. "Forever."

* * * * *

*For more island romances in the
Hawaiian Reunions miniseries
from Anna J. Stewart,
visit www.Harlequin.com today!*